Murder
in the
Monashees

Roy Innes

NEWEST PRESS

Library and Archives Canada Cataloguing in Publication
Innes, Roy, 1939-
Murder in the Monashees / Roy Innes.

ISBN 1-896300-89-8

I. Title.

PS8617.N545M87 2005   C813'.6   C2004-906678-1

Cover and interior design: Ruth Linka
Cover image: J. Alleyne Photography
Author photo: Lynne Young

Canada Council   Conseil des Arts   Canadian   Patrimoine
for the Arts   du Canada   Heritage   canadien

NeWest Press acknowledges the support of the Canada Council for the Arts and the Alberta Foundation for the Arts, and the Edmonton Arts Council for our publishing program. We also acknowledge the financial support of the Government of Canada through the Book Publishing Industry Development Program (BPIDP) for our publishing activities.

NeWest Press
201–8540–109 Street
Edmonton, Alberta T6G 1E6
(780) 432-9427
www.newestpress.com

1   2   3   4   5   08   07   06   05

PRINTED AND BOUND IN CANADA

To Barrie

Chapter 1

The funeral director paused, but only for a moment, when the man told him that there would be no service for the boy and that he would be the only one attending.

"John's mother died a few years back," he explained. "There's just him and me."

If the director wondered why there were not at least some friends present, he said nothing. He led the man into the small chapel where a coffin was set on two brass biers, the lid open.

"I'll leave you," the director said. "Just push this button by the door when you are through. Your son's ashes will be at the front desk by eleven o'clock—you just have to sign for them. Thank you for choosing Victoria Memorial Services and please accept my sincere condolences."

He had the presence of mind not to offer his hand; he simply turned and left the room.

The man stood over the body of his son, repressing the urge to shake him awake as he had done so many times before on their hunting trips. The morticians had done a good job. There was no deathly pallor; colour highlighted his cheeks. He looked at the boy's chest, half expecting it to expand with life as it did when he was born.

She left it too late. He'd taken her to the hospital once. "False labour" the nurse said, and his wife was mortified—always apologizing, his wife—never wanting to be "a burden" to anyone. The boy was born in their bed. He knew what to do. It wasn't much different than a calving but that first breath was a long time coming. When it did, and he felt the life in his hands, he was overwhelmed by emotion. The hardness melted at his very core and he cried. His wife understood. He looked at her then in a new way and she was happy.

Now, tears ran down his face, stopping as the hardness returned. He'd done the right thing this time. His wife's funeral was awful. The preacher droned on and on about God and Jesus and going to a better place. There were so many people there—people who barely gave her the time of day when she was alive. All that "sympathy for your loss" shit and pats on the back. Even John was embarrassed by it, and he at least had done some church time at his mother's insistence. He never went— "Big fairy tale," he'd said, then regretted it when the boy stopped attending. She said nothing, but it hurt—you could tell.

He wasn't going to share John anymore with anyone. At least in death the boy was his and he planned to keep it that way. *I don't need sympathy,* he thought. *I have the memories, and John's ashes. His spirit will be with me now, only me.*

The killing didn't bother him. As long as he could remember, killing was a part of living. He shot his first deer when he was a mere boy. He remembered the animal trying to crawl away using its front legs, its hind quarters paralyzed by the bullet that broke its spine. His father stood beside him shouting, "You shot a foot too high—missed his lungs. Now you got to bleed him." The boy pulled his hunting knife from his belt and, dodging the frantic animal's thrashing antlers, sunk the blade repeatedly into its neck until he found the carotid artery. Brilliant red blood spurted in a fountain, spraying the front of his mac. The buck's head sunk slowly into the snow, tongue protruding and eyes glazing over. "Good man," his father had said. "Man," and he was only twelve! He wouldn't let his mother wash the shirt for days.

He laughed at the shit that was peddled about the psychological trauma to the American GIs from all the maiming and death they were forced to witness. He felt fear, sure. He could have taken a hit many times but he didn't. He watched them fall all around him but he came through without a scratch. He looked after himself—no buddies to worry about. He made no friends. His motto was "He who watches his own back lives the longest," and that stood him in good stead. He watched the TV on Memorial Day when the President, eyes bright with tears, spoke before the wall that listed the dead. "Cry you hypocritical bastard," he'd said to the screen, hoisting a beer can in mock salute. "But you don't see my name there—too bad." He knew, too, that there was at least one name on the wall that needn't be, if the stupid bugger hadn't taken his second lieutenant's bar so seriously.

The ten-hour drive from Victoria should have exhausted him but he was wide-awake when he pulled into his driveway. He backed the pickup to the door of the garage. It was dark and he didn't want to chance being caught in someone's headlights from the road when he unloaded the body. He unlocked the big door and pulled it up, annoyed at the noise the mechanism made as it rolled onto the rails above. He dropped the tailgate of the truck and pushed aside the sports bags. The little asshole was neatly wrapped up in the orange tarp and swinging him out of the box and onto the concrete floor was a simple maneuver. He closed the door quickly, listening for the lock to engage as it banged down. He felt for the light switch above the workbench and turned it on.

He untied the yellow poly rope and spread the tarp open. He stood gazing down at him and felt his rage boiling up again. The look of fear on the shit's face when he realized his life was about to end; the whimper when he grabbed him as he tried to run; the crunch when his neck broke—all so satisfying, so pleasurable—but there was an expression there now of serenity, of peace that wasn't right. He grabbed an end of the rope and, pulling it taut between his hands, fell to his knees and jammed it viciously into the corpse's mouth, wedging it open.

"Now talk you son of a bitch. Talk!" he shouted, pressing with all his weight. "Tell me again what a rapist I am. Tell me again."

He pulled up on the rope.

"Laugh, will you? Laugh. Tell me I'm too stupid to understand. Tell me that again too."

He liked this new expression. His fingers deftly anchored the rope with a square knot at the top of the head. He reached for his knife and cut off the long end.

It still wasn't enough. He walked across the floor and pulled an axe from a rack on the wall. He returned to the corpse and placed his foot on the chest. He paused for a moment, then swung the blade down, once, then once again, severing the head from the torso.

He felt calm returning. His pulse was still racing but as he stood there, holding the axe, his heart slowed and his rage ebbed. He could think rationally now and decide what to do with the body.

Chapter 2

The Monashee Mountains in southern British Columbia are more foothills of the Rockies than true mountains in a picture-book sense. They don't have sharp, snow-capped peaks, but are spectacular in their own way. The late Fall is particularly beautiful when the needles of the larch trees turn a brilliant yellow. Typically they grow in bunches amongst the pines, spruce and fir, creating a canvas of dark shades of green splashed with gold. Many second- and third-growth plots within the older unharvested stands give a variation in texture. The creeks, running deep and then shallow and falling into gorges, add blues and whites to the palette as well as sound and motion to break the stillness of the forest. A photographer gazing upon all of this would be annoyed, however, by two jarring, man-made blemishes. First, ugly brown scars of logging roads cut into the greenery as they snake their way to the peaks, and second, just below one ridge, a dot of fluorescent orange glowed unnaturally. Zooming in, the camera would reveal this dot to be a toque warming the head of a hunter lying prone in the snow. Russell Montgomery was mumbling to himself as he peered through his rifle's scope at a thicket seventy-five yards ahead of him. Behind it, he knew, was a large mule deer stag.

"I've spent three hours tracking you through two feet of snow, you bastard, and now you're mine," he muttered.

The buck, up to this point, had been in control, easily staying out of range. It was too easy, perhaps; its primitive mind, underestimating the danger, had allowed the gap to close. Montgomery was breathing quickly, partly from the exertion but more from excitement. His eyeglasses were beginning to steam up but he didn't want to take the chance of clearing them and missing his opportunity for a shot. His mitts were off, toque pushed back, and his elbows jammed into the snow to steady his rifle. Hurry up, for Christ's sake, he thought, I can't hold forever.

He expected the animal to emerge slowly, affording him a perfect target as it lifted its great head to sniff the wind.

But to his surprise, the buck exploded from cover in huge lunging leaps, and headed straight up the hill. His trigger-finger jerked, sending a bullet on a trajectory that missed by a wide margin. Instinctively, he chased after it, chambering another cartridge as he ran, but he had gone only a short distance when a snow-covered branch caught his foot and pitched him face first into the slope.

"Shit!" he exclaimed, extracting himself, the rifle, and finally his glasses from the powder. After brushing himself off and retrieving his gloves, he was ready to abandon the hunt but hope flickered. He shouldered his gun, trudged ahead until he reached the animal's track, then followed it up a short rise where it met the switchback of the logging road above. He stopped there, scanning the slope that rose beyond, hoping he might still locate the buck, but there was no chance. The entire hillside was covered by second growth fir, twenty feet high and densely packed. His quarry had vanished.

"Shit, shit, shit, shit! Seven days in the best deer hunting country in BC—I see one lousy buck and can't even get a decent shot off."

Montgomery was the picture of dejection as his shoulders slumped and he turned to begin the long descent to his vehicle parked below. He was cold now. The rush had worn off and the wind was blowing directly up the hill, stinging his face and chilling his neck and arms. He was worried about falling again, especially going downhill when it was so easy to twist or even break an ankle. He was concentrating on following the trail he had broken on the way up, paying scant attention to his surroundings, when just inside the treeline, a few yards from where the buck had taken cover, he caught a flash of red out of the corner of his eye. He stopped and looked, trying to figure out what it was, and when he couldn't he traversed towards it. As he neared, he thought he was seeing a bundle of discarded hunting clothes—a red plaid coat and khaki wool pants—and was shocked to discover that the clothes were on the body of a man. But most disturbing of all was the absence of the head. It was a decapitated human corpse. Montgomery recoiled in terror, falling backwards and striking his head against a tree. Stunned momentarily, he saw trees and sky whirl above him. As his eyes refocused, he suffered yet another shock. Grinning down at him, six feet from the ground, was the corpse's head, lashed to the trunk with a yellow poly rope placed between the teeth, which was pulled back and tied upwards behind, creating the macabre expression. Just above the head, pinned by a large hunting knife, was a piece of waxed cardboard upon which was written a sign in large black letters:

DON'T FORGET THE TROPHY

Panic clutched at his chest as he scrambled to his feet and ran pell-mell down the slope, the concern of falling lost in his haste to distance himself as fast as possible from the scene. He felt as though he was in the midst of a nightmare, being chased by an unknown demon, his flight slowed by frequent tumbles in the snow.

Chapter 3

RCMP Corporal Paul Blakemore was parked at his favourite spot—a sharp right-hand bend in the Crowsnest Highway at the end of a two-kilometer passing lane—a reprieve after ten miles of hairpin, follow-the-leader curves marked by a solid, no-passing, centre-line. Christ himself would speed down that straight stretch to get by the ubiquitous slow-moving campers, the ass-ends of which were such an irritation to the faster vehicles. Blakemore could fill his "dance card," as he liked to call his book of citations, in less than an hour. His radar picked up the speeders well back, and when they slowed at the sharp curve sign he could easily flag them down with no danger to himself.

The town of Bear Creek, Blakemore's latest posting, suited him perfectly. He loved the rural setting, the fishing and hunting. The people were down to earth, which allowed him to do his policing straight from the shoulder without the pussyfooting crap that he had to swallow in the big city. He would be content to spend the rest of his life, both professional and private, in this community if it was up to him. The problem was his wife, Barbara, who didn't share his enthusiasm. She was an urban creature, without children to occupy her, and found many days long and boring.

Blakemore was pondering this weighty subject when a call came over the radio.

"Central to Corporal Blakemore. Standby for instructions. Do you copy? Over."

He never failed to be amused by his partner's radio formality. Aside from the odd trucker or "Reever" (Recreational vehicle driver) they were the only two on that frequency.

"Yah, Ernie, what have you got?"

"Proceed to Whipsaw Corner Store. Hunter reporting probable homicide."

"Homicide? You mean the usual shoot your buddy instead of the deer accident? Okay, I'm on my way."

Constable Ernie Downs lost it. Radio decorum went out the window.

"Jesus, Paul, this is a big one. Corpse is in two pieces. Someone cut his head off. Christ, maybe I should get Vancouver in on this right now. We're out of our league."

"Don't you dare Ernie, my faithful Malamute. If the story is true, we could bring a touch of glory to our little detachment—impress the big city boys and show them they're not the be-all and end-all. I'll check back with you when I've investigated. Stay where you are and keep the citizens off my back till I've had time to get a real hold on this."

He shut the radio off. Ernie needed to calm down. He also didn't want word of this leaking out on the airwaves too soon. The Whipsaw hot stove league would be spreading the news quickly enough. Blakemore was right. By the time he reached the small general store, a sizable crowd had gathered. He was surprised that they had actually waited for him before charging out to the hills to view the body.

The store, owned by "Old John" Koodekoff (to distinguish him from "Young John Koodekoff," the manager of the sawmill) was named after the creek that bisected the lot. The back half was useless since the beavers periodically dammed the waterway below, submerging it a great deal of the time. The store, with living quarters above, was on higher ground and to date the floods had not reached it. Old John was indeed old, but at eighty-five his mind was clear and he had no difficulty holding his own with his regulars who loved to linger and argue with him on any topic from politics to sports. Local gossip was his first love, though, and in this he outdid even his gregarious wife. His version of events reached gospel proportions. The phrase "If

you heard it from Old John, it must be true" was the stamp of authenticity that raised rumour to fact.

When he saw the squad car pull up in front of his store, he was ready. Blakemore spoke to none of the crowd assembled outside, nodding only to one or two as their eyes met, and headed straight for the door. Old John pulled it open before his hand reached the latch.

"Stand back, stand back," he shouted to no one in particular. "Let the police through." To Blakemore he said, "Follow me, Paul, your man's in my office."

The interior of the Whipsaw Corner Store was a totally disorganized jumble of hardware, sporting goods, confectionery, pet foods, and, it was rumoured, a few crocks of homebrew white lightning under the counter. There were no recognizable aisles; the merchandise appeared to be placed at random on an assortment of tables, boxes, and rickety shelves. A long glass-covered counter against one wall supported a cash register and a lotto terminal (the only feature that gave a touch of today to the establishment). Old John's "office" was no more than a small clearing around the pot-bellied stove where a few straight-backed wooden chairs were placed for his customers along with one moth-eaten old Lazy-Boy rocker, his personal throne. The fact that he had seated the frightened hunter on the rocker meant that much hay was to be made in the old man's world by virtue of this unusual event. He positioned himself at the Mountie's shoulder.

"Corporal Blakemore, this is the unfortunate gentleman who discovered the horrible crime."

The hunter, Montgomery, was still in a state of shock. He brightened, however, when he saw the familiar RCMP uniform and leapt to his feet.

"Thank God you're here, officer. It was horrible."

Blakemore looked at him with clinical interest. He ordinarily trusted his first impressions to smell out criminals, but this man fit no pattern he recognized. If anything, he looked like an accountant or a banker dressed in hunting attire. He was of average height but gave the impression of bigness. His double chins, however, indicated his bulk was made up more from fat than muscle. He was prematurely bald, having doffed his toque in response to the considerable heat radiating from the stove. Wisps of reddish hair stuck out in all directions from around his ears and his horn-rimmed glasses magnified his eyes like a Mr. Magoo. His chubby face was flushed and beads of perspiration dotted his forehead.

"Okay sir, now just calm down and start from the beginning. Please sit."

Blakemore had learned his interviewing skills well. He deliberately removed his overcoat, took out his notebook, and pulled up a chair beside the agitated man. Montgomery sat on the edge of his chair, fidgeting with his toque, as he regarded his inquisitor. The policeman was tall and built like a centre line-backer, though there was the suggestion of a paunch from too many hours of sitting in a squad car. There was a touch of grey in his dark hair and Montgomery guessed him to be around forty. He moved slowly in a benign way but his eyes were hard, reflecting experience and a no-nonsense approach to his job.

"What is your name and where are you from?" Blakemore began.

"Russell Montgomery. I'm up here with my two buddies for a week of hunting and I run into this nightmare. God, what did I do? I've been working my ass off in a lousy office in downtown Vancouver. I deserve a break. Why did I have to be the one to stumble on the headless hunter?" He abruptly reached for his wallet.

"Here is my business card. My home address is on the other side."

"I understand your distress, Mr. Montgomery, but you are the discoverer of the body and, like it or not, you are a very important part of this investigation. Now, where are your friends?"

"They're up in the hills somewhere. We split up first thing this morning. They took the other vehicle to hunt the lower clearings for whitetail. I wanted a big muley, and so I went higher up. This is our last day. They'll stay out till dark." A frightened look came over his eyes as a horrible thought entered his mind.

"I don't have to go back up there do I? Good God, give me a break." But Blakemore was not into mercy at this point.

"I'm afraid you do, but I'll call my partner. He'll contact your friends when they return to town. Where are you staying?"

"At the Thunderbird Motel. The rooms are booked under my name. But really, I've told you everything. Couldn't I just show you the trail and let you take it from there?"

"'Fraid not," replied Blakemore. "I'm a one-man patrol here today and you're with me till I'm a lot wiser about this whole affair." Montgomery's shoulders slumped.

Blakemore rose and faced the townspeople who by now had crammed into the little store. He saw no point in continuing his questioning in front of this crowd, and he wanted to get out of there before his nemesis from the Bear Creek *Bulletin*, Heather McTavish, arrived. He was amazed that she hadn't sniffed this one out yet.

"Listen up, folks," he announced, looking hard at the closest of the eavesdroppers. "Mr. Montgomery and I are going up now to the site of the crime. No one is to precede us and no one is to follow us. The route must be kept clear for Clyde Groat and his volunteers in the inhalator truck. They'll bring the body out. If Doc Benson is available, he'll be asked to come too. I

repeat. If anyone obstructs our route up or down, they are in deep trouble."

With that he donned his coat, indicated that the unhappy man was to do the same, and then led him through the grumbling crowd to his cruiser.

"Hop in Mr. Montgomery and lead me to your corpse," Blakemore said, in a tone a bit too jocular from his hapless passenger's point of view.

As soon as the location Montgomery gave him was clear, he radioed Ernie.

"Looks like you were right Ernie. We've got a live one here, so to speak," he chuckled into the mike. "Get on the blower to Clyde and tell him to take a few of the boys in the meat wagon to pick up the delecti. Tell him to bring along the camera stuff. I want to get pictures of the untouched scene. Also, see if you can track down the Doc. He'll have to do the coroner thing anyway and he may want to see everything first-hand. Oh, and one more thing. My man here came up with two buddies. Names?" He held the mike in front of Montgomery for a response.

"Matt Abelman and Joe Black."

"Did you get that okay?"

"Roger," replied Ernie.

"They're staying at the Thunderbird. Should be back at nightfall, but you'd better check there now. They may have gotten bored freezing their balls off. They're hunting the meadows above Koodakoff's place. The body is a couple of hundred yards straight up the slope from the gravel pit on the Whiskey Creek Road. I'll park the limo there. The boys can follow our tracks to the scene. Got that all okay?"

"Roger," said Ernie.

"Don't scare Abelman and Black off. I've got their buddy here, but you never know. Joe Citizen doesn't like to be

involved in a murder investigation and I want them close and fresh. Got that too?"

Montgomery felt dread gripping the pit of his stomach. The Mountie was obviously planning to climb the ranks on this case, using him as a toehold. That lousy office in Vancouver was beginning to look like a far-off oasis.

Blakemore made good use of the ride to continue his interrogation of Montgomery. He had him go over his story completely without interruption, then proceeded with his questioning.

"What did you do after you found the body? Did you move anything? Walk around a bit?"

"Hell, no," responded Montgomery. "I was so shit-ass scared that I damn near flew down the hill getting out of there. It took me three hours to climb up but I'll bet I made it down in thirty minutes straight across all those switchbacks. I jumped in my Bronco and booted straight to the Whipsaw store. I wasn't hanging around for anybody. For all I knew, the wacko who did this could still have been there. He obviously had a thing for hunters and I wasn't going to be his next victim."

"Did you see any sign of someone being in the area? Tracks in the snow? Vehicles parked by the road anywhere?"

"No, nothing up to that point. That's why I was hunting there. It looked as though I was the only one around, and with the fresh tracks of a buck I thought I had a good chance of nailing one without its being spooked. After I found the stiff, though, I was conscious of nothing other than getting back to my vehicle."

Silence followed for a few minutes as Blakemore ruminated. Finally he decided to change his tack.

"I'm a hunter too, you know. I can sympathize with your situation. What do you do in Vancouver?"

"Would you believe? I'm a computer softwear designer. Hunting is as far away from my everyday life as you can get and

that's why I love it. The fresh air, the tracking, and with a bit of luck a kill. I've been coming up here for a few years now, and I've rarely been skunked. It's given me real bragging rights with my co-workers back home. This year's been a bummer to say the least. I thought for sure I would bag that big buck."

Blakemore was amused. Hunters are an amazing breed. Once you get them onto the subject they forget everything else. The headless corpse had vanished behind Montgomery's deer.

"What do your two buddies do? Are they keen hunters like you?"

"We've known one another since high school, but this is their first year hunting. I guess all my crowing twigged their competitive spirits. We've been that way, competitive I mean, since we first met. They both took the CORE course last summer, and since they got their licenses they figured they could shoot rings around me this fall. Ableman's a lawyer and Black's a fireman. They both work in Vancouver."

"You've been up here for a week, you said," Blakemore reminded him. "Did you or your pals meet any other hunters on the hill? Is there any chance that the dead man is someone you may have seen before?"

"That face would not be recognized by its own mother. It's too horribly distorted. But, no. We heard the occasional shot fired, but once we spread out on our day's hunt, I didn't and the other two guys didn't mention seeing anyone."

Blakemore returned to his thoughts. There was only one week of the buck season left, and with the cold conditions the city hunters tended to stay home. The locals, if they had not already limited out, deigned only to "road hunt," enjoying the warmth of their heated cabs. It was not unusual, then, that Montgomery and his friends were the only ones legitimately out on the hills at this time. That, of course, raised the probability that someone

had been there for illegitimate purposes, or that the body had been dropped there, the deed being done somewhere else. The cardboard sign implied a deer-lover's revenge, but that was just too bizarre to be a possibility. He chuckled to himself thinking that the most likely suspect in that regard would be Miss Roberts, the chief librarian at the high school, she had read *Bambi* as a child and never got over its impact on her. She wrote letters to the editor of the Bear Creek *Bulletin* every year at the start of hunting season. In fact, the local hunters didn't even need to read the Provincial Hunting Regulations to know the opening day. Miss Roberts's protest letter always listed it.

He pulled into the gravel pit and radioed Ernie to confirm that his instructions had been carried out. He and a reluctant Montgomery then made the climb back up the slope, following the tracks made by the descent of the frightened hunter. Blakemore led the way, scanning the entire hill for any sign of other human tracks. He saw none. Fifty yards from the crest, Montgomery shouted ahead to him.

"It's right ahead of you, just off to your left. You can see the red of the coat."

"Okay. I see it. Now you stay just where you are. I don't want any new tracks in here."

Blakemore took a roll of yellow tape out of his jacket pocket and strung it up to trees and shrubs for three hundred and sixty degrees around the sight, encircling an area sixty feet in diameter. As he did so, he again noted the absence of any tracks other than Montgomery's. His advance to the torso, the impression of his fall, and his headlong descent were clear. The buck's tracks led into the thicket, straight out, then up to the crest of the hill. In short, all of the visible signs completely coincided with Montgomery's story. There was absolutely no other sign, either of the dead hunter's trail or that of his killer. The body was

completely exposed, without any snow cover. The last snowfall was two weeks past. The corpse appeared to have been placed there from the heavens and probably within the last two weeks.

Chapter 4

Dr. Zachary Bensen, age twenty-seven, currently feeling eighty-seven, slumped back into a dilapidated chesterfield that graced the so-called "Doctors' Lounge" of the Bear Creek Hospital. Only the fatigue etched in his face marred his movie star good looks—wavy black hair, chiseled features, and deep brown eyes. He'd removed his small, dark-rimmed glasses and gazed blankly at his surroundings.

The couch took up a large part of the space leaving precious little room for the rest of the furnishings. There was an end table supporting a dictating machine and an ashtray. The anti-smoking campaign had cleaned out the rest of the hospital, and so this room was the last haven for the tar and nicotine addicts. A surprising number of the hospital staff were in that category. There were two old battered lockers, only one of which was functional with the other used to store the OR "greens." A laundry hamper on wheels contained a few of the discarded uniforms, but by and large the floor collected most of them. A metal trolley, supplied by the kitchen, was more organized. It was covered with a clean white cloth upon which was gathered a supply of cups, saucers, spoons, milk, sugar packets, and a large coffee urn. Despite the suspicions of those who worked the graveyard shift, the coffee in the urn was changed frequently. Zachary gratefully poured himself a cup. Abruptly, the most dreaded fixture in the room jarred his peace. The phone rang.

"Hello," he answered. "Dr. Benson's ghost speaking. Dr.

Benson has been up all night with a difficult delivery. He came in here a moment ago and died on the couch."

"I'm sorry Dr. Benson. I wouldn't bother you but it's the Queen's Constable Ernie and he's in a real flap. Would you please talk to him? It does sound like a life or death situation, I think."

Mary Sloan, the hospital switchboard operator, was Zachary's favourite person in the whole institution. On the telephone, she was a master. She was level headed, compassionate, and handled every situation with a finesse that should have made her the hospital CEO rather than a very nice person stuck in that god-awful cubicle behind the reception desk.

"Only for you, Mary, only for you," he said, emphasizing the fatigue in his voice. He hoped that she would add this on to his Brownie points. "Put him on."

"Hello Ernie. This had better be good. I'm really pooped out here."

"Doc, thank God I've got you. We've got a gruesome murder on our hands. Dead hunter with his head cut off. Paul has gone up to the scene with the guy who found the body. He wants you up there ASAP. Jesus, Doc, please hurry. This should be big city stuff but you know Paul. He likes throwing away the book, and on his own up there he could make a real mess. We could end up looking like hicks. You've got that forensic stuff down pat. We need you up there."

"Calm down Ernie. You're not all that far from 'that forensic stuff' you studied at the Academy. I've got great faith in the RCMP. They wouldn't have turned you two loose if you weren't qualified, would they?"

In truth, Zachary had his doubts about Ernie, who had a penchant for avoiding direct responsibility—preferring to do the bookwork, so to speak, and leaving the heavy stuff up to his partner. Rumour had it that Ernie's father, "Chuck" Downs,

a retired RCMP sergeant, had pushed his reluctant son into the Force, snuffing out his son's real desire to be an artist. The word "gay" was whispered in certain quarters of the community. Paul Blakemore, on the other hand, despite his "one of the boys" attitude, was regarded as a shrewd, perceptive individual with a real enthusiasm for policework.

"It's been seven years since those classes and neither of us has been in charge of a murder investigation," Ernie argued. "The last one I even saw was three years ago when I was a rookie in Vancouver. Doc, you've got to go up there."

"Where, by the way Ernie, is 'up there'?"

"Twenty minutes max, Doc, just north of town. I've already got Clyde standing by with the inhalator van. He'll pick you up at the hospital in five minutes. In fact, I think he may be waiting at the ambulance entrance right now."

Zachary gave up at that point.

"Ernie you sonofabitch, you owe me for this. I'd better not get a speeding ticket for the next ten years."

"You got it Doc." A sigh of relief came from Ernie as he quickly hung up.

Chapter 5

Zachary wished that the passenger seat of the van would tilt back to allow him a few precious minutes of dozing, but the inhalator service was not built for comfort. It was crammed with equipment. George Smith, who ordinarily rode in the front passenger seat, was jammed in the back with Karl Reinhart, the ranking Advanced Life-Support Attendant. George was junior in seniority but his considerable bulk dictated the usual seating arrangements. Zachary had glanced longingly at the stretcher when he stepped into the vehicle, but noticed that the blankets

and mattress had been removed, leaving the stainless steel plate. It looked like an autopsy table.

He glanced at Clyde Groat. The inhalator was a converted Econoline van poorly designed for anything but pavement driving, so maneuvering it on gravel required considerable skill. Clyde gripped the steering wheel with both hands and his eyes never left the road. He was clean-shaven and had taken the time to put on his first responder's uniform—dark slacks and white shirt with the two gold bars indicating his captain's status. Most of his contemporaries sported a two-day growth of beard and rarely wore anything other than their work clothes. Bear Creek was lucky to have him as their volunteer fire chief, thought Zachary. He knew there had been some dissention amongst the citizens when the logger ran for the position. He was a young, big-boned Doukabour with short, brown, curly hair and an open, easy-going manner that belied the seriousness and dedication within.

Paul was making a second circuit around his taped perimeter when he heard the engine of the inhalator van groaning up the road below. He started back down the trail but stopped when the engine sounds continued, then began to fade.

"Damn," he swore. "They're taking the switchback to come out above!"

He turned and charged up the hill.

"Where the hell are you going?" Montgomery yelled.

"Stay where you are," Blakemore shouted as he tried desperately to reach the crest before the van. He did his best to choose a route through unbroken snow, avoiding even the deer tracks. He didn't make it. The van passed above him, proceeded for half a minute, then turned around and arrived just as Paul stepped onto the road.

"Don't get out," he shouted as Clyde braked to a stop and rolled down the window.

"Why not?" Clyde retorted.

"I've got to check this stretch for any clues, you moron, before your size twelves screw up the whole country. Glad to see you Doc," he added as he spotted Zachary.

"For Christ's sake, Paul," Clyde complained. "It hasn't snowed for weeks now. There are all kinds of vehicle tracks on this road. Have you forgotten how many hunters were up here before that? The Wilderness Watch guys use this road a lot. The turn-around behind me is one of their favourite check points."

"I know," countered Blakemore, "but I'm looking for the tracks of a vehicle parked near here, footprints leading over the bank, signs of something being dragged, blood . . ."

"Okay, okay. Don't get your shit in a knot. All right, men. Nobody moves till Sherlock says so."

Blakemore gave him an unprofessional finger, then meticulously scanned both sides of the road, above and below, stopping about twenty yards on either end to string his yellow tape at eye level completely across the road, tying it to trees on either side. He walked back to the van and double-checked the area around it before finally opening the passenger door for Zachary and the two attendants.

"All right. You can get out and gather up all your stuff, but when we head down stay single file behind me. Why didn't you come up from the gravel pit like I told Ernie?" he added, directing his question to Clyde.

"Obviously you've never had to carry this ton of equipment, or a dead body anywhere. Down, for your information, is a helluva lot easier than up. I'm going to take the van back to the pit now so your pretty yellow ribbon below is going to get busted," he said, grinning maliciously.

"Shithead," replied Blakemore, his humour returning, knowing that the tape would be retied. Clyde was actually one

of the first real friends he had made after arriving in Bear Creek.

Montgomery was more than relieved to see the procession winding down the bank towards him. He was cold and wanted out of there in the worst way. He had spotted the equipment carried by each man and feared that a great deal more time was going to be spent inside the yellow ring. His morbid curiosity measured zero. He wanted none of this and told Blakemore so the moment he approached.

"Officer, is it really necessary for me to stay here? I've got nothing more to add to your investigation. I want to get back to my room and my friends. Couldn't you radio for them to come and get me or, better still, call a cab from town? I certainly don't mind the expense."

Blakemore pulled him aside and spoke in a low, authoritative voice.

"Look Mr. Montgomery. It's too bad that you got involved in this, but you are and at the moment you are involved up to your eyeballs. The only signs of a human being around the body are yours. Unless I can find an explanation for that, you are the prime suspect in this murder. Now George, the big guy over there, has brought a thermos of coffee that I know he'll share with you. I'm afraid that you're stuck here for the time being."

Everyone had overheard the conversation, of course, and when Blakemore turned away from the stunned man, George hurried over with his thermos in hand. Montgomery looked anything but a maniacal killer at this point. His jaw had dropped and what little colour he had in his face had drained.

"Here," said George, pouring steaming coffee into a Styrofoam cup then handing it to him. "Maybe you'd better sit down. There's a dry log."

Montgomery obeyed, still in shock. He held the cup in both hands, letting the heat warm his fingers. His benefactor was

indeed large, probably six feet six, and judging from the strain on the seams of his jacket when he moved, his clothes covered a massive body. His face, which was long and lean, suggested that muscle rather than fat made up the bulk. It was expressionless. He looks retarded, thought Montgomery, like there's no one home up there. Since he was, however, the only one available to talk to (the partner totally occupied with the stretcher) he finally blurted out.

"He can't be serious! He's kidding, right?"

"Paul can be a bit of a joker, but you'd better do as he says. He's also got a short fuse and he isn't much fun when he gets mad," was George's attempt at reassurance.

Montgomery's mind whirled as he watched the policeman and a young man who looked like a skinny Clark Kent carrying a large black doctor's bag step inside the taped ring and approach the body.

"Jesus," he thought. "I've just been accused of murder! I'm in the middle of the great Canadian outback, captive of this cop who acts more like a Mississippi sheriff than a Mountie, and drinking coffee with George the Giant. Abelman! He's my only hope. If they don't lynch me right here and now, Abelman will rescue me. I'll speak to that young doctor when he's through. He's probably my best bet for a little compassion. He'll get Abelman on my case. Case! Shit, I'm already thinking like a criminal. This can't be real. I must be having a nightmare."

He sat there brooding, although the thought of Abelman cheered him slightly.

"You weren't exactly Mr. Tact with that poor bugger back there," Zachary said to Blakemore as they carefully approached the body. "He doesn't even look like a hunter, let alone someone who could commit a gruesome murder."

"You never know," replied Paul. "Ever see pictures of mass

murderers? Most of them were everyday, nice-guy-next-door types and I wasn't fooling about the tracks. You'll see."

The body and the head had no particular effect on Zachary other than a clinical one. His internship year was at the Detroit Receiving Hospital where, particularly on his Emergency Room rotation, gruesome was more often the norm than the unusual. This one wasn't even bleeding.

"In fact," he said out loud, "the absence of blood here is remarkable. I don't see any under the head or around the torso."

Blakemore nodded as he furiously photographed every conceivable angle, being careful to keep his own tracks out of the photo. He allowed Zachary to approach the body only when he was finished, and even then he had the camera at the ready to snap anything that might be uncovered during the examination.

"There are a number of peculiar things here, Doc," he said, and pointed to the snow around the body. "There's no sign of drifting or melt. The neck is fresh meat to the bears. Not touched. The head is like a bird feeder to the ravens. They should have at least plucked out the eyeballs by now. They're experts at picking apart a carcass. I'd say that this body was dumped here in the very early morning hours today. My suspect over there got to the Whipsaw store just after eleven. He claimed to have come down directly after finding the corpse, so we're looking for time of dumping and time of death. Keep both of those in mind won't you Doc, when you look all this over? Oh, and don't laugh. The third question is the cause of death. There should be blood spattered all over the clothes if he really died from the neck chop, but there isn't a drop. I suppose some deranged bugger could have cleaned it all up and dressed him in fresh clothes. Jesus! That would be weird."

"That's sharp reasoning," responded Zachary. "I guess you're not just a pretty face."

"You mean you actually had doubts?" Blakemore asked, feigning hurt feelings.

Zachary donned his rubber gloves and examined the stump of the neck.

"Done by an axe, I'd say—a very large and sharp one. Two blows from the side—one straight through the spine and the second through the windpipe. Chop chop. It takes a cold bastard to do that so efficiently. He certainly knows how to handle an axe, or has extraordinary hand-eye co-ordination. The human neck is a tough structure to get through that cleanly."

"Yeah," agreed Blakemore. "The thing hanging in the tree has no dangly bits either. You could use it as a book end."

"I can't see any other sign of trauma—broken bones, bullet holes, and the like. The legs are drawn up from rigor mortis I presume, but I'll be damned. Feel this," Zachary exclaimed as he poked the neck with his finger. "It's frozen solid!"

Blakemore chose to check this finding by prodding the corpse's shoulder.

"You're right. But the daytime temperature up here is barely below freezing, and overnight probably not much more than minus six. One night isn't enough to freeze a body like that. I'll bet this thing was lying in somebody's freezer before it was brought up here. This is going to raise hell with your setting a time of death, isn't it?"

"I'm afraid so, Paul."

They directed their attention to the head.

"Is it frozen too?" Blakemore asked.

Zachary confirmed that it was.

"How'd he get that happy smile on the face?"

"The killer must have arranged it with the rope before freezing it. God! Can you imagine the hate that went into an act like this?" replied Zachary. "Not being satisfied with murdering the

poor soul, he had to add mutilation and ridicule to the corpse."

"By the way, what do you think about the sign, Paul?" he added.

"Either this was done by some animal rights loony, or more likely it's a dumb attempt to make us think that. Headquarters keeps a close tab on the real whackos and I'm sure we would have been notified if one has strayed into our jurisdiction. The knife's interesting. It's one of those cheap mail-order things that's advertised in kids' comic books—'exact duplicate of Rambo's own, genuine camouflage paint, and trail-finding compass on the handle'—that kind of come-on. I'll dust it for prints but I don't have much hope I'll see anything."

They both stood for a few moments, deep in thought. Finally a shout broke their silence. Clyde had arrived on the site and his impatience with the apparent halt in progress was obvious.

"Come on you two. I'd like to get back before dark and I'm sure as hell not planning to rig up floodlights."

"Okay, okay," answered Blakemore. "Bring on the stretcher and the Baggies, but watch where you're stepping. I want as little as possible disturbed."

The three men, Clyde, Karl, and George, worked efficiently, transferring the torso into the body bag, zipping it closed, and finally hoisting it onto the stretcher. Blakemore, himself, took down the head, carefully placing it into a large plastic bag. The knife and sign were handled similarly to avoid smudging any possible fingerprints. There was nothing significant under the body when it was removed, and all there was in the snow below the head were pine cones, needles, and bits of bark. It seemed that the body and its severed head had been placed in this remote spot as if by a Divine hand.

But Blakemore was not into divinity. Montgomery was still the most likely candidate. "Never ignore the obvious," his

instructors had stressed. "It saves so much needless investigation."
There were nagging questions, however. How did he manage to
transport the body, even downhill from the switchback? There
were no signs of anything being dragged and there was only the
one area where he claimed to have fallen that he could have set
down the heavy load. He didn't appear to be that strong, but
with the adrenaline rush of fear it was possible. Where did he
store the body? He was familiar with the country, having hunted
there for "a few years," and could have arranged a hiding place.
Blakemore made a mental note to check the rental lockers that
were available in Bear Creek and vicinity. A good number of
hunters liked to use them, especially if they lived in apartments
or small homes. Some of the units were large enough to hang,
butcher, wrap, and quick-freeze their kill. But no matter how
much he wanted everything to fit, one observation wouldn't go
away—Montgomery's demeanor. His shock appeared genuine.

They descended in single file, Clyde leading the way,
followed by George and Karl carrying the body, Zachary, then
Montgomery, and finally Blakemore who continued to scan the
snow for tracks. When corpse and equipment were loaded into
the inhalator van, the ambulance men got in and headed back
to town. Zachary joined Blakemore and Montgomery in the
police cruiser.

"I'm going to drop you off at the store to get your vehicle,"
Blakemore said to Montgomery. "But I want you to come
directly to the station. You can follow me there."

"Why do I have to go there? You're not putting me in jail
are you?"

"No," replied Blakemore. "But there are some formalities in
confirming your ID and there may be further questions after the
Doc and I do a first run over the body to see if we can determine
its identity and so forth. Maybe you know this guy."

"I'll cooperate, of course, but I want to contact my friends, if they're back."

"That's all right with me, but I'd suggest that you phone from my office. The pay phone in the store won't be very private."

Montgomery was going to argue, but this was Rome and he wasn't going to antagonize one of the lions. Besides, Abelman was getting closer.

Chapter 6

With Montgomery obediently following in his Bronco, Blakemore continued to think out loud, hoping for some input from Zachary as they headed for the station.

"It's too bad that I couldn't let him phone from back there, but one of his buddies is a lawyer and I'd like to delay that meeting as long as possible. I really wanted to get a look into the back of his vehicle but I noticed that the door locks were down and he wasn't likely to unlock it before going inside. I might have better luck at the station. I'll let him park inside the impound lot. Maybe he'll leave it unlocked there."

"Shouldn't you get a search warrant organized first?" inquired Zachary. "With a lawyer so close, you might be well-advised to do so. You know that you've been damn lucky that this guy hasn't started to demand his rights. Eventually the scare is going to wear off."

"Don't worry. If I find anything I'll throw him in the slammer and have lots of time to get an official OK."

They drove the rest of the way in silence. Zachary was beginning to feel the fatigue again and so put his head back for a few minutes of dozing. Blakemore left him alone.

The Bear Creek RCMP station was of grand dimensions considering the size of the town. That, and the fact that two

full-time officers were posted there, caused some ill feeling in a few of the larger communities along the highway. The unit functioned well, however, and the workload they handled was surprisingly large. A high chain-link fence behind the building enclosed the impound lot. Contained within it were two stolen vehicles, a few wrecks, a couple of bicycles, a trailered boat, and sundry articles that could be stored outside. The inhalator van was backed up to the rear entrance. No one was in it. The crew was either reporting to Ernie or they were in the process of depositing their cargo in the morgue. He pulled to a stop alongside the van, got out, and motioned to Montgomery to park on the opposite side, away from the street. He followed and opened the driver's door of the Bronco.

"Your car will be safe here," he said to Montgomery. "We'll go in the back way. I'll introduce you to my partner. He may have already spoken to your friends, but there is a private phone you can use in my office." He casually slammed the door after Montgomery stepped down and led him into the station. Zachary held the door open for them.

They entered a wide corridor. On the left were a pair of huge heavy doors, above which was the sign MORGUE. On the right was a blank wall, interrupted only by a large cork board cluttered with wanted posters, regulations, government bulletins, transfer opportunities, and a Ducks Unlimited calendar with the deer hunting season highlighted. At the end of the corridor, Blakemore turned abruptly to the right. Montgomery followed, his heart skipping a beat as he saw what was behind the blank wall—a steel-barred cell with the usual spartan bunk, lidless toilet, sink, and large drain in the middle of the floor. It was windowless. Facing the cell, however, was a wall of glass. A large office-reception area spread out on the other side and there, sitting with coffee cups in hand, were the ambulance crew and

a Mountie who was the antithesis of Blakemore. He was thin, almost delicate, with a fair complexion and sporting a perfectly trimmed pencil mustache. His eyes were soft, friendly, thought Montgomery, like someone trying to please. All had turned to observe the arrival of Blakemore and his suspect. Zachary had gone directly to the morgue.

"What took you so long?" Clyde challenged. "We're all done. Just getting ready to take the van back to the firehall."

Blakemore ignored him and spoke to Ernie.

"This is Mr. Montgomery. Were you able to locate his friends?"

"How do you do, sir," said Ernie who, much to Blakemore's annoyance, acknowledged Montgomery first before answering his question.

"Yes, I just contacted Mr. Abelman. He's on his way over."

Damn, thought Blakemore. He was relying on the phone call to give him time to search the Bronco. Before he could form an alternate plan, a man who turned out to be David Abelman threw open the front doors and swept his six foot four inch frame to the reception desk in three great strides. Long strands of salt and pepper hair stuck out from under his British tweed racing hat, which seemed incongruous with the rest of his attire—a plaid hunting jacket, blue jeans, and Sorel boots. His intense, thin face and hawk-like nose gave him a predatory countenance that, to say the least, was intimidating. He appeared blind to everyone there except Montgomery.

"Russell, what in God's name has happened to you? When the officer phoned I was afraid that you had been killed."

Montgomery almost leaped over the counter in his haste to stand beside his saviour. The words spilled from his mouth.

"Dave! You wouldn't believe what I've just gone through. They suspect me of killing some poor bugger I stumbled on up in the hills this afternoon. Jesus, get me out of here!"

Ableman drew himself to his full height, glowering at the two Mounties.

"If that statement is true, gentlemen, you had better do a lot of explaining. First, have you laid any charges against my friend?" He directed the question to Ernie, sensing a weak link there.

"No sir. Of course not, sir. Corporal Blakemore will explain. Go ahead Paul."

Blakemore gathered himself. He noted that the inhalator crew members were showing no signs of leaving. They weren't going to miss the drama. In addition, the expression on Montgomery's face was turning from fear to belligerence, suddenly buoyed up by his large compatriot. The tables were turning.

"That is true. No charges have been laid, but the circumstances are such that Mr. Montgomery is a very plausible suspect and I would think it unwise of him to feel he can ignore that fact. We would request his cooperation in remaining in Bear Creek until we've completed more of our investigation."

"This is absurd. Russell wouldn't hurt a fly."

He doesn't have any problem blasting away a four-point buck though, thought Blakemore.

"Unless you have a court order to detain him," Abelman continued, "I'm taking him back to our motel where he isn't harassed, to let him tell me the whole story."

"This is a murder investigation, and a gruesome one at that," replied Blakemore. "I have the authority to detain Mr. Montgomery if I wish, but I'll give you a break. My office is through that door to your right. There's a private telephone line in there that you're free to use. The coroner at this moment is examining the victim's body, and I'm sure when he is finished there will be a few more questions we'd like to ask your friend. After that, he's free to return to the motel."

Abelman hesitated. He looked at the fear returning in

Montgomery's eyes, and decided that ticking off this cop would be a mistake. After all, he, David Ableman, trial lawyer of some stature, would be present during any questioning. He would have Russell well tutored before that.

"Very well," he said. "I hope that it has been noted how cooperative my client has been."

Blakemore observed the rapid change from the word *friend* to *client*. A lawyer is a lawyer, he thought.

"It has been duly noted, Mr. Counselor. By the way, where is the third member of your group, Mr. Black? I would have thought that his concern for his friend would be as great as yours.

"He hasn't heard any of this yet. He dropped me off at the motel and went for a beer. I wanted to have a nap."

Ernie rounded the counter and opened the office door. Abelman entered, followed by Montgomery who was now regretting his outburst as he glanced back at Blakemore's expressionless face.

As soon as Ernie closed the door, Blakemore turned on his heel and headed out to the Bronco. He paused for a moment to open the morgue door and speak to Zachary.

"Don't get going too far, Doc, I want to be in on your examination. I'll just be a second."

He didn't wait for a reply, but went straight to Montgomery's Bronco. He pulled open the driver's door, released the electric locks, and then opened each door in turn, leaning in to examine every inch. There was nothing of note in the cab—a couple of topographical maps of the area, road maps of the province, flashlight, radar detector, compass, empty potato chip bags, pop cans. In the glove compartment was the registration, which checked with the information that Montgomery had given.

The back was more interesting. The rear seats had been folded down. In the well behind the front seat were a .30-06

hunting rifle and two boxes of 180-grain cartridges. The bolt was forward and the clip was inserted. It was probably loaded.

"Good for a quick citation," he mused.

On the deck created by the folded-down seats was an assortment of travel gear, a spare tire, shovel, jack, tire chains and, neatly folded in a corner, a large plastic tarp. He lifted it and felt his heart leap. Underneath was a large double-bitted axe!

"Well, well and what do we have here?" he said, straining forward to examine the cut surfaces. He was disappointed to see that they were clean with no sign of hair or blood. He turned his attention to the tarp. He unfolded it carefully. It was old, with a few nicks in it, but the greatest revelation was the obvious stains of dried blood on its surface. An attempt had been made to wash off the blood but the creases held the particles quite noticeably in a number of spots.

"This is more like it!" he reveled, taking out his pocketknife. He cut out a two-inch square of the stained area. He saw nothing more on the floor and so refolded the tarp, hiding his knife cut, and placed it back where he found it. It was then that he spotted the rope. It was coiled up behind the spare tire—a yellow poly, with one end cut and the other end heat-sealed. A length had obviously been cut off.

"Do I have the other end, I wonder?" he said, feeling the rush of discovery. He headed back to the morgue.

Zachary was examining the corpse's head, which he had propped up with two sandbags. He jumped when Blakemore burst through the swinging doors.

"Damn it, Paul. You startled me."

"Sorry, Doc, but I need a fast read on this," he said, holding out the piece of tarp. "There's a blood stain on it and I have to know whether it's human or animal. Mr. Montgomery may become a guest in my little jail. Can you do it quick?"

"Taken from the Bronco, no doubt," accused Zachary. Blakemore nodded, showing no remorse.

"As a matter of fact, distinguishing between the two is quite simple. Hold on."

With that, Zachary took the fragment over to a bench where a modern binocular microscope was set up. It took him only a few minutes to transfer flakes of the dried blood onto a glass slide and prepare it for viewing.

"Well?" said Blakemore, impatiently.

"It's not human blood," Zachary replied, staring down the eyepieces. "Probably left over from deer he killed in previous seasons. Your theory just developed a large hole."

"Shit, I'll have to let him go, unless"—and he looked hopefully at the corpse—"our silent friend here has a message on him somewhere. Have you found anything yet?" He decided not to mention the cut rope.

"I haven't done much yet. The head has some interesting features though. Look at the teeth. See that? They're metal implants. All of his natural teeth are gone, probably from an antibiotic resistant infection, and these were put in their place. It costs a fortune to have that done. Most people wear plates. The technique was developed in Germany. A few centres in the States picked it up but the only one I know doing it in Canada is a high-priced dental surgeon in Toronto. There's money in this boy's past somewhere, I can tell you."

Blakemore made a mental note to follow up on this. That kind of money in someone this young either came from doting parents, in which case missing persons would have him listed soon, or from the drug trade. The RCMP "narc" division would help his investigation along that line.

"He's young for sure," Zachary continued. "There are no age lines on what's left of his neck, around the eyes or brow. His

hair is totally blond with no greying. If necessary, though, I can determine his age accurately with X-rays, but why don't you go through his pockets? An ID would save a lot of work."

Blakemore proceeded to do just that. They were empty.

"He's been picked clean. Funny, though. Labels are still on the clothes. The Eddie Bauer coat could have been bought anywhere, but the pants are BC made. I recognize the company. It's a family run business, catering to hunters. Based in Kelowna, I think, but their stuff sells all over the province. Good chance, then, that this is a BC boy."

"Here's something," Zachary called as he continued to examine the head. "I removed the hat and guess what? No 'hat head' indentation of the hair, meaning he wasn't wearing a hat when he was killed. This was put on after. And see this. Bits of tree bark in the hair on the back, and if I'm not mistaken there are fine blue strands as well—from a carpet, I'd guess. See how they spring back? Let's have a look at them under the microscope."

Blakemore bent down to look closely as Zachary extracted a few of the fibres with a pair of forceps.

"Doc, would you get some of that bark too?"

"Why? It's probably from the tree he was pinned to, wouldn't you say?"

"That was a pine tree. Most of that bark looks like alder to me. Where do you suppose that came from? Strange."

Zachary agreed. Under the microscope, Blakemore's suspicion was correct. The bark was alder, not pine. The coloured strands were definitely nylon, from an inexpensive carpet, probably a shag variety.

"Boy! This head sure as hell moved around a lot after it was dead," Paul exclaimed. "Indoors and out. I wish it could still talk. It would be a fascinating story."

He continued to speculate.

"Shag carpet wouldn't be inside a vehicle, unless the body was wrapped in it. Any sign of those blue fibres on his coat and pants?"

A thorough search by them both found none. The bits of bark on the clothing were all pine.

"Reconfirms that it's highly unlikely that he was wearing those clothes when he was killed, eh? It also means that the body was moved from the death site to where it was dressed. I wonder how far apart those points are. Surprising how well everything fits him. Probably his own, wouldn't you say?"

Zachary nodded.

"The alder is puzzling," Blakemore continued. "At some point in the transfer the back of that head went from shag rug to a surface covered with alder bark. There's lots of alder around here but it grows lower down in the river valley. It's kind of a useless tree so far as timber is concerned, but it's a popular firewood. You see stacks of it in anybody's yard who has a woodburner in the house, which is pretty well everybody in Bear Creek. Maybe the body spent some time in a woodshed."

"Give me a hand, will you?" interjected Zachary. "I want to remove the clothing and see if there's any sign of trauma—bullet holes and so forth, and then my real work begins. I must try to accurately estimate a time of death, frozen or not, along with determining the precise cause of death. Those are always at the top of the list when the questions start flying in court."

Getting the clothes off turned out to be much easier than Blakemore expected. Zachary simply worked from the back, using a pair of powerful shears to cut through all the garments, from the neck to the bottom of the spine, then down each of the limbs. Everything came off in one piece. The naked body lay before them.

The victim was indeed young. In fact, if it had not been for

the pubic hair, it could have been the body of a child. There was absolutely no sign of trauma. No bruises, stab wounds, bullet holes, or even needle marks. Both men had looked specifically for the latter, BC being noted for drug-related homicides.

"I'm afraid this is going to be a tough one, Paul," Zachary sighed. "Why don't you leave me to it? I'm going to call an old teacher of mine in Vancouver. He's chief of forensics at the General Hospital and it might be best to ship the body to him, if he'll take it. The cutbacks have hit his department hard and he doesn't have the Telethon raising money for him."

"Okay, Doc. Mr. Lawyer is probably getting impatient. I'll take a set of prints, though. This stiff may have made a mark on the criminal rolls. I'll send them to both the Provincial and Ottawa Bureaus. I should get an answer back pretty quick."

"By the way, Doc," he added. "I'll bet that body and head together don't weigh more than one hundred and twenty pounds. He's short and skinny. Montgomery could have carried him."

With that, Blakemore turned and swept out through the swinging doors.

Chapter 7

Dr. Peter Meuller was finishing up his dictation and looking forward to the weekend. His wife, who was singularly responsible for his precarious sanity these days, had booked two wonderful seats for the opening night of *La Boheme*. Ordinarily, he avoided crowd scenes, preferring instead an intimate dinner at one of their favourite restaurants, but he had gotten hooked on opera as a young man, and this performance was special. Richard Margison, the Victoria-born tenor, was singing the role of Rudolfo, and for Vancouver Opera to persuade him to do it was a coup extraordinaire.

His desk phone rang.

He answered it, only because it was his private line. Probably his wife, he thought, although a few of his selected colleagues had the number. He prayed that it was not one of them. Forensic medicine was not the nine-to-five job that his fellow pathologists enjoyed.

"Hello, Mueller here."

"Dr. Meuller. It's Zachary Benson. I'm terribly sorry to bother you at this late hour on a Friday, but. . . ." The dreaded "but" thought Meuller, although he liked Bensen, remembering him as one of his most intelligent and attentive students. He was disappointed when Zachary chose to go out into the boondocks and do general practice rather than continue in Forensic Medicine. "I need a go at living medicine before I commit myself to the dead," was the reason the young man gave.

"I can really use your help," Zachary began and went on to give a complete summary of the case finishing with, "Is this something that you would be willing to take on?"

"Zachary, it's great to hear from you, but the answer to your question, I'm sorry to say, is a definite no. I'm snowed under here with work and my staff's been cut by 20 per cent. There are times when I even have to do the technicians' jobs, from slide preparation to opening the skull. Besides, I know you can handle this yourself. I'd be pleased to advise you and will do my best to facilitate any lab services that you may need, but, aside from that, I'm afraid that you're on your own."

"I understand completely. In fact, your being unable to take the case actually makes it much easier for me. Any flak that I get from the lawyers can be parried by a built-in excuse. I'm it for this place, so far as forensic opinion is concerned, and they'll have to take it or lump it. Quite frankly, I'm looking forward to the challenge."

"Atta boy!" replied Mueller, relieved. "I admire your attitude—now, a few suggestions."

"Anything you can give me will be gratefully received, I can tell you."

"First, you have no time to lose. For a body, even this small, to freeze through and through would take close to thirty-six hours in a standard chest freezer. Use an electric scalpel to get into the abdominal cavity and check the liver. It would be the last organ to completely freeze. If it hasn't, you know the body was probably in the freezer less than thirty-six hours. You can then use the conventional decomposition factors to accurately calculate the time of death. Second, the cause of death itself must be determined. Poisoning, of course, is to be considered, and for that you know the routine blood samples that need to be taken. When you have them, my lab will do the analysis for you."

"Suffocation," Meuller continued, thinking out loud. "But a young man would have put up a fight unless he was drugged. Better double check for trauma. Is there any sign of a struggle? Any bumps on the head, broken fingernails, and so forth. Get X-rays of the skull and neck. Any fractures? Examine the cut ends of the large veins and arteries of the neck. Be absolutely certain that he didn't bleed to death. If the cuts were done post mortem, there should be full diameter blood clots at the ends. Otherwise, maybe the axe blow really did kill him."

Zachary listened in admiration.

"I'll get right on to it. Once again, my sincere thanks. May I call on you again?"

"Any time, Zachary, and I mean that. Good luck. You can do it. Have confidence. I trained you, remember?"

"Yes sir," said Zachary, surprising himself with his degree of enthusiasm. He hung up the phone and proceeded directly to

his task. He was relieved that Blakemore had not returned. He could concentrate better working on his own.

Chapter 8

Blakemore had a stroke of luck when he returned to the central desk. A large mirror was installed above the front entrance that allowed the duty officer to deal with clients at the desk and yet monitor the jail cell behind him. Just before he crossed in front of the cell, he glimpsed an unwelcome figure in the mirror. Heather McTavish, the pride of the Bear Creek *Bulletin*, was engaged in an animated conversation with Ernie. He jumped back before she saw him.

"Thank God for little mercies," Blakemore muttered under his breath. He quickly backtracked through the rear entrance, around the building, and re-entered by way of a private entrance to his own office. Montgomery and Abelman looked up, startled by his abrupt appearance. He put his finger to his lips to silence them.

"There's trouble for us all out there in the reception area right now," he said, speaking in a hushed voice, "in the form of a particularly aggressive newspaper reporter. She would probably sell her own mother to have her name on this story when it blows."

Montgomery paled.

"Oh no!" he exclaimed. "This could ruin me. I just landed the job in Vancouver and my new company survives on PR. They'll have a shit hemorrhage if my name hits the papers mixed up in this."

"Officer, my client is completely innocent of any wrongdoing here. It's your duty to protect him from any such public exposure," Abelman said, again rising to use the full effect of his height.

Blakemore choked back his anger. It was belligerent behaviour like this that made him dislike the legal profession as a whole, and trial lawyers in particular.

"That, counselor, to put it plainly, is a lot of horseshit. Your client is fair game for the lovely lady out there and so I suggest that you sit down and listen to my proposal."

"Dave, please," Montgomery beseeched. Abelman sat down, his eyes blazing. If it wasn't for Russell, he thought, I'd love to get at this Mountie Dick and tear him to legal shreds. Intimidation was something he used, not suffered.

Blakemore spoke directly to Montgomery, ignoring the lawyer.

"Here's what I want you to do. You're not wise to make the drive to Vancouver tonight, particularly in your present frame of mind. I agree that to ensure your anonymity you need to get out of Bear Creek, and you should do so as quickly as possible. But, I do want one more question session with you when the autopsy is completed and after I've had a chance to recheck the site where the body was found. I plan to be up there early tomorrow morning. If you travel as far as Silverton, less than an hour's easy drive, you can stay there overnight. Do you know the Pancake House on the West Side of town?"

Montgomery nodded.

"I'll meet you there at ten o'clock for a late breakfast. Even at that time it's usually packed so you might want to get there a bit early to reserve a table. No one will pay any attention to our conversation. The noise level is pretty high. You understand that I'm giving you a break here don't you? Don't disappoint me."

"I won't, I promise," Montgomery replied quickly, before Abelman had a chance to speak. "Just let us out of here, please."

"You're free to go."

The frightened man bolted for the door, followed by his

lawyer moving at a more dignified pace and pausing at the threshold to leave with a parting shot: "I hope that we meet in court, Corporal. You'll find that I'm a different kettle of fish there."

A smelly kettle of fish anywhere, thought Blakemore, as he rose and gathered Montgomery's coffee cup, which Ernie had so graciously given him. Might as well send the prints on this to the same place as the stiff, he muttered, pleased with himself.

Heather McTavish possessed an interesting background. Her parents operated a successful dairy farm in the Okanagan, and Heather, the youngest, was their only girl. Three brothers preceded her and they were the reluctant forges of her personality. She was a tiny child but soon discovered that a sharp mind and quick tongue more than leveled the playing field with her brawny siblings. This talent readily converted to the schoolyard and she became, in short, a holy terror. She feared no one. At the age of sixteen, however, her raging hormones took over, and to satisfy her cravings she was forced to sublimate her domineering personality. Adolescent males, she soon realized, seemed to have a "dumb blond nymphomaniac" fantasy, and if that was what it took for mutual gratification she could play that role as well as anyone—despite her red hair. Her staunch Presbyterian parents, however, found this new persona quite intolerable and fought hard to reverse it. Heather ignored the curfews, the dire predictions that she was on a fast track to perdition, and continued to revel in her sinful pleasures. But intolerance eventually won out and so she chose the common solution taken by so many of her contemporaries in a similar situation—she ran off to "the Coast."

Only there a short while, her brain soon regained its fine function, her mouth caught up, and she found herself a leader

in the cause to right the world of all its wrongs. She chose Victoria as her "headquarters" and took part in protests from the Carmanah Valley to the steps of the BC Legislature. Her face appeared with amazing regularity in the newspapers and clips on the six o'clock TV news. It was a good down-on-the-farm face—wholesome and innocent—a poster face for the cause. One of the opposition MLAs (Green Party) saw her attraction and tried to recruit her into conventional politics. Her response was that it was too slow and boring a way to achieve her ends. She was an activist and proud of it.

But at age twenty-one she was burnt out—too much politics, too much back-biting. She left Victoria, headed east, avoiding the Okanagan, where her parents lived (she didn't want that life either) and settled in Bear Creek. Why she stayed there was a mystery. Most likely it was because she met Ethel Roberts, the high school librarian. They literally bumped into one another at the Public Library, an institution dearly loved by each. They got talking about one of their mutually favourite authors, Ernest Hemmingway, and his life as a reporter. Heather liked the image and eventually a position became available at the *Bulletin*.

"If I were younger and more adventurous, I'd jump at that job," Ethel had said with a sigh. "It's ground level, for certain, but oh, it could lead onward and upward."

"I have no qualifications to be a reporter. I've never even been to college," Heather lamented.

"You're bright and obviously well read. Quite frankly, there's no one around here that is qualified either. Most of the paper's existing staff couldn't write their way out of a paper bag. They also have a complete lack of ambition. They haven't changed their style in all the years that I've lived here and that, I'm sad to say, is measured in decades."

Heather was encouraged, and at Ethel's suggestion she wrote a few short essays to serve as a sort of portfolio. Armed with those and a slightly edited version of her years in Victoria, she went for an interview. To her amazement she was hired on the spot.

Over the next few years she proved her worth. Her writing style was eminently readable and somehow she could create a story out of nothing. Her confidence and enthusiasm returned. She, once again, had a passion in life.

This was the personality that faced Blakemore as he stepped out of his office into the reception area. Her outward appearance was disarming. She was cute. There was no other word to describe her. She had a round baby face complete with dimples and the remains of childhood freckles spread in a butterfly pattern over her nose and cheeks. Her body had the curves of a well-developed woman but at four feet eleven, "cute" was the image she projected. From puberty onward she considered this a handicap and perhaps it explained some of her aggressiveness. She wanted to be taken seriously, but people she met seemed to have an inordinate urge to pat her on the head. Blakemore was not one of these. The prep-school girlish appearance did not fool him. He knew how tough a customer she was.

"Corporal Blakemore, how nice of you to drop in," she said sarcastically. "Your partner here has been most informative." Ernie avoided his gaze, suddenly finding something very fascinating on the wall above his head. "I'm a bit disappointed that I had to receive the news of this awful murder from a reliable source at the Whipsaw Creek Store. You must be aware that the citizens of this community deserve to know that there's a maniac loose in the area."

Blakemore simply couldn't understand how this little red-headed dynamo could get his goat so easily, usually within seconds of their meeting. She knew his buttons, and no matter

how he tried to hide them she always found the right one to push.

"Now don't get your back up, Heather. There was no time and, quite frankly, no need to bring the press in on this so early. In my judgement, to do so might even have compromised the investigation."

"Bullshit," she said. "Neither I nor the public are as dumb and irresponsible as you suggest. Now what's transpired so far and where's the chap who found the body? Surely you didn't let him leave. That would raise a serious question of judgement, for sure."

Blakemore shifted, uneasily. Damn this creature. Why should he have to deal with her? After all, he was the law, and she, at best, was a pain in the ass.

"This is a police matter, Heather. I'm in charge and what I say goes. You just want to sell your papers, but my duty is to see that justice is done." He immediately hated himself for that statement. It was weak, defensive, and he knew he was going to pay for it.

"I'll ignore your personal accusation," she countered, "but let me tell you, Mr. RCMP federal police officer, there are some constitutional laws in this country—freedom of information to name a big one. My readers and I have a right to know what's going on, particularly if there's even the slightest danger to our welfare. A crazed killer on the loose is not something to be hushed up."

"I'd drop dead if anything could be hushed up in this town, but okay, okay. What do you want to know that Ernie hasn't already told you?"

"That's more like it," said Heather, moving in for the kill. "First, I want an interview with the hunter who reported the body."

"Sorry, I did let him go. He already has a lawyer who insisted

that I do so. There wasn't enough to lay any charges and so I had no choice. He's long gone, I'm afraid, back home to Vancouver," he lied.

"All right, I'll let that go for the moment."

Blakemore knew that she undoubtedly had Montgomery's name from Ernie and was confident that she could track him down with relative ease.

"Do you have the name of the victim?"

"No. There was nothing on the body."

She hesitated, obviously weighing her next request.

"I'd like to view the body."

"That's completely out of line and you know it," retorted Blakemore, exasperated.

"Maybe not," she returned. "Have you forgotten the composite sketches that I arranged for you when you couldn't get an ID on that runaway kid who drowned in the river last year? You know damn well that the media are your best means to reach someone who can identify the victim. Your photography skills, by the way, are terrible. I have a better camera and know how to use it, particularly to get something that an artist can work from."

He was beaten. It was true that an identification was crucial to his investigation, and trying to get a police artist in Vancouver to do a sketch would be a time-consuming affair. He also had to agree, reluctantly, that he was no Yousef Karsh with the camera.

"It may be too late. Benson has already started the autopsy, but I'll take you to the morgue. A composite is a good idea but it will be an artistic challenge. The face is really distorted. Your artist did a good job last year on the kid, but his face wasn't as damaged."

"Cory Fleming is a talented artist," Heather reassured him. "Don't let the fact that he lives here fool you. A little luck and his work will sell in the big centres, I can tell you."

Chapter 9

Zachary had not gotten to the head when Blakemore and Heather arrived at the morgue. He was just completing his assessment of the frozen liver. He was mildly surprised to see Heather, but once he observed that she was not the least bit fazed by the sights before her he accepted her presence completely. In fact, something inside him lit up when he saw her. Perhaps it was the contrast between the coldness of the morgue and the radiance of a very pretty woman. He had met her only once before, when she interviewed him shortly after his arrival in Bear Creek. He remembered that it was all business on that occasion—free publicity for his practice and a fill-in article for her newspaper. He was amazed that he hadn't noticed her attractiveness then.

"Welcome to my den of horrors, Heather. Nice to see you," he said pleasantly.

She smiled and nodded to him but didn't speak. Her eyes turned to the corpse and its head.

"Okay, Doc," Blakemore interjected grumpily. "What have you found out since I was here?"

"Paul, I'm sad to say that the body is completely frozen, right to the centre of the liver. There will be some decomposition, but in a frozen body it takes place at an extremely slow rate and so the time of death is going to be a very approximate figure."

Heather interjected. "You mean that the victim has been lying out there long enough to freeze solid? That must take a very long time. It hasn't really been that cold over the past month, even up on the hills. Doesn't seem possible," she said.

"We have formed some theories," Blakemore blurted out.

"Which you will share with me, no doubt," she shot back.

"Up to you, Paul," Zachary interjected, watching with amusement the obvious annoyance on Blakemore's face.

"Sorry. All is speculation at the moment, and I don't want any rumours spreading around on that basis," he replied, stubbornly.

She hesitated for a moment, then decided to let him off. She walked over to the bench where Zachary had propped up the head and gazed at it for a full minute. Finally, she spoke.

"The face is distorted, all right, but, you know, there's something familiar about it. A faint bell is ringing at the back of my head."

"You mean you might know this person?" Blakemore exclaimed, incredulously.

"Perhaps, but it's not at the surface right now—maybe when I see Cory Fleming's composite after he straightens out the distortion."

With efficiency born of much practice, she then proceeded to set up her camera and take a series of portraits and profiles of the head.

"What else can you give me here, Doctor Bensen—weight, approximate age, height, etc.?"

"Weight, 122 pounds, height five feet five inches, and age mid twenties, I'd guess. I can be more accurate, of course, when I've done the X-rays."

"Thank you," she said. "I'll have to develop these prints myself and get them over to Cory. He usually goes cross-country skiing on the weekends and so I doubt that he can complete a sketch before Monday afternoon at the earliest. Let's try for Tuesday's edition of the *Bulletin*. See you later." With that, she removed the film from her camera and disappeared out the doors.

"I like her," Zachary remarked. "She's really attractive. Redheads are special."

"She's a bloody bomb," said Blakemore, "looking for a place to explode. I shudder to think what she's going to write in her column tomorrow."

Chapter 10

At precisely 10:05 Saturday morning Blakemore entered the Silverton International House of Pancakes. One full hour combing every inch of the area where the body had been found proved fruitless. He had hoped that Montgomery's tracks might reveal that he was carrying a heavy load, but the snow was not deep enough to use depth of compression measurements.

He spotted the two men drinking coffee in a corner booth. *Two* men. Damn, he thought to himself, where is the third guy? I should have insisted that he be there as well.

"Good morning, Corporal," Abelman said, pre-empting Blakemore's question. "Joe couldn't stay overnight. He had to report to work this morning in Vancouver, but here is his phone number, which I have written on the back of my business card."

Blakemore glanced at the card as he accepted it, noting that Abelman's law firm was situated in the elegant Pacific Bank Building in downtown Vancouver. He removed his heavy parka and the regulation fur hat that few of his fellow officers deigned to wear. He liked it though. It was warm, practical, and radiated an image of the Old Northwest spirit. He ignored the stares of the patrons around him as he sat down beside Montgomery. The latter visibly flinched and crammed himself into the corner of the booth as far away from Blakemore as he could get.

A buxom waitress appeared, having spotted the familiar Mountie as soon as he came in. Her original hair colour was indeterminate, but at the moment she was a blond. Her eyebrows consisted of two garish arcs of ochre that were, in fact, subdued when compared to the screaming crimson lipstick that adorned her large mouth. Her nylon uniform struggled to contain the volume of flesh that threatened to pop the buttons holding it all in. Her age could have been anything from forty-five to

fifty-five, but at one time in her life she probably had more than her share of admirers. Despite the obvious fact that the woman's figure had slipped a bit, her femme fatale confidence showed no sign of waning. Blakemore, as she confided to her fellow waitresses, gave her "a case of the hots" each time he came into the restaurant, and it was understood that no matter where he sat his table was hers.

"What can I getcha, big boy?" she offered, in her best Mae West voice. "Coffee, tea, or me?"

"Coffee, for sure," he replied. "Only Brits and preachers drink tea, and you know you're too much woman for me. I've got to practice on my wife a few more times." A huge grin broke the serious expression he had hoped to maintain for his interrogation.

"Aw, I could be a wonderful teacher for you. Your wife would thank me," she crooned, gently pressing her thigh against his arm.

"Sally, honey, you're making me feel faint. You'd better bring me some food. What's the special this morning?"

"Okay, it's back to business," she said, pretending to be miffed. "The special is two eggs, any style, toast, hash browns, and bacon or ham. Coffee's free. But you know, I can get them to make you something even more special, same price."

"What's that?" he asked, curiosity aroused.

"An oyster omelet. Guaranteed to get your pecker up." She laughed uproariously.

"You are outrageous, Sally, really you are," Blakemore said, fighting for control. "Bring me the regular special, eggs easy over, brown toast, ham, and a large shaker of saltpetre."

"What are you two having?" he said, turning his attention back to his companions at the table.

"We've already eaten," replied Ableman.

"They had a Vancouver breakfast," explained Sally. "Coffee and a muffin each. I feel sorry for their wives." With that she retreated to the kitchen to place her order, her buttocks moving, as Blakemore often described, "like two pigs humping under a blanket."

Abelman quickly brought the atmosphere back to earth.

"All right officer, let's get on with it. Russell and I are busy men with people relying on us. We don't have either the time or the inclination for frivolity this morning."

Blakemore tightened. Okay, it's time for hardball.

"Very well. First, then, where does Joe Black think he's getting off by leaving the vicinity of a murder investigation? As a fireman he should be aware of his duty under these circumstances. If this was an arson case, and he was officer-in-charge, I'm damn sure he wouldn't allow anyone to bugger off if they might have pertinent information. I have half a mind to phone his superiors and have his ass kicked straight back up here."

He heard Montgomery gulp, but focussed his gaze directly at Abelman. The lawyer shrugged, returning Paul's gaze with an insolent smile.

"Joe Black is a captain in the Vancouver Fire Department. Relatively speaking, he outranks you by a considerable degree. I doubt that your phone call would create much in the way of ass kicking. If anything, you might find yourself protecting your own rear. Now, I repeat, let's stop wasting time and get this over with."

Paul was stymied. In truth, he didn't have any great searching questions for Montgomery and he was tired of dealing with this arrogant son-of-a-bitch lawyer. He decided to be honest and a bit of a son of a bitch himself.

"Actually, I don't think that Mr. Montgomery here is likely to give me any more useful information at this time. I am

disappointed that Mr. Black chose to leave prematurely, but it may be better after all to interview him privately. You're free to go, then."

Out of the corner of his eye, he saw Montgomery beam. Abelman exploded.

"What? You mean you have delayed us, caused my client unnecessary stress, expense, and this is all that you have to say? I think that if there is to be any conversation with superiors it will be me to yours. Russell, we are leaving right now. I'm sure the RCMP will cover the breakfast tab, at least."

"You're cheap dates. Two coffees, two muffins. No problem. I'll pay for it out of pocket. Won't even ask for reimbursement. You're my guests."

He pulled himself out of the booth to let Montgomery go and watched them disappear out the front door. He slid back in and waited for Sally to return.

Chapter 11

Saturday, under normal circumstances, was almost a day of rest for Zachary, unless he had an expectant mother on the go. The evening before, he and Blakemore had left the morgue shortly after Heather. He was too exhausted to continue the post mortem, and by then Blakemore was long overdue at home for his wife's supper. Zachary, as her personal physician, knew she had forgone her monthly trip to Vancouver this weekend in a deliberate attempt to find some time when she might be able to have some meaningful communication with her husband. He, in turn, had promised not to go hunting. Zachary was treating her for depression and was only too aware of the problems in the Blakemore household. This dinner was special, he knew, because she had discussed it with him at the last counselling

session in his office. In fact, she had asked him what he felt was the best way to approach her husband. He cursed himself for not reminding Blakemore to leave sooner. There were no messages on his answering machine, however, and if the evening had been a total disaster she most likely would have called. He decided to leave well enough alone and not call her. She did have another session booked for the coming week. He also fully expected that Blakemore would be contacting him soon to push for autopsy results.

Reluctantly, he drained the last of his cappuccino (made in a decadent machine that cost him more than three hundred dollars), put aside the Toronto *Globe and Mail* crossword that he used to jump start his brain every morning, and got ready to return to the body in the morgue.

He was feeling strangely down this day and, driving the short distance to the police station, he began to ruminate. He was twenty-seven years old and from the age of eighteen he had been totally immersed in Medicine—pre-med, medical school, internship, and now general practice. His childhood was a happy one, his high-school years filled with the usual adolescent girl-chasing, underage drinking, pot-smoking, and general hell-raising, but Medicine had turned him into a workaholic, fixated individual. Everything was clinical now—even his speech, which for the most part was controlled, scientific, and deliberate. He was dismayed to realize that in the entire year he had been in Bear Creek he hadn't made a single close friend. Yes, there was the banter with colleagues, hospital personnel, and the Mounties, but other than the "meet the new doctor" night when he first arrived, social occasions were few and far between. I know I have been working day and night, he conceded to himself, but that can't explain it all. People perceive me as a medical machine, he reasoned, not a person. That's not fair, but it's my

own doing. Look at Blakemore. He's been accepted so well and he's a bloody cop with twice the social hurdles that I, the *doctor*, should have. He vowed to change, to loosen up and find himself some life outside his profession. If he did not, he knew the risk of depression was a real one. Too many of his overworked colleagues suffered from that disease—some fatally.

He was still deep in thought when, two blocks from the station, he spotted Heather McTavish. She was seated at a table by the window in Keats' Korner, a tiny bistro-book store that served remarkably good coffee and was a hang out for what Bear Creek had in the way of a literary crowd. He parked his car in front and went inside. This morning he was pleased to see that there was no crowd. She was alone, intently reading a newspaper, a coffee cup at her side.

She didn't notice him until he stood beside her and spoke.

"I see you have the same morning addictions as me. Coffee and a crossword puzzle," he said.

She looked up, pencil poised.

"Well, good morning to you Dr. Benson," she said with a smile that he felt all the way to his groin.

"Yes, I hate to give up on this but I'm stumped on one last word. It has six letters. The clue is, 'I return in a lost vase, doctor examined.' Perhaps the answer is a medical term. What do you think? I'll buy you a coffee if you can solve it."

He leaned over her shoulder to see the word in question and breathed in the fragrance that emanated from her hair. It shone like the finest red silk.

"I'll accept the challenge, only because I want to join you. You've just about solved it yourself and you're right, it is a medical term. Look. You only have four letters to fill in:_E_ _N_ . *Urn* is another word for vase and so if you 'lose' it from the word *return* see what is left: ret. Add *in a* and there's the

word. Also, cute hint on the *I* for an *eye*, don't you think?

She saw the solution immediately.

"R-E-T-I-N-A. Retina, of course. Part of the eye. I really should have gotten that, but a deal's a deal."

"Wendy," she called to a dark-haired girl behind the counter. "Bring Dr. Benson a latte and put it on my tab." She motioned for him to have a seat beside her.

"I think the milk neutralizes any ill effects of the coffee. Don't you agree?"

He looked into her eyes. They were an extraordinary emerald green and twinkled now with mischief. She was obviously baiting his medical discipline. He quickly squelched the biochemical arguments that were forming in his mind.

"If that helps to explain why you're so beautiful, I'd be the last person to argue the fact."

She had no control over the blush that sprang to her face.

"That's a remarkable riposte for a lazy Saturday morning, Dr. Benson. Are you always so quick-witted?" she laughed.

"You're being kind. That was a totally corny remark and I wanted to make a good impression. Please call me Zach. I really enjoyed your visit yesterday. Paul's quite a guy, isn't he?"

"I have to agree with that," she said, rolling her eyes.

Zachary chuckled.

"You know," he continued, "I really haven't made an effort to socialize since I came here. In fact, if truth be known, my social life has been non existent for years. I'm out of practice, no pun intended. That's my excuse for being so gauche, but I might as well put both feet in by asking you out for dinner tonight. What do you say?"

Heather was torn. Zachary was a handsome man and she'd always had a soft spot for the self-deprecating approach, but she wasn't sure whether she was ready for this. She loved

her work and so far had not really missed the role of sexual partner since she left the Coast. She had to admit, though, that her social life, unrelated to her work, consisted almost entirely of long conversations with Ethel Roberts and the denizens of Keats' Korner. Why not, she thought. Might be good for me and, besides, I could really get the inside scoop on the autopsy findings.

"Cory Fleming has gone away for the weekend. I was going to grab a burger and watch him work on the composite this evening, but that's off, so I'm free. Where shall we go? Want to start the tongues wagging in Bear Creek, or would you like to make the drive up to Nelson? The Chateau de La Femme, I've heard, does a marvelous rack of venison. You're not a vegetarian are you?" she said, with mock concern.

"No. I grew up in northern BC. Moose and venison were staples for my family. I love the taste of wild meat. Nelson's fine, although I never worry about the gossips. That's all part of small town life and for the most part is pretty harmless. I don't plan to work past six o'clock at the morgue. I'll make reservations for eight o'clock. Shall I pick you up at seven? It's about a forty-five minute drive."

Chapter 12

When he arrived back in Bear Creek from Silverton, Blakemore headed straight to the Rod and Gun Club. His futile search for clues at the crime site and the essentially useless meeting with Montgomery and Abelman had not affected his good mood. Last night had started out as a disaster. He was an hour late. Barbara had the table set with their best wedding china and crystal. There was a magnificent flower arrangement for a centerpiece and the red wine was breathing in a carafe. The

roast, however, was overdone and the vegetables were turning to mush—all because of his lateness. She was in tears. He felt a wave of remorse pass over him with an intensity of emotion that he hadn't felt for years. She had worked so hard to make this dinner a success and he, the supreme asshole, had spoiled it. To his astonishment his eyes filled with tears, and that was enough. They dissolved in one another's arms as Blakemore croaked apologies and made promises he hoped he could keep. They stayed up well into the night, baring their souls, and restating their mutual love. He described the murder case and told her it could be an opportunity for advancement if he could solve it. The hope in her eyes gave him a twinge of guilt, but the way he was feeling at that moment made him resolve to make amends for her misery.

Morning light, however, brought back a degree of sobriety, at least on his part. Barbara, as usual, was up early. Saturday was her volunteer day at the hospital gift shop and she had to pick up the flowers from the wholesaler's before the shop opened. The weekend was when the most sales were made and she took particular pride in doing up the totals at the end of the day. Her shift almost always beat out the rest of the week, even the Sunday group. The only downside of her hospital auxiliary work was the age of her fellow volunteers. They were all much older than she was. Most of the younger women in the town, it seemed, were mothers involved in child-related activities—lessons, sports teams, and the like. They were definitely not into hospital volunteering. She envied her husband's ability to fit into the community so well, but no matter how hard she tried she really did not feel at home in this town. But Paul's news of the murder case, and the possibility it might lead to a promotion, had really buoyed her spirits, and so it was with a light heart that she kissed him goodbye before she headed out.

Chapter 13

As Blakemore pulled the cruiser into the Gun Club he was disappointed to see that Ernie was not there. Although it was true that Ernie was off-duty on the weekend, he had agreed to attend a Saturday morning "shoot." Blakemore reasoned that the members of the Bear Creek Gun Club were the conservative backbone of the community and he wanted the RCMP presence to form some sort of bond with them. This bond had paid off in other postings and he wanted the same here. He would speak to his junior later.

"Hey Paul! You gonna shoot some trap today or are you just going to fire off that horse pistol of yours?" Clyde Groat's familiar voice taunted him from the shooters' shed.

"Bet your ass I am. Brought my Browning beauty. Got a new choke that's going to give me ten out of ten every time," he shot back.

"Ain't the machine, Paul, it's the operator. No fancy choke's going to beat reflexes and a shooter's eye," Clyde countered.

"We'll see," said Blakemore as he pulled the shotgun from its case, removed the trigger-lock, gathered his box of number eight shot shells, and proceeded to the club house veranda where there was a long row of guns propped up in the rack. He added his to the others.

"Who's the range warden today?" he asked the group already assembled.

"Karl Rienhart," one of the members replied.

He liked Rienhart, and since Karl was a member of the inhalator crew they came in contact often. Blakemore admired the cool efficiency that Karl displayed even in the worst of crises. He also appreciated the way he ran the shoots at the club. He brooked no deviation from the rules so the shooters could

feel safe on the firing line and going forward to retrieve their targets. He was ex-military brass, retiring here instead of to the Coast. That in itself was unusual, but unlike most officer retirees who tend to retain their self-serving officiousness, he chose community service instead. If he had any residual desire to give orders, his position as senior First Responder with the Volunteer Fire Department gave him many opportunities. People listened to Karl with respect, not antipathy.

At that moment, Karl stepped onto the veranda and announced that the trap shoot was to commence. He was hatless despite the cool air, and with his silver hair cut in a neat brushcut, ram-rod posture, and commanding voice, one could easily imagine the image of him addressing the troops. One of the members' sons scurried out to the bunker housing the trap-launching apparatus and disappeared down the steps, pulling down the "hold fire" flag when he was ready. Blakemore had to hurry since he was listed as one of the first five to compete on the line. He jammed ten shells into his pocket and took his position. Karl, who stood at the rail of the veranda directing the competitors, clipboard in hand, had called out his number—"Blakemore, station five."

"Damn," he said, catching his breath. "No time to steady the nerves today."

"Tough shit," countered Clyde who was also in the first five. "Makes for a level playing field—you with your secret weapon and all."

Before Blakemore could respond, the number one shooter shouted "Pull!" The red phosphorescent clay disc appeared in a flash, arcing straight away from the bunker. A second later, a loud boom resounded and the target shattered in the air, pieces flying in all directions. "Pull!" came again from the second station, and again a hit. Clyde Groat, occupying station three, had a tough shot as the red clay streaked sideways, requiring a wide swing of

the gun's muzzle, but he got it with ease. Number four was a miss and a curse from the shooter.

Blakemore delayed for a second, giving himself time to draw a breath and focus his concentration on the front edge of the blockhouse where the clay pigeon would first emerge. His problem in the past had been the use of a full choke, which constricted the spread of the pellets until they had traveled a considerable distance. He had a tendency to pull the trigger quickly, and unless he was on the target perfectly the wad of pellets would simply pass by the target. With his new choke screwed into his gun, the spread was rapid, right from the muzzle—but if he didn't pull the trigger quickly enough, the spread would be too great to break the clay farther out. He had to take the pigeon just off the top of the bunker.

"Pull!" he bellowed. The bird flew straight away from him, the easiest of shots. He got it, watching it explode in a shower of red fragments. He tried not to sneak a peak at Clyde, although he knew that his hit had registered.

His success continued. He broke both clays from each of the five positions, for a perfect score of ten. Clyde, to Blakemore's dismay, equaled his feat. Tiebreakers involved alternate shots by the finalists, taken at progressively longer distances from the bunker. His heart sank. The distance would do him in because of the pellet spread, and he dare not change the choke.

Clyde beat him on the very first extra target.

"Good try, Paul," Clyde said, condescendingly. "You really are improving."

"Go f— yourself," replied Blakemore, ever the good loser.

The rest of the morning went on like that, with Clyde winning all of the trap shoots, but Blakemore, as usual, had no difficulty reigning supreme in the target pistol events. The satisfaction, though, was not there. Pistol shooting was too much like his

job—a routine that he had long since mastered. Trap, however, was a challenge, and he wouldn't be satisfied until he won that as well. Beating Clyde would be the icing on the cake.

It was a strict club rule that no alcohol was allowed on the premises at any time during or after a shoot. When the day's events were over, most of the members left to carry on the camaraderie in the Bear Creek Legion (open to veterans or anyone who even knew a veteran). Clyde had drawn weekend call for the inhalator and so stayed with Blakemore at the club to help Karl close up and drink the last of the coffee that had been provided.

"How's the murder investigation proceeding?" Clyde asked him as they leaned back in the seedy lounge chairs that were arranged around the oil stove in the centre of the tiny club house.

"Any suspects yet?" added Karl, who was filing away the results of the day's competitions. "You really don't think that hunter from Vancouver did it, do you? He looked like a pussycat to me—scared to death when you gave him the lecture."

"Can't rule him out completely," said Blakemore. "As I told the Doc, you can't tell a killer for sure by his looks. We haven't got an ID yet on the victim. I have a feeling that that'll be a huge step in solving the case. Heather McTavish is getting a composite done that'll get on to the newswires early next week. Hopefully we'll get an answer soon after that."

"Heather McTavish!" exclaimed Clyde. "You must be desperate. I thought you avoided her like the plague."

"I usually do, but she is a pipeline to the news media and I've got to be practical. 'Be resourceful' is one of The Force's commandments and I always go with the Force."

"Sure you do," said Clyde with a laugh, turning to Karl. "What do you think, Karl. Do we have Corporal Do-right in Bear Creek or no?"

Karl grinned. He wasn't going to get between these two. He remained neutral.

Blakemore's rebuttal was cut short by the sound of Clyde's pager. His own radio sounded a moment later. It was dispatch from Nelson, which took over on the weekends when the Bear Creek RCMP office was closed.

"Code 12. Corporal Blakemore, Bear Creek. Code 12. Do you copy?" The voice blared from the portable unit on his hip. Code 12 meant a fire with human life involved.

"Blakemore here. I copy. What is the location?"

"Report of an explosion and fire at lot twenty-five, Merryweather Drive. Fire unit has been dispatched from Bear Creek VFD."

"That's Ethel Roberts's place," interjected Clyde. "Christ! Let's go. George has station duty today so he'll already be on the scene with the truck. We can go straight there."

All three men bolted from the room, Karl pausing momentarily to lock the clubhouse door. Blakemore switched on his siren and sped off, Clyde and Karl right behind him.

A full block away from the house they could see the flames. Blakemore vaguely remembered that Ethel lived in a small house situated on a large, treed lot at the very edge of the forest. He knew, too, that flames of that intensity meant the home was no more.

George was there, standing helplessly in front of the inhalator van. The pumper truck was pulled onto the sidewalk in front. Three firemen struggled to direct a stream of water from the single hose onto the flames. It was a futile task. There was a large hole in the roof of the one-story structure and through this, like a Roman candle, shot the greatest intensity of the heat and the fire. It reminded Blakemore of the "burning schoolhouse" fireworks that were so popular at his childhood Halloweens. Fortunately,

the huge trees that surrounded the house were larches. Being the only species of coniferous softwoods that shed their needles in the winter, they were not as likely to "crown fire" as the firs and pines. The firemen were watching them, however, occasionally directing short bursts of water in their direction.

"It was over before we got here," George said, as Blakemore, then Clyde and finally Karl, rushed towards him.

"Must have been her propane heater that went up," he continued. "I understand from neighbours that she had a small back-up unit in her crawl space in case the power went out to her electric heaters."

"Is she in there?" a soft voice spoke behind them.

The men turned. Heather McTavish stood there, her red hair reflecting the light from the fire contrasted sharply with the pallor of her face.

"We think so, Heather," answered George. "We checked and no one saw her leave the house this morning. She's not at the library and she was expected there at twelve-thirty. Apparently she does a children's story telling session from one to two o'clock every Saturday."

"Yes she does and she wouldn't miss it," Heather said, tears welling up in her eyes. Her shoulders sagged and she began to sob.

The men, uncomfortable, looked down, not knowing what to do. Except for Karl who stepped forward, put his arm around her, and spoke gently.

"Heather, we know how much Ethel meant to you. This must be a terrible shock. We have to stay here because we're all on duty and we'll bring her body out if she's in there. But is there someone we can we call for you? Reverend Hutchings? Someone from the *Bulletin*?"

"No," she said, struggling for composure. "I want to wait

here until we're sure. Please carry on with your work. I'll be all right." Please God, she thought, let this be a nightmare and Ethel be safe somewhere.

She watched in horror as the fire peaked, then ebbed as the wooden skeleton collapsed and the firemen's hoses began to take effect. Steam replaced flame and finally Clyde, now in full gear, gave commands.

"Okay, George, you and I are going in. Watch the floor. We may have to cut our way through. There's no basement, thank god, just a crawl space, but be careful."

They donned their helmets and Karl helped them on with their air tanks, turning the valves when they clicked the face-shields down. Clyde led the way, wielding an axe; George followed carrying a fire extinguisher. They entered the pall of smoke, their yellow forms moving like ghosts.

Firemen, thought Blakemore, even volunteers like these, are something else when the crunch is on. They're like well-trained soldiers going over the top, seemingly oblivious to the danger, resolute, their weapons ready for the fight.

Brief flashes of yellow, the sound of axe smashing wood, and the intermittent hiss of the fire extinguisher were the only signs of the men's progress as the onlookers squinted to see.

To Heather it seemed like an eternity, but in truth it was less than fifteen minutes when they emerged and made their way back to the pumper truck. She knew, even before Clyde removed his helmet and spoke directly to her. Despite the bulky suit, his body language was obvious.

"I'm sorry, Heather," he said.

She closed her eyes and bowed her head for a moment, then straightened with a sense of purpose reflected in her tear-filled eyes.

"I'm going back to the *Bulletin*. Ethel's going to have the best

obituary that's ever been written in this place. She was my best friend and I'm going to make sure that everyone knows what a great lady they had living in their community."

"I don't need anyone to drive me. I have my car and you're all needed here," she added, pre-empting their offers.

Chapter 14

Zachary leaned back and stretched. Two hours of bending over the corpse, examining, collecting his samples, and wracking his brain for the truth in this case had left him exhausted. There were few things that he knew for certain. The clots at the ends of the blood vessels were full diameter and so there was no doubt that the head had been cut off after death. Normally a strong reflex spasm is nature's attempt to prevent blood loss from the ends of severed veins and this was especially true of the more muscled arteries, making for compressed clots. There was not the slightest sign of struggle. No bruising, nothing under the fingernails (surprisingly well manicured), and no needle marks. When he had opened the chest and abdominal cavities he found no internal bleeding or contusion. The organs were all typical of a healthy young man. His examination of the brain cavity would have to wait until X-rays for fractures were done, but he could not feel any bumps or see any lacerations. If I could ignore the severed head, he said to himself, this is one of the healthiest and most peaceful corpses I've seen lately.

He reached for the phone to arrange for the X-rays. The morgue at the police station did not have that facility and so these had to be done at the hospital. It rang just as he went to pick it up, startling him.

"Dr. Benson, this is Mary at the hospital. A terrible thing has happened. Ethel Roberts burned to death in her home just after

lunch today. They'll be bringing you her remains when they have the fire out. Clyde asked me to track you down."

"My God!" he exclaimed. "How did it happen? Is anyone else hurt? Should I come to the hospital?"

"There was talk of a propane tank explosion, but I don't think anyone knows for sure. No word of anyone else injured. I gather it was too late to do anything more than just dump water on the flames. No one was rushing in to save her; it was that far gone. Are you going to stay at the morgue? I have no idea when they'll be able to get the body out. I don't think it'll be soon."

"No. I'm going to find Heather McTavish. She'll be taking this hard. But keep in touch with me. I've got my pager on. When you hear that Ethel's body is in transit, I'll come back here to the morgue."

Chapter 15

Heather tried to focus on her computer screen but was blinded by tears. Memories of Ethel tumbled through her mind. They had so much in common and they could fill the many evenings over tea and cakes with conversations that never lagged. Literature, the environment, travel, human behaviour, the mystical and the mundane—they reveled in expressing and listening to each other's views. She was my dearest friend, Heather lamented. She lifted the clouds from my mind and I feel lost without her. What will I do?

She barely felt Zachary's touch on her shoulder. She had not heard him come into the office. When he spoke there was such a depth of feeling and understanding in his voice that she knew she would be all right.

"I'm no substitute for her, Heather," he said, "but you need a friend right now and I want to be that person. Let me take you

home. Tomorrow is soon enough for you to write Monday's articles."

He gently took her arm. They went in his car to her apartment and there she poured out her grief. Zachary was well aware that talking is the best therapy in these situations and skillfully encouraged her to release her feelings. It worked. Heather actually began to feel better to the point where she agreed to his suggestion that they keep their dinner date that evening.

"We'll hold our own personal wake for Ethel," he said. "I know she would have approved. I'll finish all my chores this afternoon and pick you up at seven. Your car is safe at the *Bulletin* office. We'll pick it up later."

He had barely reached his car when the pager beeped. He drove directly to the morgue. George and Clyde were already there, unloading their grisly cargo.

"We found her on what was left of her chesterfield," Clyde said as they carried her body into the morgue. "She must have been napping. Funny though—you'd think the explosion would have wakened her or at least thrown her body into a corner somewhere. It's usually a drunk smoker we find lying on a couch like this. Ethel sure as hell wasn't in that category."

"The frame and seat straps of the chesterfield were steel, so we just lifted her with that," explained George. "We thought it would make it easier for you too, Doc."

"Thanks, George," replied Zachary. "It does, but I've got a favour to ask. Would you wait here until I've done a quick examination of the remains. We'll need X-rays to have absolute proof of her identity. She likely had her dental work done by Dr. Thompson or his partner. I'll ask for her films to be sent over to the hospital. You could take her as well as our hunter in one trip."

"No problem," said George. "I'll stay. No one's waiting at

home for me. Why don't you go Clyde? Doc and I can move everything OK."

"Might as well," agreed Clyde. Despite his position, death and bodies upset him. He left with no reluctance. George retired to the waiting room of the RCMP office where Ernie was manning the desk. Ernie had the same distaste for the morbid as Clyde and he avoided the morgue as much as much as he could. He preferred to simply read the autopsy reports.

Zachary was masked, gowned, and gloved when he removed the improvised plastic body bag that covered Ethel's remains. He had seen many burned victims in his training and so went quickly to his examination. The body was not totally charred as he had expected. The firemen's water barrage had preserved a surprising amount of flesh. There were even some intact portions of her clothing along her back. Zachary recognized the bright flower design of her library smock. He agreed that it was odd she would have lain down after dressing for her reading session. He found nothing else untoward, however, and thought to himself that he'd examined two bodies now that died violent deaths and yet showed no signs of struggle.

Chapter 16

Blakemore was delighted. On the way back to the station from the fire he spotted Cory Fleming filling his car at the Texaco service station. He drove the cruiser into the bay beside him.

"Hey, Cory. Has Heather spoken to you yet about our new stiff?"

"No," he replied, quizzically. "I was planning to be away over the weekend, but the damn car broke down. I've been over at my brother's place fixing it for the last two days. What's up?"

"Go home and get your paints. I've got a high paying

government job for you. We need a composite like the one you did on the drowned kid last year. The corpus is in the morgue. I'll wait for you there." With that he put the cruiser into gear and sped off, leaving Cory no chance to respond.

I'll show Ms. Carrot-top some police efficiency, he gloated to himself, mindless of her recent trauma.

He was not happy to discover Zachary's arrangements to move the bodies to the hospital.

"Leave the head with me," he pleaded. "I'll bring it up myself later."

"You know that's totally against regulations, Paul," retorted Zachary.

"But this is a much better place for the artist to work. The hospital is too distracting for him."

"The morgue there is just as quiet as this one, but rather than have Cory Fleming running all over the place, I'll acquiesce this once. But God help you if you do anything other than just expose the face for him. I don't want anything altered."

"Jeez, Doc," whined Blakemore. "Do you think I'm a total idiot? I wouldn't tamper with evidence."

Zachary softened. "I know you wouldn't, Paul, but please be careful. My neck is the one that goes in the sling if there's a screw-up."

"No fear, Doc," said Blakemore brightly. "I'll look after this head as good as my own." Somehow that was not encouraging to Zachary.

Chapter 17

Sunday was a workday for Heather Mctavish. The *Bulletin* published Monday through Saturday, and so Sunday was spent dealing with the accumulation of two days' news as well as the

weddings, socials, sporting events, and so forth that took place on the weekend. Ethel's death was to be the front-page feature and she would persuade the editor to print a blow-up of one of Heather's favourite photos of her. Her mind was clear and her focus sharp. Zachary's kindness and what turned out to be a memorable dinner were exactly what she needed to get on with life and duty. Although she had dominated 99 per cent of the conversation, Zachary's presence was comforting. Perhaps there could be a relationship there, but at the moment she was all business. Blakemore's arrival, triumphantly waving a folder containing Cory Fleming's composite drawing, was not a welcome intrusion.

"Got something for you here, little lady," he said, grinning like the proverbial Cheshire cat.

"Thought I'd just facilitate things a bit. I got 'hold of your artist friend yesterday and persuaded him to do a rush job on the composite. I suggest you stick it on the front page, blown up and all that."

"Fuck off," she said. "Ethel Roberts is going on the front page. Why don't you go and get a thousand Xeroxes of your picture and hand them out yourself on a street corner?"

"Now, now, Heather. No need to get crude. I know Ethel was your friend, but I'm just trying to do my job. You put the picture where you want, but I would appreciate it being in tomorrow's paper. Leads cool off fast and I really want to solve this case."

"All right," she answered, only partially mollified. "Leave it on my desk and I'll deal with it. Now bugger off and let me get back to my job."

He left, slightly miffed, although he knew that Heather would be certain to feature the photo, even if it was not on the front page.

Sunday duty was normally light except for the odd traffic

accident. He usually filled the day by catching up on paper work in the office, leaving the last hour before supper to catch a few speeders in his radar trap. With the homicide and Ethel Roberts's death, the paperwork today was going to be considerable. Resigned, he headed to the station, although he really wanted to go over to the hospital and see what Zachary was up to with his X-rays. He had returned the head as promised and was amused at Zachary's undisguised relief when he handed it over.

The phone was ringing when he unlocked the door to the station. Must be Barb, he thought. Citizen calls on the weekend were all funneled through central RCMP dispatch in Nelson, which in turn contacted him on his portable radio. He was surprised to find that the caller was Heather McTavish.

"Paul," she said, obviously excited. "I've just looked at Cory's drawing. I recognize the man. I crossed paths with him a few years ago in Victoria. At the time he was an environmentalist of the most fanatic variety. I knew him only as Dietmar. He was German and had a small group of devotees that would have fit in well in any terrorist organization. He was highly educated, articulate, but in the opinion of the larger, more moderate group that I belonged to, he was a loose cannon that would eventually harm our movement. We had a brief meeting with him in an attempt to tone him down, but he rebuked us saying that pacifism never won a war. He and his group were responsible for most of the tree-spiking and the vandalism of forestry equipment. I believe that he was a student at the University of Victoria, but I have no idea what he studied or where he lived. I do know that he spent most of the summers in the forests and existed like a guerrilla fighter in wartime, moving clandestinely from district to district."

Blakemore couldn't contain his excitement.

"That's terrific, Heather. Keep thinking about him. Are you

sure you didn't hear his last name or the names of any of his friends?"

"No. I've tried to remember. In fact, I think that he deliberately tried to conceal his last name for whatever reason. None of his cohorts volunteered any personal information. I tell you they were just like any underground organization—secretive and dangerous."

"People like that get noticed, whether they like it or not, Heather. Authority and the law have a way of marking them and sooner or later they turn up in active dossiers. Tomorrow I'll send the composite and the name Dietmar to RCMP Vancouver. They'll patch it around the world. I'll bet you we have a full ID on our corpse within a couple of weeks."

His estimate was wrong. It took exactly forty-eight hours.

Chapter 18

On Monday, Ernie was back to work. He was the first to arrive at the station, as usual. He liked to be well-ensconced in paper-work when Blakemore came in. They had been partners for two years now and Ernie blessed the happenstance that brought them together. His previous postings right from the academy had all been unhappy ones. The rumours about him were true. He hated being a policeman and became one only to please his father. It was also true that Ernie was gay, a fact he discovered late in his teens. Academically, the RCMP curriculum was no problem, and physically, thanks to his father's insistence that he be active in team sports, he could keep up with the best of the recruits. But his heart was not in any of it and he became a loner. He spent his spare moments in basic training listening to classical music and honing his considerable artistic talent by finding subjects to sketch in the barren Regina environs. Needless to say, this

alienated him from his contemporaries who were, for the most part, gung ho, testosterone-hyped, go-gettum jocks using their time off for beer nights, golf, pick-up hockey games, and the like. In short, Ernie eschewed this male bonding and in doing so paid the price. He suffered hazing and eventually ostracism, making him bitter and chronically depressed. With the low self-esteem that came with this, he had little self-confidence and lived each day with fear that he would screw up and tarnish the family name. His father was two thousand miles away in Kingston, but Ernie felt his influence as though he were standing beside him.

Blakemore was a huge surprise. When they first met, Ernie perceived that his new partner would be a carbon copy of the officers he had worked with before. To his astonishment, Blakemore simply overlooked his weaknesses, and from day one they were a well-knit team. He was still unhappy being a Mountie, but working with Blakemore eased his chronic depression and the dread of facing each workday.

He was worried, though, about his failure to show up at the Saturday Gun Club shoot. He had concocted an excuse but he knew that Blakemore would see right through it. He had planned to go and would have if it weren't for Jim. Friday night at the cabin had been special and they couldn't bear to part the next morning. They had found one another, he and Jim, last summer at the Banff School of Fine Arts where they were both enrolled in three-week courses—Ernie in free design and Jim in playwriting. Jim lived in Nelson, working in his father's sporting goods store. Their lives were so similar from youth to adulthood that they bonded instantly. It was the lakefront cottage, owned by Jim's parents, that gave them a sanctuary to be together. The Gun Club commitment, unfortunately, was no competition.

When Blakemore wheeled in just before nine, however, he had only the hunter case on his mind. He brought Ernie up to

date on the events of the weekend, showing him the copy he had made of Cory Fleming's drawing.

"Ernie, old buddy, I want you to do your magic with your scanner. This and the fingerprints need to be sent to Ottawa. Ask for them to be run through Canadian files but be sure they patch everything through to Interpol as well. Vancouver will want a copy of all reports as well as the composite, but hold off on that till tomorrow, will you? I want the results sent directly here first. Use your way with words to convince them, eh? We've got a major breakthrough here and we deserve first crack at it. Can you do it?"

Ernie didn't want to argue and disrupt all the good vibes.

"No problem," he answered, "using that piece of computer junk, as you called it. Remember you wanted to send it back to Central Supply in exchange for a better office chair?"

"I know, I know," admitted Blakemore. "I've been wrong before, although I can't remember when; it was so long ago."

Ernie took the sketch over to the computer while Blakemore went to his office to fetch the prints he had taken from the hunter. The ones from the coffee mugs could go later. Dietmar was the top priority and he wasn't going to risk some clerk confusing the two.

The day went quickly for both officers. Blakemore, like it or not, had to catch up on his reports before he started forgetting details. Mercifully, there were few interruptions—rare for a Monday. Ernie handled most of them over the phone or at the desk. It was almost as though Ethel Roberts's death had subdued everyone, putting minor annoyances and infractions in perspective.

Blakemore left messages at the hospital and Zachary's office for him to call, but he knew that Monday for a general practitioner was generally the busiest day of the week and so he didn't really expect a return call until late. He did hope that Zachary would

be able to read the stack of tissue slides that he prepared over the weekend. The time of death would be another big step forward. The blood samples for poisoning, drugs, and so forth wouldn't even arrive at Meuller's lab until early Tuesday. He had no idea how long it would take to analyze them.

By quarter to twelve, his grumbling stomach was too much. He contemplated taking Ernie to lunch. He hadn't forgotten his not showing up at the Gun Club and knew there must have been a very good reason why. Ernie usually was a man of his word. He had noticed a subtle change in his partner since the summer holidays. He no longer dropped by the Blakemore home on the weekends—a disappointment to Barbara who enjoyed his company.

Blakemore came to a decision.

"Hey, Ernie," he called down the hall. "Let's do lunch together today. I know you brought your carrot sticks in a bag, but I'm buying, so how about it? We'll put the 'gone fishing' sign on the door."

Ernie's heart skipped a beat. He sensed "let's talk" in the offing but couldn't think of a plausible reason to refuse.

"Okay," he lied. "That would be a nice change." In truth, the idea of a "heart to heart" with Blakemore was not something he wanted. They had never discussed one another's personal life and he didn't wish to start now. As well, unlike most policemen, he did not like the attention the uniform drew from the staff and customers in restaurants. He preferred to eat in private when on duty, reading a novel, and listening to classical music on his Walkman. There would be no privacy in any place that Blakemore chose. But he was wrong.

"You know, I've never been to the Leland for lunch. It's a bit posh but, hell, you only live once and I feel like a treat. We're going there," Blakemore said with authority.

Chapter 19

The Quality Inn chain of hotels, The Leland being one, is a success story in the province. They were built on the premise that winter travellers wanted more than a simple bed, shower, TV set, and drink machine down the hall. For years that was all one could expect in smaller towns and cities along major BC highways because the corporations believed that summer tourism was the only thing that could support their investments. The Quality Inn group bucked the trend, building efficient, small hotels, complete with cocktail lounges and upscale restaurants. They made nothing but money and the Leland was no exception. It was always busy for dinner, but aside from a few business people lunchtime tended to be quiet.

"Give us a corner table, will you?" Blakemore asked the young hostess. "Somewhere peaceful."

"All our tables are private," she returned, looking a bit apprehensively at the two uniforms, "but follow me, I'll seat you in the Library."

Blakemore followed, admiring her youthful buttocks as she led the way. Ernie's gaze was directed elsewhere and he was pleased to note that only a few of the tables were occupied. As usual, everyone looked up as they walked past. The 'Library' was a tiny room with shelves of books, two easy chairs and a reading lamp in one corner, and a table for two in the other. I can imagine how much in demand this room would be by romantic couples, thought Ernie. It was perfect. Jim would love it.

"Your waitress will be here shortly," the girl said, looking at their uniforms rather than their faces. "Have a nice meal."

Blakemore watched her sway back to her post while Ernie looked over one of the menus she left. Their waitress was a big

lady with a jolly disposition who had no problem looking them both in the eye.

She reminded Blakemore of his mother.

"Nice to see two fine young upholders of the Law choosing our humble establishment for your lunch," she chirped. "I highly recommend today's special—salmon, poached in a cream dill sauce and served with white asparagus, wild rice, and baby carrots. Coffee and dessert's included—frozen chocolate mousse drizzled with raspberry preserve—all for ten dollars."

"That sounds wonderful," said Ernie, "and I'll have decaf coffee, black, thank you."

She beamed and turned to Blakemore who hadn't bothered to look at the menu.

"Nope. I want bulk. I'm hungry as a bear. Bring me a T-bone steak, two baked potatoes with all the fixings, hold the salad and substitute baked beans or corn. Extra bread, butter, and make my coffee the real thing. I won't have dessert, I'm on a diet."

She coughed.

"I'd love to cook for you," she said, with a laugh, and headed to the kitchen with their order.

Blakemore went right to the point.

"Ernie, I know it's none of my business, but I've got to tell you that Barbara and I are worried about you. You're becoming a damned hermit, avoiding people. Missing Saturday's shoot is one good example. That was a real opportunity for you to mix with some fine citizens. Also, Barbara's a bit hurt that you haven't been dropping by. She's bugged me a number of times to invite you over for dinner and I have, but you've turned us down. Just tell me to bug off if the reason's too personal, but if it's something I can fix I really want to know."

Ernie's emotions went for a spin. The look of concern in Blakemore's face was genuine and hearing that he had slighted

Barbara filled him with guilt. He lived with the self-loathing that was part of his depression, but at this moment he absolutely despised himself. It wasn't really he and Jim against the rest of the world. The Blakemores were not the enemy. It was time to be honest. He was tired of hiding and being afraid.

"Paul, I'm sorry. I'm terribly sorry," he blurted out. "You're absolutely right and I'm afraid to admit that I have been acting that way for a long time. I didn't go to the Gun Club because I was with someone special this weekend and I didn't want to leave him. Paul, I'm gay, and I've found someone to love. I don't know how this will affect the partnership between you and me, or how Barbara feels, but that's how it is and I'm relieved that it's out in the open—at least between us."

"Well!" said Blakemore, after a long pause. "That's one hell of an excuse. You realize that you're putting me in a bad spot. You'll be out on your ear if the Force finds out you're gay, and I suppose that I'm obligated to report you. But I won't. I don't always follow the rules as you're well aware, and I'm not a bigot. That might surprise you. But I'm truly not. I grew up in the West End of Vancouver at the time that gays were choosing that as the Canadian San Francisco. I've been propositioned more times than I can say in my young tight-ass days."

Ernie blinked in amazement, struggling with the image of his partner being hit upon by a man.

"No, don't laugh," Blakemore admonished. "It's true, but you know it never bothered me. In fact, I enjoyed kibitzing with them. I actually got invited and went out to more than a few gay parties. I knew I was the token straight, but the fun went both ways. I enjoyed myself. It's my considered opinion that any guy who feels threatened or who ridicules gays has a problem with self-confidence—sexual or otherwise. Nothing like putting someone down to feel big yourself."

"You've been a good partner, Ernie," he continued. "Some of your predecessors were real lulus—dumb shits or back-stabbing ladder climbers. You and I work well together and, quite frankly, I couldn't care if you fucked goats. I've also decided that this conversation never took place."

Ernie couldn't speak. He fought back the tears, reached across the table and touched Blakemore's arm. The goat-fucking image was a bit harsh, but the message was clear: this was a friend.

"Right, then," Blakemore said, as he spotted the waitress bringing their meal. "It's all fixed. Let's eat."

Chapter 20

Zachary saw his last office patient at five-thirty and contemplated the stack of charts in front of him. Iris, the office nurse, wanted those charts completed and with billing codes filled out on her desk when she arrived Tuesday morning. She made that clear to him as she put on her coat to leave.

"We've got to keep up with the billing, Dr. Benson," she admonished. "I don't want to get behind with them. You know how the Medical Plan likes to nit pick and the resubmissions are a lot of work. Before you get started on that, though, you'll notice that I've put the call back charts on the top. The patients' questions and lab results are pinned on the front. When you've contacted them, just put the sheets back inside the front cover. That way I know they've been spoken to and I won't have to start all over again with the forgetful ones."

"Yes, Mary," he answered, wearily. "Sometimes I wish I was on salary and just had to deal with a single paycheck at the end of the month. I don't mind the phone calls, but I hate all those billing codes."

"So would I. It would make the bookkeeping a snap," she

retorted. "But the majority of your colleagues would hang you for that statement. Oh, by the way, there's one extra call for you. Corporal Blakemore called this morning but said not to bother you and it would be okay for you to call back at the end of the day."

"Fine, Mary, I'll call him later," Zachary replied, and bid her a goodnight as he tackled the stack of charts. The corporal could wait. Anyway, Blakemore should be on his way home for dinner with his lovely wife if he had any sense. Heather jumped into his mind at that point and he had to consciously block that delicious thought as he reached for the first chart.

At 6:45 he was done. He locked up the office and headed for the hospital. The adrenalin from the day's office grind hadn't worn off yet. He wasn't the least bit hungry and so he decided to look at the specimen slides from the hunter. The lab had called earlier in the day and left a message that they were ready for viewing. If he had any energy left, he would also clean out his in-file at X-ray and thus avoid a reprimand from Sally on Tuesday morning when he had arranged to be present when the technicians X-rayed his two coroner cases.

Visiting hours were just starting when Zachary arrived at the hospital, so to avoid being button-holed by a patient or a relative he entered the lab directly through the back door. All the lights were on but none of the staff were evident. A bell on the reception desk had a sign saying 'Ring for assistance.' The night duty technician was probably on the wards drawing blood, he thought. A large folder with his name on it lay beside the bell. Blessing his good fortune for the privacy, he took the folder, which contained his slides, into the microscope viewing room. It wasn't often that he had his pick of the scopes, the technicians having priority, and so he sat down at the big Zeiss binocular scope—the Cadillac of the lot. Its optics were beautiful.

He loved pathology. Most of his fellow medical students

hated the subject, preferring the clinical bedside courses; but he admired the truth, the final diagnoses that were revealed by the autopsies and the tissue slides. He examined his collection with care, not skipping a one. When he was finished, he had an answer once again and called Blakemore.

"Good evening, Paul. I'm sorry to disturb you at home, but I've got something more for your hunter case. The tissues show that autolysis was well in progress before the corpse was frozen. In fact, there are fourteen to sixteen hours' worth. Either the killer had a tough time making up his mind about what to do with the body, or it was transported unrefrigerated a long time or a long distance."

"I'll be buggered," responded Blakemore. "This case gets curiouser and curiouser. Thanks, Doc. Once more, you've got my eternal gratitude. Now for Christ's sake, go home. I'll bet you haven't even had supper yet. Do you want to come over here? Barbara's got some great leftovers. She's nodding her head as I speak."

"No thanks, Paul, but tell Barbara I'll take a raincheck. I've got some X-rays to read and some in-house paperwork to do before I leave. It'll be late when I finish. I'll grab something in the hospital cafeteria. Despite rumours, their food's good. Most of it is catered from Zelda's Deli, an establishment of which I'm sure you're aware."

"You're right there," said Blakemore. "Her perogies are to die for, covered in real sour cream. Okay, Doc, but get some rest. We don't want any burn-out in your direction. You're too valuable."

Zachary felt a twinge of guilt as he hung up. He could have accepted the invitation, but Barbara was his patient and he was experienced enough to know that socializing, particularly with marital problem cases, was not a good idea. The microscope work had given him real eye fatigue and he had no desire to

look at an X-ray light box or read patient files, but the perogy talk had whetted his appetite and so he headed for the cafeteria.

Chapter 21

Ernie opened up the precinct office Tuesday morning feeling lighthearted and ready to face the day. His talk with Blakemore had lifted a veil from his world and gave him a whole new lease on life. He hummed Beethoven's Ninth as he readied himself for the day's work. He was not prepared, however, for the phone call that came in just before eight. The caller identified herself as secretary to Chief Inspector Ward, the Commander of the RCMP in British Columbia.

"The Inspector wishes to speak to the officer in charge. Is that you?" she asked.

"No," he replied, feeling his stomach flutter. "That would be Corporal Blakemore, but I'm afraid that he's not here. May I have him call you back? I expect him in at any moment," he added, hoping that she would say yes. No such luck.

"Jane! What the hell is the hold-up? Put Constable whoever on the line," boomed a voice in the background.

"Yes Sir!" she said, and in a blink Ernie was ear to ear with his supreme boss.

"All right, Constable, I'm going to start off by telling you that I have just had my ass blistered by phone all the way from Ottawa. The Attorney General for Canada has just had his ass equally blistered by phone from Germany. Seems a set of fingerprints has gone through our computers that belong to the beloved son of Herman Klaus, billionaire industrialist and probably one of the most influential men in all of Europe. His son, it would appear, is very dead and lying in your little precinct. This is not good news to either Herman, Canada the Safe, or to the RCMP, who are responsible for

the protection of the inhabitants of and visitors to this fine land. The fact that there was a Canadian rap sheet on the fair-haired lad apparently has been lost in the translation. In Herman's eyes the boy was approaching sainthood for his fight against Canada's rape of its forests. Father wants answers and Father wants them now. As the plumbers say, "Shit runs down hill," and at the moment, Constable, you are at the bottom. What is going on?"

Ernie felt his sphincter tighten. Damn Paul. He knew that Vancouver should have been notified the day the body was found. He fought for composure.

"Corporal Paul Blakemore is actually the officer in charge here and he is leading the investigation into the death of the unfortunate young man and I'm . . ."

"Don't try to pass the buck. I'm talking to you right now and I know damn well that this is the biggest thing that's hit that one-horse station of yours, so don't plead ignorance with me. Give me a report!"

"Yessir!" The word "report" saved him. He visualized a courtroom and a judge. Pavlovian response took over. He related events, findings, and investigations from beginning to end in a controlled, professional manner.

"Very good, Constable," said the Chief Inspector when Ernie had finished. "Almost sounded like you switched on a recording, but you've told me exactly what I wanted to know. That's good police work you've done so far, but I think you need help. I'm sending Inspector Coswell from the Vancouver Homicide Unit and some of his technical people to bolster things up in your area. They'll arrive late this afternoon. The Inspector will arrange for transfer of the body to our forensic man in Vancouver who's got a few more bells and whistles than your local MD. By the way, I want you to phone up that chap, Benson wasn't it? Tell him to leave everything as is. Our man will take it from here.

Be politic about it though. Don't want to ruffle any feathers. I don't need to speak to your partner. I think you comprehend my instructions well enough, but you might mention to him that I want Inspector Coswell to have the utmost cooperation from all concerned. Okay with that, constable?"

"Absolutely Sir. You can rely on us to do that 100 per cent."

"Good. I'm sure you will. That's all then," replied Ward, abruptly hanging up.

Ernie sank back in his chair, pausing for a moment to allow the tightness to release from his chest and regain his normal breathing before putting a call in for Blakemore.

Chapter 22

At precisely the same time that Ernie was dealing with his superior, Zachary was standing in front of a row of fluorescent view boxes studying the X-ray films of the decapitated corpse. The only sign of trauma was the neck. The spine had been neatly severed, the vertebrae showed splintering and chipping of the bone where the axe had struck. But there was something else. He stood back. There was something wrong with the pattern. He remembered one of Paul Meuler's teaching pearls: *always look for a pattern. Everything is cause and effect. The position of bone fragments, the size and depth of a wound, all explain the action that caused them.* The damage from the chopping action was obvious, but higher up the X-rays revealed a more significant injury—a compression fracture involving the anterior spine. Only one force could have caused that—extreme forward flexion of the neck, not blows from an instrument. Zachary had seen more than his share of this kind of broken neck from various causes— gymnastics, hockey, diving accidents. The cause of death was no longer in doubt. He must tell Paul.

"You've got a stack more to read Dr. Benson," admonished Sally, the Radiology clerk, as she watched him head for the door.

"I'll do them later," he called back over his shoulder.

"Sure," she muttered. "Meanwhile I have to look at a jammed 'unread' file." Sally thrived on efficiency and abhorred procrastination. Dr. Benson was in for one of her famous nags the next time she laid eyes on him. This feeling was reinforced when Charlotte, the day staff technician, poked her head out of the film processing room and said, "Did you find out from Doctor Benson whether or not he needed anymore views taken of the two coroner cases? We still have them in here and would sure like to see them out."

Sally had forgotten that request in the haste of the doctor's departure.

"No," she lied. "He rushed out of here before I could get the words out of my mouth. But don't worry. I'll have Mary at switchboard get him right now." Sally felt somewhat mollified by this since she did not often have the opportunity to have her name broadcast over the hospital public address system.

"Dr. Benson. Please call Sally in X-ray. Dr. Benson, please." Mary's calm voice reached all corners of the hospital.

Zachary paused. Crossing Sally was not something he wished to do but he wanted to reach Blakemore before lunch. He was booked at noon to assist Dr. John Taylor, the general surgeon, on a cancer case that would probably take three or four hours. It was now 11:40. He shut Mary's repeated paging out of his ears and slipped into the Surgeon's Lounge and went directly to the phone, nodding to Dr. Taylor who was already changing into his greens.

"I'll be right behind you, John. I just have to make a quick call."

As he expected, Blakemore was still at home and picked up the phone himself.

"What's up Doc?" He never tired of the Bugs Bunny phrase, particularly when he was in a good mood. Heather McTavish's identifying the corpse was a breakthrough that he hadn't expected so soon.

"I've got the cause of death on our hunter, Paul. He died of a broken neck. I know that it's remote, but do you think that it's possible that the death was accidental, and we are dealing with a sick fanatic who came upon the body by chance and used it as an anti-hunting message? It would explain the absence of any sign of a struggle."

"It would have to be a sick fanatic all right, but I guess it's a remote possibility. If you needed a population to look for sickos, the animal rights groups are fertile ground. It would be ironic though. I haven't had a chance to tell you yet, but I have a probable ID on our corpse. He was an environmentalist fanatic. Heather remembered him from her past life as an activist."

"Heather knew him? That's remarkable. I'd really like to hear all about it but I have to go. They're waiting for me in the OR."

"Okay, Zach, and by the way, don't sweat the final paper work. You've given me lots to go on right now. Take a breather. You've been great."

Zachary felt a glow of pleasure. Genuine thanks from a hard-noser like Paul was high praise indeed.

"No problem. Anytime," was his slightly embarrassed reply.

"Anytime" might have been overdoing it a bit. Paul would remember that when he needed his next favour.

Chapter 23

Inspector Mark Coswell was not a happy man. Old ramrod Ward had insisted that no time be wasted getting his homicide expert into the Bear Creek investigation and airflight was the only

option. Amongst Coswell's weaknesses was a recurring affliction—motion sickness. Busses, cars, trains, boats, and especially airplanes triggered uncontrollable nausea and then vomiting. Every drug and device known to man had failed to work with him. Motion was comfortable only if he was on foot or if he had his hands on the steering wheel. Somehow the latter took his mind off his stomach. At this moment, however, as the 20-passenger De Havilland wafted down the final narrow approach to the Castlegar airstrip, its wings perilously close to the huge fir trees looming on either side, Coswell had his face jammed into an airlines "barf bag" and was heaving up his stomach contents.

Blakemore, standing at the Arrivals gate, wearing (at Barbara's insistence) a freshly laundered and pressed uniform, scanned the faces of the deplaning passengers trying to identify Coswell. He was totally taken back when the most unlikely candidate proceeded directly towards him. He was fiftyish, short, balding, over-weight, and had the sickliest countenance—pale and sweaty. He was wearing a light, khaki raincoat, open in front to reveal an ample paunch barely covered by a red woolen sweater, baggy blue jeans held up by an unseen belt, and, on his feet, black Nike trainers.

"Blakemore, I presume," he said, extending a clammy hand. "Good of you to come and get me. Would you do me one more favour and get my bags off the conveyor? There are two—both black, soft leather with a red fluorescent tape on each handle. Here are the tags."

With that he abruptly strode over to the waiting room and plopped down on one of the seats.

Blakemore, still speechless, did as requested, pulling the bags off as they came bumping by on the continuous running belt. By the time he lugged them over to where Coswell had sat down, the colour had returned to the Inspector's face, or at least

to his nose and cheeks, giving them a rosy glow. Goodly amount of alcohol has been through those arteries, Blakemore thought to himself.

"Thanks a lot. Paul, isn't it?" Boswell's remembering his Christian name from the mass of information the man was undoubtedly given prior to leaving Vancouver was not lost on Paul. He nodded.

"Nice to see the Force so well represented," he continued, "by an officer who obviously takes pride in his appearance. I'm afraid I went to seed right after my rookie year. Fitness has never been a passion with me, although it seems in vogue with my staff. Once I squeaked through the height requirements I decided that exercising my brain rather than my body would do me better, and I think that's proven out with time. My doctor doesn't agree, but what does he know?"

Blakemore's mind was reeling as he tried to get a handle on the personality who had just stormed into his world. Coswell rambled on.

"The lab boys are coming up in their van and should arrive sometime tomorrow. The airlines people wouldn't let them on with their equipment—too heavy. They'll look after themselves, though, so don't organize anything special for them. In fact, they're a bit on the geek side and best left to their own. Just point them at the murder site, or anything else for that matter, that you think they should go over." Nice politics in the word "you," Blakemore mused.

"I noticed on the map," Coswell went on, "that Bear Creek is twenty miles east of here on Canada One. I presume you have one of those great issue Cherokee 4x4s. I've always wanted to drive one—OK with you? They give us those clunky Tauruses in Vancouver that drive like buses."

Blakemore barely had time to say, "Sure, no problem," when

Coswell jumped to his feet, gave him a big grin, and said "Great. Off we go." He headed to the automatic exit doors, leaving Blakemore to carry out his luggage.

For a man whose driving was probably 99 per cent city-based, the Inspector guided the 4x4 at exactly the legal grace ten kilometers over the speed limit navigating the curves, traffic, and ice patches with great skill. Blakemore, to his surprise, was beginning to feel a strange respect for this remarkable officer. His de-briefing was even more skillfully done.

"I read the report that your partner gave the Chief. Ward's secretary used to be a courtroom stenographer before she hired on with us and so she took down every word, listening of course on the same phoneline. If you reach into the right hand pocket of my raincoat the report is there. Pull it out, would you, and give it a read? See if you have anything to add or subtract."

Paul did as he was told, reading Ernie's familiar prose with the aid of the trouble light from the glove compartment. He had to concede that his partner had a talent for report-writing far superior to his own. The facts were all there and none of the speculations.

"No," he said. "Ernie's got it exactly right."

Coswell shot a brief glance at him then returned his attention to the road as the headlights of the Cherokee reflected off the centre line marking the curves ahead. He was silent for a moment, then, continuing to stare straight ahead, he said, "Good. We have a baseline. Now, what are your off-the-record ideas? I confess that I read your profile at head office and so I know you've been a presence in this Bear Creek jurisdiction for three years. You must know just about everyone in the area. Do you think the murder could have been done by a local?"

"Well, I don't rightly know. I don't think anyone 'round here is a killer personality, but who can tell what evil lurks in

the minds of men?" he said, attempting humour using the old radio show quotation.

"Quite right," replied Coswell. "But let me put it another way. What line is your investigation taking right now?"

Blakemore was flustered. He sensed that he could not outwit this man. He recalled an embarrassing episode when he once gave evidence before a sharp trial judge. Blakemore was certain that the accused was guilty as charged and so tried to verbally manipulate the facts. It happened early in his career, and the judge's rebuke, plus the blot on his record, scarred him deeply. He decided that he would play ball with Coswell. Perhaps, if he made himself really useful to this investigation, he would at least be 'mentioned in dispatches.' Despite the bitterness creeping over him, he answered.

"I think there has to be a local connection. Even if the killing was done at a considerable distance from here, the body was planted on that mountain as a message for some person or persons in this municipality. Whoever did it, I think that person wants to see the reaction to that message. Someone is harbouring a bellyful of hate. I only hope that it's a singular act and the murderer is satisfied. If not, I think that there will be more violent acts if he or she is not caught soon."

"Has there been anything like that—further violence I mean?" Coswell sensed that Blakemore had made a silent decision to cooperate and he wanted to keep that going.

"No. There was another violent death but that was an older woman who was burned to death in her house. It was an accident caused most likely by a propane tank exploding."

"She wasn't the president of the local Animal Lovers Against Hunting was she?" the Inspector returned, half facetiously.

"Funny you should ask that," Blakemore said. "She actually was outspoken in her anti-hunting sentiments, but she was

an old sweetie. You kind of expected her to be against killing anything. She really offended no one."

"Just poking," Coswell was quick to reply. "It's my suspicious nature—the result, I guess, of too many years in homicide investigations."

A lot of success in those investigations, Blakemore thought to himself, or he would not have risen to the rank of Inspector. His comment also brought a twinge of guilt as he recalled how quickly he had accepted the circumstances of Ethel Roberts's death and never really considered it anything but an accident. He made a mental note to at least re-examine the scene and be sure he got Zachary's autopsy report.

"I'm really fascinated by the lack of any human trail to the body of the dead man on the mountain," Coswell continued. "Do you have any theories as to how that could be? Is it possible that there was an isolated snowfall that covered up the tracks of the person who dumped him there? I notice that it was at a considerably higher elevation than the town."

"No. We had three solid weeks of cloudless skies prior to the time the body was discovered. No fresh snow anywhere, including the mountains. There is a possibility that the body was there more than three weeks, but I think that's unlikely. The nights have been cold but some of the daytime temperatures have been quite mild and, as was mentioned in the report, there was no sign of animals getting at the body. There are just too many scavenger species up here, both birds and mammals, to have left a feast like that alone."

"How then? Helicopter? That seems a bit Hollywood but stranger things have happened."

"I thought of that, but when one of those things comes down over pine and fir trees the downdraft litters the ground with cones and needles in a pattern that is unmistakable. There was

nothing like that up there. He wasn't pushed out either. The head tied to the tree squelches that idea."

They drove on in silence for a few minutes: Blakemore waiting for further questions; Coswell warming to the puzzle.

"That has to bring us back to the hunter who found the body. Could he have performed some sleight-of-hand, covered his tracks, anything to explain the findings? I understand that you had no choice but to let him leave after his statement. That lawyer friend of his was a pain, I'm sure. The only other thought I'd like to run past you is the possibility that all three hunters were involved in the murder. Three men might have been physically able to create the scene that you found."

"Yes. That's a possibility," agreed Blakemore, "and I was annoyed that I couldn't follow up on interviewing the other two men individually to compare stories. They're all back in Vancouver now."

"I'll see that you get your wish, believe me. The Chief Inspector isn't going to spare anyone in this case including Abelman, who, by the way, I have crossed paths with in Vancouver. He's a real bastard in the courtroom, sharp as a tack. I can't imagine him being dumb enough to be an accomplice in a murder, but, as you so aptly said, 'Who knows what evil lurks in the hearts of men?' By the way, I'm impressed that you are familiar with the old *Shadow* series. That show outdates us both, but I was a real crime buff when I was a kid and I suspect that you were too."

"I was," Blakemore confirmed. "The Vancouver Library has those old Lamont Cranston broadcasts in the archives. I listened to every one of them." He was beginning to relax now, surprised at how easily he was being led. Coswell picked up on this and abruptly changed the subject.

"They have me booked in something called the Thunderbird Motel. Do they have a restaurant? As you can see, I really like

my food and I didn't get a chance to eat before my flight," he lied, knowing that his ample breakfast was residing wherever the airline disposed of the barf bags.

"I'm sorry," Blakemore returned. "I completely forgot to tell you that you're to come to our house for supper. My wife, Barbara, is a terrific cook, and she insists that I bring you as soon as you arrive. She's expecting us around seven. It's quarter to now so we'll be right on time."

"That's really above and beyond the call of duty, but I accept wholeheartedly. I only insist that we find a liquor store. I want the wine to be my treat. I am a bit of a connoisseur of the grape, honed, I might say, from an early age. My father owns a vineyard in Kelowna," he explained.

"You and Barbara will hit it off, then. My wife's older brother, whom she adores, writes about wines for the *Vancouver Gourmet Magazine*. I'm a bit of an ignoramus, but the two of them are teaching me some taste."

"Eric Vogel? I read his column religiously. He is *the* authority on BC vintages. He knows of which he speaks, I can tell you. I'll really have to choose carefully tonight. I hope there is a good selection here."

"There is. Sales are surprisingly good in Bear Creek, despite its woodsy population. Tourists returning back East or to the States buy a lot."

Coswell was not overstating his determination to pick a wine to impress Barbara. When they pulled into the one provincial liquor outlet in town the Inspector was in his element. He quickly won over Rodney, the manager, and the two of them went over every shelf, it seemed, bottle by bottle.

"My father owns the Castilitoni Vineyard in Kelowna," Coswell pre-empted, further impressing Rodney, "and so I know those wines well. We'll have one of his late harvest Reislings as

an aperitif, but I would like something spectacular for the meal. Paul, do you know what the main course will be?"

"Never mind," he said, before Blakemore could answer. "We'll get reds and whites."

Twenty minutes later, they checked out of the store with the Castilitoni Reisling, a Mission Hill Private Reserve Chardonnay, a Quail's Gate Pinot Noir, and a Blue Mountain Champagne as a "digestif."

"I'm actually partial to the whites," Coswell explained. "BC's are amongst the best in the world. The reds are coming on strong, though, particularly the Pinot Noirs."

The ride from the liquor store to the Blakemore house took less than ten minutes as Coswell continued with his dissertation.

"You're probably wondering why I picked a Pinot Noir instead of a Cabernet for the red. I think the subtleties of taste in the former are more pleasing, although a face full of bouquet from a spicy Cab is not to be scoffed at. The Chardonnay is really a stand-alone wine and there are probably better whites if one chooses the food first, but I have always felt it was the Queen of the whites and I've never tired of it. The Mission Hill Vineyards put BC on the world wine map in 1993 with that one Chardonnay. It won the Gold Medal, you know, at a major event in Paris. The Blue Mountain Champagne is as good as anything that California has produced. Their Pinot Gris is even better, but none of it gets into the liquor stores. The restaurants and private buyers get it all."

"That's it," interjected Blakemore. "The last house on the right—the white one with the holly tree in the front yard. Pull right into the driveway. Barb's left her car on the street."

Although this wine enthusiasm was not really shared by Blakemore, he was relieved that his wife would have no trouble being included in the conversation this evening. Hunting and

shoptalk usually dominated the rare occasions that he invited anyone for dinner.

Chapter 24

Barbara greeted them at the front door. She was wearing a black three-quarter-length cocktail dress, black pumps, a pearl necklace (borrowed from her friend Mandy), and had done her face to perfection. She was absolutely stunning. Blakemore barely managed the introductions. Coswell, too, was speechless for a moment but recovered quickly.

"I am very pleased to meet you, Barbara, and I can't begin to tell you how much I appreciate your inviting me to dinner. Please excuse my appearance. I'm not a good flyer and I try to reduce the pain by wearing the most comfortable things I own. I've brought a little contribution that I hope is appropriate. Paul's told me that Eric Vogel is your brother. I've never met him but I have great respect for his knowledge. All of my choices for tonight are recommendations from his columns."

Barbara melted. Blakemore knew how nervous she was about meeting Coswell and he was truly happy for her. She had gone to an unbelievable amount of trouble to make a good impression. As they moved into the living room, he saw the fresh flowers on the mantel, the coffee table books arranged perfectly, and, out of the corner of his eye, he saw the dining room table set once again with their wedding china and best crystal. The odours from the kitchen were sublime and he was sure that he saw Coswell sniff in that direction.

"Paul," he directed, "Why don't you open up the Reisling? It should be served at slightly less than room temperature and the trip in the jeep will make it just about right. I want to get to know your lovely wife."

The evening proceeded like a dream. The dinner was perfect and the wines complemented both the food and the company. Barbara was the centre of all the conversations, from wine appreciation to growing up in BC and the trials of families living within "the Force." The purpose for Coswell's visit to Bear Creek was never raised until Blakemore dropped him off later at his motel.

"I hate to mention business after such a great evening, Paul, but I'd like to get together early tomorrow morning with you and your partner. I notice this place opens for breakfast at six-thirty. That okay with you?"

"Sure," he replied, lying through his teeth. Ernie was the morning person. Blakemore did not get up to speed till eight o'clock at the earliest. He preferred the late shift. His only satisfaction would be phoning Ernie when he got home to inform him of this unusual start to their workday. Ernie would lie awake all night worrying and would probably look as bad as Paul at that ungodly hour.

Chapter 25

He threw the paper into the stove and watched her face burn. "Ethel Roberts will be sorely missed, dedication, molding of young minds, a saint. . . . blah, blah, blah." She molded John and Anne all right. Turned them against me—her and her hoity-toity ideas. Why didn't she mind her own business and leave us alone?

It was easy to kill her. Easier even than the Kraut kid. Also, she had to go. She would have found out for sure. John should never have brought him up here last summer, lecturing me in his snooty foreign accent about logging and hunting. Sure I got mad and said things, but having them get up and go over to Ethel's place and leave me alone on the last night John was here—that was too much. That airy-fairy

environmental talk would be right down her alley and I'm sure she encouraged them. She knew I'd be mad, but that didn't stop her from keeping them there for hours while I sat at home waiting.

Anne knew how I felt and it made her last days even tougher. Ethel Roberts was responsible for that—coming between a man and his wife and a man and his son. She caused us a lot of pain we didn't deserve.

He remembered sitting in his son's apartment again and how his heart lifted when he heard the hated voice on the answering machine. "Hey John, Diet here. Would you believe I'm going to be on the six o'clock TV news? I'm doing the interview this morning. I need a few hours sleep, but after that how about we go out to O'Douls around seven? I'm an easy walk to the Palace so I'll just come over and take a chance you're in. Hope to see you later, bye for now."

He'd waited, feeling his rage return. Seeing and hearing the arrogant bastard on the TV screen added fuel to the fire and his resolve hardened. Luring him into the apartment had been so easy. "John's in the can," he told him and held the door open, smiling. Dietmar was obviously surprised to see him but entered without hesitation. He'd taken only a few steps when he became aware of two things—the open bathroom door and his own voice on the TV. He called out John's name and in a terrifying moment he knew his fate was sealed.

The reporter friend—Heather McTavish—was someone who needed watching. I wonder how much she knows, he thought. Her and Ethel were thick as thieves, I've heard.

Debbie was not a happy lady. She opened the Thunderbird Cafe weekday mornings, but aside from the inhalator crew that would occasionally show up if they had a late call, there was rarely a customer before seven. That gave her lots of time to brew the coffee, tapping the first pour for herself, and then enjoy it while she waited for Molly, the cook, who usually ambled in sometime around seven. This morning, however,

there were two men standing at the door waiting for her to unlock it at precisely 6:30. Ernie she recognized. The other, she soon discovered, was a veritable cyclone that blew through the door giving orders almost immediately.

"A fine good morning to you, my dear," he said, crossing the room directly to a corner booth that was unofficially reserved for the local tradesman. "Coffee straight up please, and two menus. I and my colleague need to stoke up for a powerful day of crime work."

"Just coffee for me, Debby. Black," said Ernie, following Coswell to the booth. She was contemplating asking them to sit elsewhere, but something about the new man stilled her normally sharp tongue. She was a bit taken back by her feelings since, in this establishment, she usually ruled. She brought them the coffee and menus.

"I'll have the corn beef hash, with three eggs over easy, extra side of toast, jam, and leave room for cream in the coffee," Coswell added.

"Just the coffee for me," said Ernie. He looked like he was suffering from a two-day hangover thought Debbie.

She disappeared into the kitchen and began to prepare the order. The bowling ball head was obviously not going to wait patiently for Molly. She would have to cook this herself. The corn beef hash was pre-made, requiring only two minutes in the microwave. She cracked three large brown farm eggs on the griddle and dropped four slices of twelve-grain bread in the toaster. She grumbled to herself as the breakfast took shape.

"Paul's going to be a bit late, I see," began Coswell. "That's okay. It'll give me a chance to hear your thoughts on the investigation so far. Your report to the Inspector, by the way, was first class."

Ernie perked up. Praise directed his way was a rare treat.

"For instance. Do you have a theory to explain how the corpse got deposited up on that mountain? Helicopter was the only thing I could think of."

"That was my thought, too," answered Ernie. "But Paul said the signs don't match and the only helicopter in these parts belongs to Ross Crocker. He owns a good part of this corner of the world—ranching, logging, hunting lodge, construction, even this motel. He sure isn't anti-hunting. The walls of his lodge, I understand, are covered by trophy heads of every species of game animal from here to Africa."

"What's his attitude to trespassers? Maybe our hunter strayed onto his territory."

"No. Ross isn't the easiest guy in the world to get along with, but when it comes to hunting he's a believer in open ranges and has a soft spot for hunters, either local or foreign. His pet peeve is any form of authority that challenges his. He pretty well dominates the municipal government around here. The RCMP detachment is really the only power that he can't overcome. He and Paul have had quite a few run-ins."

"Over what?"

"Anything, really. A lot of petty complaints, the purpose of which I think is to use us against what many townspeople consider a bully. They don't like the way that he pushes developments through and ignores any protest. The latest is a block of condominiums that he's planning to put up on the shores of Cougar Creek, just north of town. That's a favourite hiking, canoeing, and fishing spot for the locals and tourists. There are some reasonable questions that are being asked and he simply ignores them."

"I wouldn't think the population here is big enough to support a condo development," commented Coswell.

"Actually it is. Retirees are moving here from the big centres

in droves. It's a good thing in many respects. These people bring their pensions and savings to bolster the local economy, which has been suffering recently because of the slump in the forest industry. They like peace and quiet and many of them get involved in volunteering for everything from local committees to ambulance work. Two of the crew who brought down the hunter's remains are good examples—Karl and George—both members of the retirement community. I personally think the condos are a good idea. These folks want small, zero-maintenance dwellings like that. Crocker might have found a less contentious place to put them though."

The sound of loud, angry voices just outside the cafe door interrupted their conversation. Blakemore entered first, followed by a bear of a man with full beard and shoulder-length hair—all completely white. He looked like a giant Santa Claus dressed in a logger's plaid shirt, denims, and Kodiak work boots.

"I'm telling ya, Mr. Corporal Mountie, it's a sorry thing that you've got nothing better to do than give me a ticket for a goddam red traffic light violation. Six-thirty in the goddam morning, for Christ's sake. There wasn't another vehicle for miles in any direction."

"Except for me, eh?" Blakemore threw back over his shoulder. "Right behind you."

"Yeah. What'd you do? Sit up all night on that side street so you could make a pinch? Why aren't you out solving that murder that everyone's talking about instead of enforcing some petty traffic offense?"

Blakemore ignored him and continued across the café to the corner booth where Ernie and Coswell sat, watching the proceedings. He hung up his coat and hat and pulled a chair up to the booth so that he was seated with his back to the room. His detractor, face suffused with anger, stomped over to the counter

and plopped his considerable weight down on a stool. Debbie, emerging from the kitchen with the corn beef, eggs, and toast on a large plate noticed him immediately. She made a detour to serve him. He ignored the order she was holding and gestured for a coffee. She balanced the plate precariously in one hand and with the other filled a cup with coffee and placed it in front of him.

"Sorry I'm a bit late," Blakemore apologized, "but that was just too good an opportunity to pass up. Good morning to you both."

"That," explained Ernie in a hushed tone, "is Ross Crocker."

"Well," Coswell greeted. "And a cheery good morning to you, Paul. That was quite an entrance."

Looking over Blakemore's shoulder, he saw Crocker's massive shoulders stiffen and knew that this air of frivolity was not being appreciated.

"Some take their punishment better than others," he said, in a voice loud enough to reach the counter, "but I'm just doing my job, eh? Have to fight crime whenever I see it."

If possible, the shoulders got even tighter and it was probably fortunate that the two adversaries were facing in opposite directions because Blakemore's Gaulic shrug was pure salt in the wound.

Ernie put a halt to the duel as Debbie deposited Coswell's breakfast on the table. The Inspector dug in immediately, making appreciative sounds as he tackled the mountain of food.

"Paul, the Inspector and I have already ordered. Why don't you get yours in now. I think I feel like something more than coffee too." Debbie, who, with a sidelong glance to be sure that Crocker was settled, pulled her order pad out of her apron and waited impatiently, pencil poised. The subject of food effectively diverted Blakemore's attention.

"Morning, Deb. Aren't you glad I'm here to brighten your day?" he said. "I'll have steak and three eggs, sunny-side up,

hashbrowns, and a double order of toast with butter but no jam. I'm on a diet. Coffee up front."

She maintained a stone-face as she turned and took Ernie's health muffin request. The sounds of pots rattling announced, to Debbie's relief, that Molly was at work in the kitchen. Thank goodness, she thought, maybe things will get back to normal here.

Now that it appeared the floorshow was over, Coswell got down to business. Customers were arriving in a steady stream, creating a noise level that gave privacy to their discussion.

"Paul, I know the Chief expects me to go up to the crime scene, but, quite frankly, I think it would be a waste of time." (And a barfy trip up switchback roads if Blakemore takes the wheel, he reasoned). "If it's okay with you, I'd like you to take the lab boys up there and supervise their investigation. You know better what's normal and what's not in that terrain. I'd like to start working on the connection between Dietmar Klaus and this community. I'm an unknown to the citizens here and I believe that gives me an edge. I can speak to both sides of whatever fences exist and the questions can be wide open. Ernie, you need to mind the station and the radio, but it would be a real help if you would also set up interviews for me. Now, put your thinking caps on, men, and give me some idea as to where and who to start with. How about the female reporter? What do you think?"

"I agree," Blakemore answered quickly, relishing throwing Coswell to the she-wolf. "As far as I know, she's the only one around here that knew him, although the composite drawing just appeared in Monday night's edition of the *Bulletin*. Heather did a good job with that, by the way. She wrote a short piece asking for anyone who had seen him to come forward. Her editor was afraid of a notification of next-of-kin legal hassle and so the name 'Dietmar' was left out. I know the family is now

aware, but I'm not sure where we stand in that regard. Is it okay to publish his name?"

"You're right to be so cautious. Nowadays, who the hell knows, eh? I'll get Chief Ward to handle that for us. I'll also ask Heather when I see her to print a follow up when we get the 'all clear,'" replied Coswell. "Maybe that will tweak someone's memory."

Ernie was wracking his brain, trying to contribute. Ethel Roberts was the only thought that came to him.

"Do you think it's possible that there may be a juvenile connection?" he offered. "The dead man was quite young. It's a shame that Ethel Roberts isn't with us anymore. The kids in this area really loved her, even the hardheads. You'll agree, eh, Paul? How many times has she been a go-between for us in juvenile incidents? Even when they left or dropped out of school, she was a resource for them. Heather and she were really close friends. Perhaps something came up in one of their conversations."

"That's a very good suggestion, Ernie," complimented Coswell. He turned to Blakemore. "What about you, Paul? Can you think of anything?"

Blakemore was, for a moment, too surprised at Ernie to answer. That was a helluva good suggestion. Where had that come from? His partner usually took the back seat when they worked together.

"I'm still stuck on Montgomery, but locally I'd look at my pal Mr. Big Ass over there. Crocker has a mean streak and he sure as hell has the ways and means of doing someone in. I don't know what the motive would be but he does have a short fuse. Maybe the Kraus family pissed him off at some time and he wants to leave them a big message. One thing I can tell you for sure—my interrogating him would be a waste of time. Good luck is all I can say."

"Gentlemen," said Coswell. "I've got to thank you both. It's

been my experience that a toehold is all that's needed to get on the twisty path to the truth. You've given that to me in a first class manner. It's a pleasure to be on your team."

What a load of patronizing bullshit, thought Blakemore. Ernie glowed.

Debbie, now totally busy with the morning clientele, came over to top up their coffees.

"Your breakfasts will be ready in a minute. Lord, but this is some morning. It's like summer tourist season and me with no help," she complained.

"You'll be fine Deb," reassured Blakemore, "but don't forget the first food out of that kitchen is ours, not Crocker's."

She frowned and retreated to the counter, almost colliding with Clyde Groat, the volunteer fire chief, who had just entered. Two burly young men dressed in the ubiquitous plaid Macs, baseball caps, and sporting two-day growths of beard accompanied him. Ross Crocker immediately intercepted them, standing up from his counter stool, and motioning for them to join him in a booth obviously reserved for him. Clyde spotted the two Mounties and waved as he followed Crocker across the room.

Ernie nodded in acknowledgement and pointed Clyde out to Coswell. Blakemore turned in his chair to look.

"Clyde's the class of that group," Blakemore commented. "The two trained seals with him, or should I say Rottweillers, are Crocker's Joe-boys. I wouldn't trust either of them any farther than I could throw them. It's odd that they came in with Clyde. They usually don't stray far from their boss's ass. Crocker must have some honest work for them to do for a change. Clyde will get his money's worth out of them; that's for sure. But I'm still puzzled. Clyde has his own selective logging outfit and his own crew. Those two aren't much use to him except as grunts."

Coswell was interested.

"You make them sound like the Mafia or heavies in an old Western," he said. "Have they been into any serious crime that you know of? I remember your comment that there were no killer personalities around here. Could they be an exception?"

"No," replied Blakemore. "I guess my objectivity gets warped when the subject of that lot comes up. We've had the usual Saturday night run-ins with them—drunk and disorderly and a few malicious damage charges, but nothing big. I might say that Crocker, though, is right there with them on more than a few occasions. He doesn't handle his booze well and goes into a wild cowboy mode when he over-imbibes."

"There is an intimidation element, though," Ernie added. "There are a lot of people around here who won't speak up on issues like the Cougar Creek project because of them. I'm not sure whether Ross Crocker has anything to do with that, other than providing the backup for their inherent bully personalities."

"I wouldn't bet on it," grumbled Blakemore.

Debbie brought a halt to their conversation as she arrived with the breakfasts.

Chapter 26

Zachary entered the hospital twenty minutes before the seven-thirty arrival of the day staff. He wanted to be at the X-ray viewing room ahead of Sally. He was feeling a bit down after Ernie phoned him yesterday afternoon with the word from Chief Ward that he was, essentially, to butt out of the hunter case. A lecture from her wouldn't lift his mood.

The hospital was not large enough to have a graveyard shift and made do with an on-call system, and so once again he had a few minutes of peace in which to read the films. Ethel Roberts's were on top of his pile. The dental films from Dr. Thompson's

office were clipped to them. He felt slightly guilty because he had ordered frontal and lateral views only of the skull to save time for the technicians. That would be enough to compare with the dental set and establish the identification, but Dr. Mueller would not have been pleased. He would have insisted on a full skeletal survey, looking for bony injury. Fire deaths in Vancouver were often suspicious, cover-ups for murder, and hence the routine. He emptied the envelopes and clipped the skull series up on the fluorescent viewboxes. He held the dental films in his hand, selecting those that represented the same projections as the hospital ones. The fillings matched perfectly. Ethel Roberts's remains were officially identified. He returned the dental films to their envelope and was writing "return to Dr. Thompson" on a sticky when Charlotte, the day technician, came in. She looked at the skull films that Zachary had left up on the viewers.

"Good morning, Dr. Benson," she said. "Whose films are those? Someone didn't do a good job showing up that fracture: they're focussed too high. It must have been Jane. She was on call last night. I'll speak to her. That's just not good enough."

"Fracture?" exclaimed Zachary. He turned and stared at the X-rays.

"Yes. The upper cervical fracture," she said cautiously, not wishing to believe that he had missed it.

She was right. Just caught at the bottom of one lateral skull film were the vertebrae of the upper neck. There was a compression fracture, identical to the one he found on the hunter's X-rays! The fire wasn't the cause of Ethel Roberts's demise: she died from a broken neck. To sustain a fracture like that, the force of the explosion would have had to hurl her backward, jamming the back of her head against the armrest of the sofa and generating extreme flexion of her neck. But that didn't fit. Her neck was in a normal resting position when he

examined her body in the morgue. He doubted that the firemen would have repositioned her, but that was possible. The other, more likely, possibility was that she was murdered and the killer had placed her body on the couch. He reached for the phone and dialed the RCMP station, not wanting to disturb the Blakemore home so early in the morning.

Nelson dispatch answered. Damn, he thought, where the hell were they? Ernie should have been at the station by now.

"They're still switched over to us," the woman said. "That is unusual. We haven't been informed of a major accident, but I'm sure they're busy somewhere. I understand that your call is important but leave it to me. I'll find them. Where can you be reached?"

"I'll be at the hospital. Tell them to have me paged," he told her.

Charlotte was staring at him. She had read Ethel's name on the requisition. He suddenly realized that news of another murder in Bear Creek was about to spread with lightening speed.

"Yes, Charlotte, there are inconsistent findings but I'm going to ask you to keep this confidential. It's a police matter and neither you nor I want to assume anything until they have had a chance to investigate. Right?"

"Yes, Doctor. I understand."

He hoped she did. A killer loose in Bear Creek was unthinkable, but that's how it looked. Fear would be the order of the day in the community. This was not crime-numb Vancouver.

He pulled the films down from the viewboxes and replaced them in their envelope just as Sally arrived. Before she had a chance to speak he snapped out instructions.

"Sally, I want you to pull the films on my other coroner's case. I'm signing out those and this file because I want them in my office for a meeting with the police. I'll read the rest of the cases later."

She opened her mouth to object, but the look on Zachary's face, and Charlotte standing there like a totem pole, made her stop. Grumbling, she did as she was asked.

His pager buzzed.

"Charlotte," he said, "would you phone the switchboard and tell Mary to direct this call to the Surgeons' lounge? I'll pick it up there."

Zachary knew that the lounge would be vacant because the OR staff would be busy setting up the first scrubs of the day. His conversation would not be overheard.

It was Blakemore returning his call.

"I just got back to the station, Doc," he said. "We had an early morning meeting with the homicide expert from Vancouver. I just left him with Ernie. They're going over to the *Bulletin* to arrange an interview with Heather. I'm minding the store here. What's up?"

"Paul, you won't believe this but Ethel Roberts's death is more complicated than a straight-forward burn case."

Zachary quickly went over his revelation in the X-ray department and voiced his suspicion of a second murder in Bear Creek.

Blakemore's mind raced. Zachary could be right about another murder, but his prime suspect, Montgomery, would be off the hook. He had to get a better hold on this or he would really be pushed to the back of the bus. He couldn't even think of a local suspect. He'd thrown Crocker's name into the ring only as a response to Ernie's good showing in front of Coswell. He needed time.

"That's very interesting, Zachary," he said calmly. "But a propane explosion is a helluva force and I can see it breaking a few bones. I think that you had better leave this with me and not spread it about. It could cause an unnecessary panic."

"I've already done that," replied Zachary, a bit miffed. "Charlotte is the only one who knows about the fracture and she won't pass it on. I asked her to keep it confidential and I know she will. Charlotte's a professional."

"Good," Blakemore said. "I've got to hand it to you Doc, there's no doubt that you're a real pro as well. I'll bet that Vancouver forensic guy, what's-his-name, isn't going to add anything to what you've told us. Remember—don't sweat the paperwork. In fact, I don't see why you have to do anything more in that regard. Why don't you leave the rest of the work up to them?"

"You of all people know I can't do that," retorted Zachary. "Reports go with the job and Dr. Mueller is someone I respect immensely. I'll make damned sure he gets the best write-up I can manage."

Blakemore winced.

"Okay, okay," he conceded. "I didn't mean to imply that you would slack off. I just hate paperwork so much myself that I think I'm doing someone a favour if I suggest they could cut down some of it."

"All right," said Zachary, mollified. "Now am I correct in assuming that everything I have is to go to Dr. Meuller?"

Blakemore seized upon the opportunity.

"I actually have not been given exact instructions regarding that. I'll check with Coswell. Why don't you just drop the bundle off at the station and have Ernie send it along with all our stuff?"

"That makes sense," agreed Zachary. "I have the hunter's X-rays ready to go and I think I'll include Ethel Roberts's as well, just for a second opinion."

Blakemore frowned but didn't object. Zachary would catch on if he pushed it. He would have to keep his eye out for the report, though. Old, efficient Ernie would have it off to Vancouver in a shot if he got it first.

"Got to run," Blakemore said. "My other line is lit up. Thanks again for your good work, Doc." He hung up, leaving Zachary holding the phone, feeling a strange uneasiness about the entire conversation.

Blakemore's second line was actually blinking. He switched over to it. The caller was Inspector Ward's secretary.

"Good morning, Corporal Blakemore?" she asked.

"Yes," he answered, feeling his pulse race.

"Chief Inspector Ward would like to speak to Inspector Coswell, please," she said, in what Blakemore read as an officious tone. Big man, big secretary, he thought.

"Not here, I'm afraid," Blakemore responded, baiting her with his terse reply. He had decided that she was uppity, and uppity in women he couldn't abide. He heard her pass the information to her boss, a click, then a loud voice boomed into his ear.

"Where the hell is he?" shouted Ward. "Never mind. Tell him he's to get the next flight back here to Vancouver. Hans Kraus has arrived on my doorstep along with the Attorney General for BC and they want a lot of information fast and they don't want it over the phone. While I got you, though, what's developed since I spoke to your partner?"

Blakemore paused, but only for a second. He was going to take a big chance.

"The investigation has been on hold, sir. We knew Inspector Coswell was going to take over and indeed he has. We've just completed a debriefing session with him and he's off with Constable Downs arranging interrogation sessions with some of the locals. I expect things will move quickly now."

"It had better," Ward growled. "Now be damned sure he gives you two lots to do on this case while he's here in Vancouver. I don't want anything put on hold. You got that?"

"Yes sir!" Blakemore answered.

"Right, then," said the Chief, and abruptly hung up.

"And you have a nice day, sir," Blakemore said into the dead phone.

He felt a brief twinge of guilt as he hung up, but resolve took over and he put in a call to Ernie. There was no answer. He and Coswell were probably at the *Bulletin*. Hopefully they hadn't met with Heather yet. Blakemore wanted another go at her first. He switched over to central dispatch and jogged the three blocks to the newspaper office, arriving totally out of breath. The police cruiser was parked in the no parking zone at the front door. He went in and found Ernie and Coswell at the reception desk. No sign of Heather, thank God. He caught his breath and relayed Inspector Ward's message to him.

Coswell suppressed a curse as the young receptionist looked on, but his scowl revealed his thoughts.

"Thank you for your help, young lady," he said to her. "Would you tell Ms. McTavish when she comes in that I will arrange to see her when I return?"

"Back to the station, men," he directed Blakemore and Ernie.

All three rode back in the police cruiser, Coswell roundly cursing his superior.

"I don't know how that old bugger expects me to get anywhere when all I do is fly back and forth to Vancouver. He's been sitting behind that administrative desk so long he can't handle a face-to-face with some victim's father? And what in the hell do I have to tell him that isn't in Ernie's excellent reports?" He grumbled on with his monologue until they reached the station. There his attitude changed and he proceeded to set the groundwork for the continuing investigation.

"Since I have to be in Vancouver anyway," he began, "I'll do the questioning of Montgomery and his two friends. Black's rank doesn't hold water with me so it's probably for the best I be

the one to handle him anyway. I'll also check out the University of Victoria angle. There may be some clues there and, in fact, I might even go over there myself. It's too bad that I couldn't talk to Heather McTavish first, but I'll leave that up to whichever of you two wants to meet with her. Try to get more details and call the results to me in Vancouver. Perhaps it would be best if Ernie does that."

"Paul," he continued. "I want you to ride herd on the lab boys. Tell them to get their asses in gear and finish up no later than noon tomorrow. I want that unit back in Vancouver as soon as possible. This hunter killing may be big stuff to the chief, but it's a drop in the bucket when you look at the investigation load in Vancouver, let alone the whole province. They're needed back home, that's for sure."

Blakemore listened in silence. He was beginning to feel pushed into the background and Ernie rushed to the fore. He would deal with that when Coswell was gone, although he would have to be careful. Coswell essentially had just given direct orders. He continued with his instructions in a tone that was abrupt and to the point. There was no soft-soaping now; he was completely in charge.

"I want you both to put your heads together and make me that list of people you think might give us some leads. Don't worry about Ward's 'keep busy' comment. You have a detachment to run here—traffic, vandals, local run-ins. Just carry on with that. I shouldn't be anymore than a couple of days on the coast. We'll get going on the questioning as soon as I get back. All clear with that?"

"Yes, sir!" said Ernie.

"Gotcha," answered Blakemore.

"Don't worry about driving me to the airport," Coswell said. "I'm going to get a rental to use up here."

"Oh, shit," he said, remembering where he was. "I guess there isn't such a thing in Bear Creek."

"No," Ernie replied, helpfully "but Castlegar has all the major companies. Hertz I know will drive one here for you and they charge very little for that. The agent who delivers it will also look after it for you at the airport when you're in Vancouver and have it waiting for you on your return."

"That's great," Coswell said. "I'd appreciate you're arranging that for me, Ernie, and damn the expense. See if you can get me one of those V-eight Explorers."

Ernie is really piling up Brownie points with this guy, thought Blakemore.

"No problem," said Ernie, beaming with pleasure.

Chapter 27

He liked cats, especially farm cats. They were cool, sitting quiet, or walking about looking like they didn't give a shit about anything, their faces expressionless. He admired their patience, waiting, waiting, motionless until the right second to pounce. He never saw one miss its intended victim. Not like dogs—noisy, bouncing around like stupid clowns, whining to be petted and useless as hunters unless they were in packs. Even then they had to run an animal down before they could kill it. They had no patience.

He was a cat-person. He could wait and plan. His victim wouldn't get away either, and the kill would be quick like the wrestler in Edmonton.

He had held his rage when the bugger tried to make out with his wife. He waited for the perfect moment in the ring—when he felt the referee's tap to release his hold. The man's big neck relaxed for a second, just enough so that a quick jerk was all it took to snap it. He rode him down to the canvass then let go. The crowd gasped as the jammed nerves

sent shock waves to the dead man's muscles and caused the body to twitch all the way to the soles of its feet.

"Tragic accident" the newspapers said—the coroner agreed. But the look in his wife's eyes, when he returned to their hotel room, was clouded with suspicion. They had been married for less than a month. They never discussed it then or at any time after.

She was one of eight sisters in a Mennonite family that was outgrowing their small farm. She was the oldest, and when he told her father that wrestling was just a sideline and he was going to settle down on a farm in BC, consent to the marriage was quickly given.

He'd told the old man the truth about the farm in BC, but his professed "love" for his daughter was bullshit. He needed a wife like he needed a car—for the convenience. She was cute, great in bed once she got over her missionary attitude, strong, and quiet. The latter two virtues were most important to him. She was just like his mother—hard-working, non-complaining, and knew her place in a man's world. She didn't disappoint him.

He was worried about the red-headed bitch from the newspaper. She was the total opposite of his wife, pushing her nose into everyone's business, badmouthing logging and construction—even the damn Mounties were afraid of her. She's sharp, though, and because she might figure everything out, what with being so buddy-buddy with Ethel Roberts, he thought it was time he dealt with her.

Heather was annoyed with herself. The alarm had not gone off because she stupidly forgot to set it the night before. She couldn't remember the last time she had slept so late. It was almost nine o'clock. She quickly dialed Susan at the *Bulletin* and was even more dismayed to hear that she had missed Coswell and Ernie. Damn! she thought, I hope I haven't blown a golden opportunity for today's column. She dressed quickly, did her bathroom ablutions, made a cursory attempt to arrange

her hair, donned her coat, and headed out the back door of her ground floor apartment. She didn't bother with her car, choosing instead to hoof it via a shortcut through the woods back of Ethel Roberts's place. As she passed the charred remains of the house she saw a lone backhoe at work and a lump rose in her throat. The debris had been gathered into a neat pile and the bucket was being used to load it into a dump-truck, creating a cloud of dust and soot that obscured the operator.

Life moves on, Heather thought sadly. Someone will build here—perhaps a family with children. Ethel would like that. As she reflected, she suddenly realized that Ethel would have an estate that needed to be settled—probably a substantial one. She lived frugally, and teachers' salaries, for some years now, were good. She probably owned the house and property outright and there would be an insurance settlement from the fire. Ethel's parents were dead, Heather knew, and she never mentioned any siblings. I'd better check with Paul Blakemore, she thought. He's probably got some information by now. I wonder who she listed in the to-be-notified or beneficiary clauses at her bank, lawyer, and the like. My name might very well be on some of them.

Heather's mood turned down again, chastising herself for such thoughts.

"But that's my Scottish, Presbyterian blood," she mused, forgiving herself. "Ever the practical. I can't help it, and Ethel would want me to settle things for her."

She stopped in her tracks.

"Damn, damn, damn," she said aloud. "I must be going soft in the head. I am her executor." She recalled their discussing the nuisance value of death to the survivors over coffee a month or so back. Ethel had mailed her an envelope shortly afterward that just got stuck away someplace. I never did talk about it, she thought. It went right out of my mind—the sin of youth,

I guess—no consideration of mortality. Now my Presbyterian mind better smarten up. I am the one responsible for dealing with Ethel's wishes. What in God's name did I do with that envelope?

She turned and hurried back along the path to her apartment, trying to picture putting the envelope somewhere. It was most likely in her desk. She hadn't cleaned it out in ages. She was so deep in thought she barely noticed that the backhoe had stopped running. The dust had settled and the familiar Crocker emblem was visible on the door of the truck. The operator was nowhere to be seen.

She unlocked the back door and went straight to the tiny den that she called her home office. The desk was even messier than she remembered. She had gotten as far as the second drawer when she heard a crash in the kitchen.

"Racoon," she thought. "I must have left the door open."

She rushed out of the den and ran into the kitchen. The back door was open. That was her last conscious thought. It happened too fast for her to feel anything more than rough hands clasped on the back of her neck, her shoulders pinned back, then the floor rushing to meet her. She did not hear the knock on the front door or see the rapid departure of her assailant out the back.

She awakened to the persistent knocking. A large goose-egg was growing on her forehead and her neck was in spasm. The knocking stopped. Heather staggered to her feet, almost falling back in a faint, but she managed to reach the front door, unbolt it, and throw it open. Ernie was walking back to his cruiser. She called to him.

"My God, Heather," he exclaimed, running up the step to support her as she swooned. "What happened?"

"I've been mugged!" she said, "I can't believe it. I've been fucking mugged. All those years in the big city and never touched.

Settle down in sleepy little Bear Creek and some asshole jumps me. Jesus H. Christ, what is the world coming to?"

Fully conscious now, she hoped that the shocked expression on Ernie's face wasn't related to her choice of words. This wasn't old redneck Blakemore. Ernie had some sensitivity. He helped her back into the apartment and settled her on the armchair in front of the TV. He then turned quickly and went into the kitchen, noted the open door, and walked out the back looking for any sign of Heather's attacker. There was no one. The woods paralleling the back of the apartment complex were only a few yards away. The assailant would have disappeared into them in a matter of a few seconds. It was also unlikely that anyone would have seen the individual: the roof of the parking lot blocked any view between the buildings and the trees. Ernie returned to Heather and looked anxiously at her face.

"Your forehead is really swelling, Heather. Were you unconscious at all? I think I'd better get you to the emergency."

"No. I was just stunned for a moment. I'll be all right."

Ernie wasn't convinced and watched her closely as he began his questioning.

"Is anything missing," he asked. "I noticed your bag on the kitchen counter, but nothing was spilled out of it. Maybe you could have a look at it when you feel up to it. It's cloth, I see, so fingerprints won't show very well. Try not to touch anything else though. I'll come back later and dust for prints."

"I'm really okay," she replied and she went to the kitchen, her neck rigid and a monster headache coming on. "No. Nothing's missing."

"My wallet's still there," she went on, opening it, "credit cards, cash, driver's licence. Nope, nothing's gone. He probably didn't have time. You must have scared him off before he could take anything."

"Probably," agreed Ernie. "But I'm surprised. Snatch and grab is an instinct with this kind of thief. I would have expected to find your bag and wallet in the bushes somewhere, after he cleaned it out."

"Why else would he attack me?" she asked, opening the fridge to get ice to make a pack for her aching head and neck. Ernie's answer was a pregnant pause. She looked at him.

"Oh no, Ernie, you don't think it was a rapist do you? In Bear Creek? You've got to be kidding," she said, reading his thoughts.

"It could have been someone trying to hurt you—a disgruntled reader, perhaps, someone from your past?" he said avoiding the rape possibility, although that was his first thought.

"Not likely an irate reader," she answered. "I don't do the editorials and gossip's not my bag. I did write that Cougar Creek protest article with Ethel, but that just pissed off Ross Crocker and he didn't exactly threaten my life over it. I'll have to ponder on my past, but there's no one in town even related to that. My old life's a long ways away."

"Maybe not as far as you think, Heather. Paul and I will keep a lookout for any strangers lurking around town. If we find anyone questionable, we'll line him up for you. I guess you didn't get a look at this guy, did you? Any part of his clothing? His shoes? I noticed some dirt leading into the kitchen from the back door."

"That could be off my shoes. I actually started through the woods out back to get to the *Bulletin*. I came back to get something, but to answer your questions in a word—no. I went out like a light bulb. It all happened in a blink. I didn't see a thing but the floor coming up and all I felt was the pressure on the back of my neck and the front of my shoulders. He lured me into the kitchen with the noise, then grabbed me from behind just as I stepped through the doorway."

Ernie walked over to the door and examined the floor.

"Look at the dirt here, Heather," he said, pointing. "That's not from your shoes. Your mugger stood there waiting for you to pass, then attacked you."

"Tell me again what you felt, when he grabbed you," he went on. "A punch or a blow or even a push is more typical."

She described her sensations to him.

"That sounds like a wrestling maneuver—a Full Nelson. A person's neck can be snapped that way. Your feet must have slipped on the floor and broken the leverage he would get if your feet were planted," Ernie postulated. "Also, being short probably helped save you in that he inadvertently lifted you and took your weight off your feet."

"How mechanical," Heather responded.

"Sorry," Ernie said. "Sometimes those classroom lectures take over."

Ernie was surprising himself. He hadn't done much sleuthing since his training. Blakemore took over most of the time and Ernie was happy to let him do so, but he was getting his teeth into this incident and he felt good about it.

"Do you remember seeing anyone when you left this morning or when you came back?"

"Not a soul," she answered. "Except maybe the backhoe guy, but I didn't really see him, just his machine and I doubt if he saw me. That was when I was on my way. When I came back the machine was stopped and he was nowhere in sight."

Ernie thought for a moment, and chose his next words carefully.

"Heather, I don't think that this was a thief. I believe it was someone trying to hurt you for whatever reason and, as I said, I want you to really think about that. In the meantime, you need protection, especially if you are going to stay here alone. I presume that is what you plan to do."

She nodded.

"Ethel was the only person I would ask to stay with me, but, you know, I'm not really frightened. I think this is all too bizarre and not likely to happen again. I'll be all right."

"No," Ernie replied firmly. "This was an attempt on your life. I know I said hurt before, but this is more than that. It was almost a fluke that he didn't kill you with his first attempt, and if I hadn't interrupted him he would have finished you off. If you can't get someone to stay with you, or stay with someone yourself, I'm going to arrange protection for you. To start with, drive your car to work and back. Park it on the street, not in the parking lot. Don't walk anywhere alone. Keep all your doors locked, and don't answer a knock unless you know for sure who it is. The hospital has push-button medi-alarms that are worn around the neck and connect to the twenty-four hour switchboard. I want you to wear one. The operator can contact us immediately. Both Paul's and my home phones are listed there. I'll personally give instructions to Mary and I know she will brief her counterparts."

"Whoa," said Heather. "I don't want to be walking around on eggshells like that, and I don't want the whole town knowing about this. Can that idea."

"But I will do the car and lock thing," she added quickly, sensing Ernie's disapproval. "And I will keep my eyes open, so don't worry about me."

He knew he was stone-walled but already had a contingency plan. He would arrange surveillance whether she liked it or not. Blakemore and he could do shifts. He pulled his card out of his wallet and wrote two phone numbers on it.

"I am worried about you, Heather," he said. "Here are Paul's and my home phone numbers on the back. The station number is on the front. Nelson dispatch will pick it up if we're not there."

He handed it to her and she put it on the counter with her purse.

"You know," she said. "I never asked why you were at my front door at nine o'clock in the morning."

"Inspector Coswell and I were actually at the *Bulletin* this morning looking for you. He wants to question you about the dead hunter again. He was called back to Vancouver and he assigned me to do the interview. Susan told me you were running late this morning and I thought I might catch you here. Good thing I did."

"You can say that again," she agreed. "I'm running late for sure now. Could this wait till later today? We could meet at the *Bulletin* around four. I really must get right over there."

"I'll take my car," she added, noting the concern on his face.

Ernie's concern was directed more at her face than her transportation. The swelling on her forehead was getting bigger and spreading downwards. She would soon look like George Chuvalo after ten rounds with Ali. If there was bruising to follow, she'd have a raccoon-face. He decided not to point that out to her.

She still had her coat on and so all she had to do was grab her purse and she was ready to go. She pulled out her keys, slipped one off, and handed it to Ernie.

"This fits both doors," she said. "Come and go as you please. I'll get this back from you when you come to the office later. Okay? Let's go. I guess you're going to follow me out to my car."

"Your darned right," said Ernie, and followed her out the back door to the parking lot.

When he saw her car disappear up the street, he quickly returned to the apartment and locked both doors. He was going to talk to the backhoe operator.

He drove the cruiser the block and a half to Ethel Roberts's place. The backhoe was sitting idle and the truck was gone. Probably gone to dump a load, he thought. He debated whether or not to wait but decided against it. Blakemore would be off to the hills with the lab crew by now and there would be no one manning the station. He needed to pick up the fingerprint equipment anyway so he could clear messages with dispatch while he was there. There were no radio calls so far, indicating a quiet morning.

Chapter 28

Bear Creek, like many of the small towns along the Crow's Nest Highway, was quite ugly in its utilitarianism. Gas stations (one for eastbound and one on the other side for westbound traffic), a Dairy Queen, a laundromat, the tourist information bureau, a Quality Inn, and a John Deere outlet bordered the highway along an access road. Parallel to this was the Canadian National Railway line. Trains didn't stop any longer, although there was an old station that functioned in the era before the trucking industry took over. A craft cooperative was now housed there. The main street was at right angles to the track crossing, where lights and barriers gave right of way to the speeding locomotives that barely slowed as they roared through. It then stretched an unimpressive four blocks to the southern town limits. Commercial establishments—the Thunderbird hotel, a hardware store, the Credit Union, sporting goods, Thrifty's, a deli, a liquor store, a second-hand-antique shop, and the like were interspersed with vacant lots and tiny, old two-room houses that were built by the first settlers. At the very end, across from the school, was the RCMP station—a stark brick structure, which, along with the chain-link fenced impound lot, was as unaesthetic

as the Federal Government could make it. Most of the area that lay within the right angle formed by the tracks and the main street was residential. One avenue, however, was an exception. Bear Creek's only stoplight marked its intersection. Located along it were the public library and the *Bulletin* office, housed in old converted mansions, vestiges of the lumber barons who lived there in a bygone era. Across the street was the firehall, an architectural contemporary of the mansions, and located where it was, no doubt, for the peace of mind of its wealthy neighbours. At the end of the block was an incongruity—the town's one and only apartment complex—The Huntingdon—twenty units in a two-story building that represented the largest new residential building construction ever in Bear Creek. A significant part of the local population, however, lived out of town, in small holdings scattered along the myriad of logging roads that radiated in every direction. These were typical rural habitations—chickens, dogs, and cats roaming the yards, with pigs, horses, goats, and even cattle corralled in many of them. Machinery, cars and trucks, some of which were functional while others were rusted and defunct, were parked haphazardly over the properties. Smoke puffed out of the chimneys, since wood was the obvious fuel of choice for heating.

The logging roads continued well beyond human habitation. Most ended in long-abandoned clear cut sites, but a few were new and led into the typical light brown of freshly logged timber patches—the pictures that the environmentalists loved to show to the world. In one of these a slash pile smoldered, and parked at the edge was a lone red pickup truck. The window on the driver's side was cracked and, on closer scrutiny, bore a neat, round hole.

Slumped sideways in the seat was a man, the side of his head pierced by the projectile that had gone through the glass. His seatbelt, unfastened, dangled beside him, and a hard hat lay on

the rest behind the seat. He was wearing Nike runners, heavy cotton pants, and a down vest over a red denim shirt. On the seat beside him was his bomber-style jacket, a patch on the sleeve with an insignia—BCVFD. He was quite dead.

He contemplated jail and a shudder ran up his spine as he remembered. Claustrophobia *was the word his lawyer had used. The dictionary said it meant "abnormal fear of enclosed spaces," but that wasn't it. He had no problem with things like that—sleeping in snow caves, hiding in deer blinds, crawling through culverts—it was the locked door that got to him. He even knew when it started, his fear.*

He was barely four years old, an age you weren't supposed to remember, but he did. They were visiting his "rich" uncle who owned an apple orchard ten miles out of Wenatchee. Three families with a mass of kids, playing hide and seek after dinner, and he stumbled upon the best place—an abandoned bunkhouse on wheels converted to a storage shed. He had trouble climbing the metal steps but made it up, pulling back the wooden door and clambering inside. A gust of wind blew the door shut behind him and although it had probably banged like that a thousand times over the years, just this once it caused the primitive outside latch to fall into position and lock him in. At first he wasn't afraid. There was plenty of light through the two big windows high up on the front wall and the stuff piled in there wasn't scary—old horse harnesses, gunny sacs, rusty milk cans, piles of hemp rope, and other items no longer of use in the modern agricultural world.

He pushed on the door, but it was locked tight. He kicked at it but that only hurt his toes. He could hear the other kids's voices but they sounded far away. He called out and became angry when no one answered. He thought they were teasing him, but he had had enough. He shouted until he was hoarse and pummeled the unyielding door with his fists until they bled. I'll kill you, I'll kill you all, he screamed. He wasn't missed until dusk. The kids thought he'd gone into the house

and the adults assumed he was still outside playing. The liquor that was consumed by the men and women dulled their concerns even more.

He became exhausted and fell asleep, face on the floor, as close to the crack of light as he could get, and that's where they found him.

His mother tried to comfort him but his father just laughed it off.

"That'll teach the dumb little bugger not to get himself locked in some place he's not supposed to be," he said to the men, and they all laughed.

He buried his head in his mother's bosom, tears of rage running down his face and his teeth grinding terribly. She said nothing.

The jail was the same. The booze had made him a child again and he couldn't control his anger. He remembered the frightened looks on the Mounties' faces when they came to investigate the ruckus. They saw his bloodied hands reaching through the bars at them, screaming obscenities. They stood back until he fell sobbing onto the concrete floor before they rushed in with handcuffs and leg irons.

When he awoke, sober, he was ashamed of himself. He wasn't the cat person. He'd acted like a rabid dog. He never touched a drop of liquor after that. Everyone, including his wife, thought it was the birth of his son a week later that had inspired his temperance, and he was happy to go along with that. The real reason was not something he wanted to admit and, like a cat, his dignity brooked no such embarrassment.

He would not be imprisoned—at any cost.

It was Clyde's own fault, getting himself shot. "Turn yourself in so I don't have to do it," he'd said as they stood facing one another in the yard. "Come with me and I'll stand beside you when you talk to the Mounties. It's the only way, believe me." He was wrong; there was another choice. He told Clyde to go ahead and promised he would follow in his own vehicle. Clyde hesitated for a moment but then, convinced his advice had hit home, returned to his truck. He glanced back only once to satisfy himself that the promise was being kept.

He knew that Clyde would be watching him and so he walked

slowly—head down, trying to look the picture of contrition—slowly but resolutely to his own pickup where his .30-30 was cradled in the gun rack. He got in and pulled the clip out of the glove compartment, jammed it into the breach of the rifle, and rolled down the passenger window. Clyde had just turned on the ignition when he squeezed off the round. He never knew what hit him, the poor, dumb, trusting son-of-a-bitch.

Chapter 29

Blakemore was fuming. He escorted the lab crew to the murder site as ordered, but he had no desire to stand around while they worked. Coswell was right; they were a bunch of nerds. One of them, however, was a ranking sergeant in the RCMP. He was a tall, bony-faced man in his mid fifties who looked the science professor type.

How the hell he got to this job in the Force is a mystery to me, thought Blakemore. The science guys are usually hired independently. Nevertheless, a sergeant he was and Blakemore had to take his orders, despite Coswell's telling him he should "ride herd on them."

The sergeant had Blakemore point out every one of the physical signs he had found—the tracks, the tree, the bark, and so forth. The three-man crew took samples and casts of everything, which seemed to take forever to the impatient Blakemore. At last their leader appeared to be finished—with Blakemore at least—and dismissed him.

"We'll take it from here," he said. "You've probably got lots to do back at the station. Why don't you leave us to it?"

"Okay," Blakemore agreed. "But let me know if you need anything further." He hoped that hadn't sounded too insincere. He decided to let the crew leave when they damn well pleased. To hell with Vancouver. He lost no time getting to the squad

car and booting it back to town. He needed to get a whole lot further ahead in this case before Coswell returned and there wasn't much time to do it. He was nagged by the realization that he didn't have the remotest clue about who a local suspect could be. He intuitively felt that Heather held the answer and hoped that Ernie hadn't buggered up his chances with her. Heather wasn't a patient lady and getting her to re-tell everything would be a chore. There had to be a connection with Ethel Roberts. Her broken neck was just too much of a coincidence.

He saw Ernie's cruiser parked at the station and decided not to stop. He didn't want to get tied up there before meeting with Heather. He continued on to the *Bulletin* office. Susan was the only one there.

"You just missed her," she informed him. "She's gone over to the Women's Institute to get the Wedding and Social calendar for the week from Hattie Crocker. She's going from there to interview some of the teachers at the school, and after that a few former students—for a follow-up piece on Ethel Roberts."

"I do hope she knocks it off early today," she went on. "You should have seen her face. It's all swollen and bruised. She had a fall at home this morning and I know she's in pain. She's a tough one, though. Probably won't quit till the press shuts down for the night."

None of this was good news to Blakemore. Hattie Crocker, Ross's mother, was as big a pain in the ass as her son. She didn't take kindly to what she considered the harassment of Ross by the RCMP and wasn't the least bit shy about telling everyone. She was a considerable social power in town, especially among the ever-growing geriatric set. He avoided her as much as he could. His rapport with Heather was never the best, as far as that went, and if she was under the weather the chances of her cooperating with him would not be good. He drove back to the station in a

foul mood. When he pulled up, he saw Ernie locking the front door. He noticed the fingerprint kit in his hand.

"What's up, pard?" he called over to him.

"Paul. I'm glad to see you," Ernie answered. "This has been an eventful morning to say the least. Let's go back inside and I'll go over it all with you."

Blakemore unlocked the door just as the desk phone rang. He walked over and picked it up.

"Nelson dispatch calling," the female operator announced. "I have a Mrs. Groat on the line who would like to speak to Corporal Blakemore."

"Put her on," said Blakemore, taking the receiver. "Good morning, Michelle. What's the second prettiest lady in Bear Creek want with an ugly old guy like me?" Michelle worked at the Credit Union and he assumed she was calling about his account there.

"It's Clyde, Paul," she said, the worry obvious in her voice. "He rushed out of the house right from the breakfast table this morning. He was reading one of the old *Bulletins* when he jumped up and said he had to go see someone quick. It must have been something he read that set him off but he didn't say what or who he was going to see. He just left with the paper in his hand."

"We saw him at the Thunderbird at seven-thirty this morning," Blakemore interjected. "He looked all right then."

"Paul," she continued, "Ross Crocker just phoned me. Clyde didn't show up at the Cougar Creek site where he was supposed to be directly after the meeting. I can't reach him anywhere. He's not at home and nobody's even seen his truck. He'd be mad if he knew I was bothering you but I'm really, really worried. He must have been in an accident or he would have phoned me by now."

"Don't worry, Michelle," Blakemore said, trying to reassure her. "We'll find him. You were right to call me. That isn't like

Clyde at all. Both Ernie and I will work on it and we'll keep you posted."

"Please do," she pleaded, almost in tears now.

"Jesus," Blakemore exclaimed after he hung up. "Work is getting to be awfully personal around here these days."

He related his conversation to Ernie.

"Yes," returned Ernie. "And I'm afraid I'm going to have to add another example."

He told him about Heather's attack, including his theory of the wrestling hold and his promise of protection.

"Holy shit!" exclaimed Blakemore. "This is getting just too goddamned bizarre." A feeling of dread was growing in the pit of his stomach. A whacko wrestler in Bear Creek responsible for both killings and the assault on Heather? Far-fetched would be the kindest word to apply to that theory. Coswell was off on a wild goose chase in Vancouver, following up on Montgomery and his friends. He'd really put himself between a rock and a hard place. Should he confide in Ernie? He immediately rejected the idea. I might as well take all the shit myself when it hits the fan, he thought, and not drag Ernie into it.

"Of course we'll protect her," he continued. "I agree with your shift idea. If it's okay with you, I'll do the first one. We'll do twelve hours apiece. Let's set up eight to eight. I don't think we need to keep her in sight at all times. When she's bolted in at night she has time to call us if someone breaks in, and during the day she has the safety of her work surroundings."

That also gives me a good excuse to contact her this afternoon, he thought to himself.

"First, though," he went on, "I'm going to find Clyde and give him shit for scaring his wife. Why don't you let me do the fingerprint thing at Heather's as well? It's probably best that you stay here to receive calls. Also, the lab crew will be circulating

through here sometime this afternoon and maybe you could chase them back to Vancouver like Coswell said. You're a lot better at wording that than I am."

"Roger," said Ernie, and gave him the key to Heather's apartment.

Blakemore returned to his vehicle, fingerprint kit in hand. He planned to drive up to the Cougar Creek site. On route, he passed the remains of Ethel Roberts's place. It was deserted—both the truck and backhoe were gone. He drove past and turned up the Cougar Creek Road.

The prospective condominium site, five miles up, was set in one of the most beautiful canyons in the Monashees. The creek was crystal clear, running fast and pure. There were two sets of falls, the largest almost thirty feet high and, below it, there was a series of ponds replete with rainbow trout. The walls of the canyon were too steep even for high-lead logging and thus spared the creek from the ravages of slash and mud, the end results of clear cutting. Helicopters, unfortunately, had again opened up these slopes to logging and Ross Crocker was using one to lift out the timber that he was clearing for the development. Blakemore could see the aircraft hovering, a long cable dangling from its belly. The men attaching the cable to the logs below were not visible, hidden by the selected trees that were being spared. Crocker's 4x4 was parked in a large clearing dug out by bulldozers. Goon number one was standing with him as they watched the helicopter work. Blakemore pulled his cruiser along side them and got out.

"Well, if it isn't the king of traffic tickets," Crocker taunted. "Aren't you a long way from your favourite traffic light?"

"Thought I would come up and watch you rape the wilderness," he shot back.

"Oh, fuck off," Crocker retorted.

"Actually, I've come on a peaceful mission," Blakemore said.

"Clyde Groat has gone missing, at least according to his wife. How come he's not here? I thought he was running this show for you."

"He is," replied Crocker. "But he didn't show up here like he was supposed to. I haven't seen hide nor hair of him since we met this morning. That's really weird. Clyde's someone I can count on and I know he needs the work. He can't make a living with that gypo business he bought off of George Smith."

Sadly, Blakemore knew that was true. George had retired at the right time, just before the price of lumber nose-dived. Clyde, who had worked his way up in the woods, starting as a chokerman at the age of seventeen and becoming a foreman at twenty-one, mortgaged everything he had to buy George's logging company. *Company* was a bit of a glorified term, since its main assets were timber licences. The equipment in the deal consisted of a logging truck, a D9 Caterpillar tractor, a hauling cradle, winches, cables, blocks, and a twenty-year-old loader. With himself and one man, however, Clyde was an efficient, selective logging enterprise. George kept his hand in by doing some of the falling for him and driving the truck full of logs to the mill in Nelson, allowing Clyde and his hireling to work non-stop. The world, however, was against him. Japan wasn't buying Canadian lumber anymore and the Americans had their own forest industry. The past three years had been bleak ones for him. Volunteering at the firehall and doing the first responder course over the winters had kept him sane. Michelle was the breadwinner and Blakemore knew how that bothered Clyde. They had married young and their two young children were in primary school. His volunteer activities saved him the ignominy of being a houseparent. The domesticated male was a rare animal in Bear Creek.

Blakemore was beginning to feel uneasy. He had fully

expected to be able to track Clyde's whereabouts from Crocker. It was well after noon, and if Clyde had gone off the road somewhere he should have been spotted by now. He returned to his cruiser and radioed Ernie.

"Ernie, have you heard anything on Clyde yet?" he asked. Crocker and his man were watching him, obviously interested.

"Not a thing," answered Ernie. "Bad things come in threes, they say. I sure hope this isn't one of them. What do you want me to do? How about paging the volunteers and organizing a search party?"

"Ordinarily I don't like to jump too fast on these missing person things and it's only been a few hours, but I agree with you. I've got a bad feeling about this. Go ahead and send out the call."

"Awe, he's probably just humping something he's got on the side," offered Crocker's grunt.

"Shut-up, Derek," ordered Crocker.

"Listen to your keeper," Blakemore added, glaring at the man, who returned his gaze with an insolent smirk on his face.

Blakemore started the engine of his cruiser, put it in gear and did a professional U-turn at speed, spitting gravel back at the two men as they watched him leave.

Chapter 30

Heather's head was really aching, despite the double dose of Tylenol. The ladies at the Women's Institute clucked over her so much that she went into the bathroom and looked at herself in the mirror. She couldn't believe how bad she looked. There was no discernable notch between her nose and her brow. Her upper lids were puffing up and she was sure she was going to bruise. With her complexion, that was going to be a sight. She decided

to delay the interviews at the school. Her face would probably scare the younger children. All she needed was a hunched back to look like Quasimoto, she thought. She left the Women's Institute, which was housed in the library, and walked across the street to the *Bulletin*. There she dashed off her social column and gave it to Susan.

"I'll work on Ethel's story at home and do the interviews tomorrow if my face goes down," she told her. "I think I can manage to hide this mess with sunglasses and some make-up if the swelling goes down."

"I think you should have a doctor look at you," Susan admonished. "You could have broken something."

"I don't think so," reassured Heather. "My forehead took all the impact and according to what I've read, that's the thickest part of the skull. In my case, it's probably really thick."

She gathered notes from her desk and shoved them into a folder that she tucked under one arm and, with her purse in the other, she headed out to her car. She was fumbling for the keys when Zachary drove by. He spotted her red hair and tooted his horn. She looked up, revealing her battered face. He slammed on the brakes and wheeled his car to the curb. He jumped out and ran to her.

"What in God's name happened to you, Heather?" he exclaimed, shocked by her appearance.

She was going to give him the shower door excuse but decided to be honest and told him the whole story. His jaw went slack as he listened. Looking down at her, he suddenly felt an overwhelming urge to protect her. He stepped forward and gathered her in his arms.

"Heather," was all he could say, hugging her tightly.

It felt nice to be hugged, thought Heather, but this is a bit excessive. He let go, embarrassed.

"I'm sorry," he said. "I'm not an emotional person, but the sight of you just made that happen. I assume you're going home. I'm surprised you even came out today. I'll follow you in my car. I was on my way to do a house call so I have my medical bag with me. I can give you something to make that swelling clear more quickly and something for the pain."

Heather was going to object, but Zachary's concern was obvious and the memory of the hug was beginning to make her feel better. She led the way in her car as Zachary turned his around and followed her.

A block away she saw the familiar blue and white of an RCMP car directly in front of her apartment. It had to be Blakemore; Ernie would have left her that space. She was right.

Blakemore was still dusting for prints when she and Zachary came in.

"Good afternoon, folks," he said pleasantly.

"Jeez, Heather. Your face looks like the front end of a bus," he added.

"Thanks a lot," she replied, sarcastically. "I thought Ernie was going to do this."

"He's busy at the shop," Blakemore answered. "I volunteered to mop up here."

"Well get your mopping done quick," she said, testily. "I've got a miserable headache."

Zachary had opened his medical bag and found what he wanted. He handed Heather two small packets of pills.

"Do you have any drug sensitivities?" he asked.

Blakemore almost chuckled at that. Environmental activists, in his experience, included more than just trees in their plant appreciation. He wondered how many Heather had tried.

"No," she answered. "I can take anything."

"Right," thought Blakemore.

"Take two of each," Zachary instructed. Heather, pouring herself a glass of water, obeyed.

Zachary turned his attention to Blakemore.

"Paul," he asked, "what do you think of all this? Is Heather in some sort of continuing danger or is this an isolated incident?"

Blakemore decided that it was now or never that he should push Heather for information, and Zachary's presence might even facilitate that.

"I honestly don't know," he replied, "but somehow I think the answer to your question lies with Heather herself. What do you say, Heather? I know you're hurting, but the sooner we get going on this the safer you're going to be."

"What can I tell you that I haven't told you already? If I thought I had anything more I certainly wouldn't be holding it back."

"Why don't we sit down in the living room?" suggested Zachary. "Those pills will click in shortly and you'll be more comfortable. Paul has a point."

One of the bonuses of living in a small community is the leeway the developers have with land. Heather's apartment was huge by city standards. The ample living room contained two large armchairs and an enormous couch, all purchased at a moving sale that she and Ethel Roberts attended just after she signed the lease. Original prints and watercolours decorated the walls. Her tastes were eclectic. The artwork ranged from abstract to local landscapes. These were purchased one at a time at various shows put on by the Craft Cooperative. A long coffee table sat in front of the couch. Its top and a shelf beneath were covered with reading material—books, magazines, and sections from two national newspapers. A cushion was at one end, presumably used as a footrest. Two modern halogen floor lamps, each strategically placed beside a chair, suggested that reading

occupied a large part of Heather's leisure time at home. She did not own a television set, but a small stereo system was set up in a corner with two miniature speakers. A stack of CDs was piled on top. Her choice of music was as varied as her art. Opera, country, metal, and jazz were all represented.

Heather settled in one corner of the chesterfield; Zachary sat beside her. Blakemore lowered himself into one of the easy chairs, sinking down so far that his knees were almost at eye level.

"Jeeze, Heather," he said. "What happened to the springs in this thing? I might never rise again."

"There's nothing wrong with the springs," she shot back. "They weren't designed to hold that much weight."

"Touché," he said.

"Come on, you two," admonished Zachary. "This is a serious matter."

"Right," conceded Blakemore. "Let's get on with it."

"Heather, I'd like you to really think back in two directions. First, Ross Crocker or someone related to his Cougar Creek development. I remember the article that had Ethel Roberts's and your name on it. That was pretty strong stuff. I think you underestimate sometimes the impact of your words. A lot of people are really hurting here, financially, and that project is a godsend to them. It means work and money to feed their families. You both could have made some real enemies there. Did you ever receive any threats after you wrote that?"

Zachary stared at Blakemore. He hadn't missed the inclusion of Ethel Roberts's name in the question. My god, he thought. This is monstrous! The two deaths and the attack on Heather could very well be the acts of a single deranged individual who is here in Bear Creek, right now. I hope that Paul knows what he's doing. The potential for further tragedy is real and Heather is in the middle of it.

He almost blurted out his concerns but held back. He would corner Blakemore later and demand some action that would ensure Heather's safety.

"The only negative feedback I got on that article," Heather answered, oblivious to the Ethel Roberts connection, "was an irate call from Ross Crocker. He called me a lot of names—shit disturber, pinko-hippy, know-it-all, and a few other choice phrases. But that was all hot air. He never threatened me."

"Maybe his attitude filtered down to one of his minions," Blakemore commented. "I wouldn't put it past a couple of them to do a little bashing if they thought you were a threat to their jobs."

"That article was a month ago," she said, "and the project is proceeding anyway. I don't think that possibility holds water."

"Maybe," Blakemore replied, frowning.

"Well, let's try another avenue then—our headless hunter," he continued. "You're the only one locally who seems to have any connection with him. Is it possible that you know something that might reveal the killer and he wants to shut you up?"

"That's a scary possibility," she said, "but equally remote, I think. I never really knew Dietmar. I only met him a few times and found out very little. He had all kinds of enemies, but no one that I was associated with. Anyway, I thought you suspected that hunter from Vancouver."

Blakemore was uncomfortable now. Zachary was giving him the evil eye and Heather was not going to be of much help if he kept on this way. He tried a new tack.

"Heather, I have to level with you. It's becoming more and more apparent that the killer is here, not in Vancouver."

Heather's swollen eyes suddenly widened.

"What?" she exclaimed. "What are you holding back you devious bugger? You've found out something, haven't you? I've got ten good reasons to be brought in on this, not the least

of which is the fact that my neck is in a sling, literally."

Blakemore told her everything. When he finished there was silence. Heather spoke first.

"Ethel's death might not have been an accident. Is that what you're telling me?" she demanded.

Blakemore nodded.

"It's a possibility," he said.

She was stunned. As the two men watched, her expression turned from amazement to seething anger. Her face reddened. She jumped up and bent forward, nose to nose with Blakemore.

"Who killed her, you poor excuse for a cop? Who the fuck killed my friend?" She looked ready to pummel him. Zachary pulled her away and held her tight. She was crying.

"He's trying, Heather," he said, trying to console her. "They're all trying."

After a moment, he felt her relax.

"I'm okay now," she said, quietly. He let her go and she sat back on the couch.

A calm had come over her and a resolve.

"What can I do to help you get this guy?" she asked him.

Blakemore seized his opportunity, unfazed by Heather's outburst.

"We have to find the link that connects all of this—Dietmar, Ethel, and you. I'm hoping we can find it from your conversations with Ethel Roberts. I'm sure there's a clue there. Think back. Did she ever mention being hassled because of her beliefs, particularly from the young and the restless? She knows every kid in this town for the last twenty years, good and bad. Did any of them turn against her, take advantage of her? Could any of them have been attracted to Dietmar and his gang? Motives for murder usually narrow down to three—money, revenge, and passion. Do any of these fit in Ethel's case?

Heather shook her head to each question, but then looked out the window struggling to remember.

"Everybody took advantage of Ethel's generosity, especially the kids. You know, she never mentioned disappointment in any of them. I'm sure there were a few, but she overlooked anything like that. Most of her stories were about the successes, and I could keep you occupied for some time talking about those. She was proud of them. If she had any jilted suitors, it would be news to me. The money angle is a thought, though. I suspect that her estate will be a surprise. She gave me a talk one night on investing when I came into a little money from an old aunt who died. I was astounded at her knowledge and the fact that she actually did on-line trading. I do remember the company, though, because I liked the name—Greenline."

"Oh, I almost forgot the reason I came back to the apartment this morning. I sort of agreed to be Ethel's executor a couple of months ago and somewhere in this place is an envelope from her with some instructions in it for me."

Blakemore's eyes lit up.

"Do you realize that's probably the only personal record left of Ethel other than what she may have kept at the school? And I somehow don't think that will be much. You've got to find it. We'll all look. Just point us in the right direction."

"I'm sure I put it in my office den, but maybe you could check this room and Zachary can look in the kitchen. It wouldn't be the first time I absent-mindedly stuck something away in a book or up on a shelf somewhere."

They began the search. She was right. Blakemore found it. She'd used it to mark her place in a book and then tossed it on the cluttered lower shelf of the coffee table.

"God, I can't believe I was so careless with something so important," Heather lamented. "I know it's addressed to me,

but go ahead and open it. You'll be a lot more objective reading it than me, I'm sure."

He did so, reading the single page silently, then handing it to her.

"There's not much there," he said. "But what do you make of the last paragraph?"

Most of the letter was composed of straightforward information—the name of her lawyer, her banker, her broker, and her safety deposit box number. The final paragraph was of interest:

You will note that I have not listed a next of kin. I have done that deliberately. I became estranged from my family in my early teens, much like you did, but for reasons I wish to die with me. One of my family has tracked me down, but under no circumstances are they to benefit from my death. My will, Mr. Fitch assures me, is ironclad, but please, Heather, do your utmost to make sure my wishes are upheld.

With all of my love dear friend,

Ethel

"This is all news to me," Heather said. "She did tell me that both her parents were dead, but she never mentioned any brothers or sisters. How strange."

She read the passage again and commented: "Something else is odd. Ethel taught English before becoming the school's librarian. Her grammar was impeccable. The error in the second to last sentence tells a lot. She must have been deep in thought, jumping from 'one of my family' to 'they.' She would never make a blunder like that unless her mind was preoccupied. She was obviously disturbed about something related to her family. Is this one relative representing others trying to get something from her?"

"If she was wealthy, and we'll soon find that out when you contact the lawyer, Fitch, we could have a motive for her killing,

but how does that fit in with Dietmar or with your attack?" asked Blakemore. "I really think that they are all connected, somehow."

"If Ethel's relative had contacted her in person here in Bear Creek you'd think word of that would have gotten around," offered Zachary. "There are no secrets in small towns, they say, especially if a stranger is involved. It may be worth your asking around, Paul, at the school or the library. Can you think of anywhere else, Heather?"

"Keats' Korner is all I can suggest. She attended readings there in the evenings. I've never seen her in a restaurant. We've had many dinners together but always at her place or mine. Outside of work, she kept pretty much to herself. I think I was the only close friend she had. I always found that strange because she was respected by so many people."

"Being a paragon is often a friendless virtue, I'm afraid," commented Zachary, contemplating his own social isolation.

"The wrestling angle is interesting," Blakemore mused. "I have to confess that I don't often read the *Bulletin*. Barbara does, though, and fills me in on anything she thinks I ought to know. She's not interested in sports, though, and I get my news, in that regard, from the Vancouver papers. Unless we have a famous Bear Creek wrestler, I'm not likely to know about it. Has anything passed your desk, Heather, about future prospects for the WWF in this area?"

"Don't be so smug," she replied. "In fact there is a wrestling program at the school. Some of the kids have been good enough to go to the Provincials. It's run by the phys-ed teacher who, by the way, is a woman. I did an article on her a couple of years ago."

"A female wrestling coach!" he exclaimed. "That's a good one." As an afterthought, he added, "Is she cute? That would

attract the boys all right. She probably has to show them the holds quite a few times before they get it."

"Asshole," she said. "She's got first class volunteers—former students, locals, and so forth—but she knows the sport herself. Grappling isn't everything; a few brains help."

Blakemore changed the subject, although the thought of pressing a thing of beauty on a wrestling mat lingered for a moment. He would add the phys-ed teacher to his questioning list when he went to the school.

"Before I forget," he said, "we've been freed up to mention Dietmar Kraus's full name in print. Would you like to do a follow-up article on the murder? The boy's father is a VIP German industrialist. You might even get a request by the big news services for the piece when it comes out. From a local point of view, it would be useful if you reprinted the victim's picture. If you want, I could get a more recent photo from the family, or the mug shot from his arrest in Victoria."

Heather was more than a little interested in doing the article. It would be picked up and international reporters would contact her. She knew exactly who Dietmar's father was—Hans Kraus, the billionaire, whose industry's acid rains had killed the Black Forest. How ironic that his son died fighting the war against the polluters, his father being one of the worst. No wonder Dietmar hid his last name.

"I could do that," she said, trying not to sound too eager. "The more pictures you can get me the better."

Blakemore's pager beeped. He heaved himself out of the chair and went into the kitchen to phone Ernie. He returned a minute later, his face clouded.

"I've got to go," he said, grimly. "Clyde Groat's been shot."

Zachary jumped up, ready to follow him, forgetting momentarily his concern for Heather.

"I'm afraid there's no need for you right away, Zach," Blakemore instructed. "Clyde's dead. Ernie's on his way there. I'd like you to stay with Heather till one of us gets back. I know you have to do your coroner's job, but it can wait for a bit. It appears to be a freak hunting accident."

Before Zachary could answer, Heather interrupted.

"We'll be right behind you," she said. "I appreciate the concern, but my job's to cover the news and I plan to be there."

Blakemore simply shrugged his shoulders. He wasn't going to take the time to argue. They left together.

Chapter 31

The return flight to the Coast was surprisingly smooth for Coswell. There was much less than the usual turbulence out of Castlegar and it was calm all the way to the Vancouver International Airport. A driver was waiting for him and he was whisked straight to RCMP headquarters.

One would expect that the building that housed the RCMP Chief Inspector for the Province of BC would be an impressive edifice. It's not. The structure is a disappointing five-story brick-façade blockhouse—ugly even in its Eastside location—situated a block from an ethnic melting pot of East Indians, Italians, Latinos, Vietnamese, and, more recently, blacks from the Caribbean and Los Angeles area. Ward's office was on the top floor with a window that faced West. He could at least look in the direction of affluence—Kerrisdale and the University Endowment Lands.

Coswell's arrival had obviously been predicted to the minute. He was quickly ushered into the Chief's office where Ward was waiting, seated behind a huge hardwood desk. With him were two men, seated at either side on heavy chairs made of the same hardwood. There was no other seating; Coswell had

to stand. He was wearing his usual travelling clothes creating an unfortunate contrast with the Chief's spit and polished uniform and the formal business attire of the two visitors. The looks directed at him prompted Coswell to remark, "I apologize for my casual dress, but the driver wouldn't let me stop off at home to change. He drove me here direct from the airport."

No one's expression changed, presumably because all three expected a member of the RCMP to be in uniform during working hours, travelling or not. Ward, frowning, introduced him.

"Gentlemen, this is Inspector Coswell. Inspector, I want you to meet Herr Hans Kraus and his assistant, Herr Schlapner."

Both men nodded; neither stood nor offered a handshake. Coswell noted the slightly pained expression on Schlapner's face at the word *assistant*.

"Pleased to meet you," Coswell said pleasantly, amused that he would never have guessed which man was which. Schalpner was the spitting image of Oliver Hardy, complete with the cookie-duster mustache, and looked very much the Bavarian beer hall proprietor who sampled a bit too much of his own wares. He held a leather briefcase in his lap. Kraus was a small, thin man with a full head of white hair, aquiline nose, and startling blue eyes.

Ward opened his mouth to speak but Kraus cut him off and questioned Coswell directly. His English was perfect, spoken with a slight British accent. Likely Oxford or Cambridge, thought Coswell.

"Have you found the murderer of my son?" he asked abruptly.

"No, not yet," answered Coswell, "but we have intensified our investigation as I'm sure Chief Ward has told you. We're expecting a breakthrough soon." He wanted Ward to share this flak as much as possible.

"As I understand it," Kraus returned sarcastically," You have only one suspect and he was let go."

"There wasn't enough evidence to hold him," explained Coswell. "But I plan to personally carry out further interrogation of him now that I am back in Vancouver. I will also make a trip to Victoria to follow up on leads there. I was hoping that you would help us in that regard."

He was pleased with himself, having turned the onus back on the father rather than continue to be the target of his obvious hostility.

"Of course," was Kraus's terse reply. Then, turning to his assistant, said, "Otto, give this man your seat. I'm sure the secretary will find you one."

Schlapner jumped up at the command and, with an icy look at Coswell, left the room to find a chair. Ward made no effort to aid him. Coswell sat down and began his questioning.

"When was the last time you had any contact with your son? Were you close?"

"As I have told Inspector Ward, my son and I have been estranged for the greater part of the past few years. He is at a difficult age—rebelling against all authority including his father. That is typical, is it not, for the young and intelligent of today?"

Coswell shrugged and nodded. Pretty typical of the young and not-intelligent too, he mused.

"He had more reason than most for his attitude," Kraus continued. "His mother died of breast cancer when he was nineteen and just beginning his university studies at Edinburgh. It was a shame, because his obtaining one of the coveted places in the School of International Business there was a moment of great pride for us. He was our only child and my wife dedicated her life to him. Her death was a blow from which he never recovered. He wanted vengeance, somehow, against a world he felt responsible. He became fixated on environmental causes

of cancer, which gave him something to fight. My world and everything connected to it became his enemy. My wife's sister was the only exception, and he did write to her from time to time. She, kindly, forwarded the letters to me. He rebuffed all my attempts to reach him and so I had to satisfy myself with this vicarious contact. There were never any return addresses on any of the correspondence, only postmarks, mainly Victoria, British Columbia. He telephoned her a number of times but, again, gave only a vague indication of where he was."

"Can you recall anything in the letters that might help us?" Coswell interjected.

"I can do better than that. I have them all with me." He motioned to his assistant, who had returned to the room with a metal chair that looked as though it came from a cafeteria and that barely held his considerable derriere. He pulled the letters from his briefcase and handed them to Coswell.

"I also contacted his university in Edinburgh. He transferred to the Science Faculty. You will note in one of his letters that he wished to become a scientist, eventually specializing in environmental research. Unfortunately, his anger affected his studies and he did not complete his first year. His professors found him argumentative and undisciplined. He would most likely not have been promoted to second year. He decided, for reasons that he did not communicate to me or his aunt, to go to Canada. He did write to me at that time and that letter is with the others. He wrote simply that he wished to continue his studies in a country that was worth saving and that he wanted his allowance increased considerably. There was also a request that I expedite his visa application. I did both without question. Since then I have been contacted twice—on both occasions by a lawyer requesting bail money and funds to cover legal fees. My son refused to talk to me despite my pleas. You will have a

record, no doubt, of the charges—resisting arrest during protest demonstrations. It was my understanding from his lawyer that he received no worse than a reprimand and a fine both times. I was surprised that his visa was not revoked, but apparently it was not."

Thanks to the wimpy Canadian justice system, thought Coswell.

"Did your son have any close friends at Edinburgh? A roommate? A Canadian connection?"

"His roommate was a Canadian—a Commonwealth Scholar from Victoria entering his third year. Dietmar's mother was especially pleased about that—a serious student to help guide her son."

And I'll bet you had nothing to do with that placement, thought Coswell. He probably paid the other kid's rent.

"They had a falling out," Kraus went on, "near the end of the term. Dietmar wanted a private room after his mother died. This was arranged. The boy's name is Jeremy Witherspoon. I presume he has graduated by now, but I have the Victoria address from his student record in Edinburgh."

"This information you have given us is invaluable," Coswell said. "With your permission, I would like to have the letters copied and, of course, leave the originals with you. I would like time to study them carefully."

"Permission granted," replied Kraus. "If you have more questions after reading them, call my hotel. They will contact me. Inspector Ward has the number." Standing and turning to Ward, he said, "You will let me know the minute your forensic specialists are finished with my son's body. I wish to take him home with me as soon as possible."

"Of course, of course," Ward reassured him, hurrying around his desk. Kraus's attention, however, was riveted on

Coswell. He had obviously made a tacit decision of trust.

"I believe that Inspector Ward is correct in his assessment of your competence, Inspector Coswell. I expect results from you soon. Please keep me informed. I cannot bring my son back to life, but seeing his murderer brought to justice will ease some of the pain."

Coswell almost shuddered as they shook hands. Kraus's unblinking stare was hard and cold. Somehow this case had risen to the top of his workload despite his altruistic remarks to the Bear Creek detachment. He had to get moving. He gathered the sheaf of letters and went to find his driver, letting Ward look after the political good-byes to the two Germans.

One hour later he was on the helijet to Victoria. Dietmar's letters to his aunt were filled with fanatical ramblings about the rape of the forests and focussed particularly on Vancouver Island. It appeared that he had been involved in some violence during the Carmanah Valley protest, which was picked up by a Victoria TV station. He was blatantly proud of his notoriety, painting himself as some sort of Che Guevera hero. Violence begets violence, Coswell reasoned, and someone with equal passion had selected the young activist as his target. Intuition told him that the motive for the murder was somewhere on the Island. Once that was established, he was sure that the trail to Bear Creek would become clear. He would start at the university. A mailing address would have been required when Dietmar registered.

For most travellers, the helijet ride to the capital city of British Columbia is twenty minutes of breath-taking scenery. It leaves from the harbour front in Vancouver, lifts over the moored cruise ships, Stanley Park, the sea wall, and then, leveling out at five hundred feet, proceeds across the Strait of Georgia. On route, the passengers have a magnificent view of the huge ferries

that make hourly crossings, a myriad of pleasure craft, fishing boats, and freighters, the tiny Gulf Islands, and finally Victoria, arguably the most beautiful city in Canada. The helijet sets down on a pad in front of one of the luxury hotels that rim the tiny inner harbour. The passengers receive another visual treat as they step out of the craft. A half dozen modern, multi-storied, architecturally splendid hotels share the harbour's shoreline with the old ivy-covered Empress Hotel and its contemporary, the BC Parliament Buildings. Float planes land and take off in the meager bit of open water, their wash gently rocking the tour boats and the Washington State Ferry moored on either side. Tourists sit and watch this spectacle for hours.

This was all lost on Coswell. He had never been in a helicopter before and assumed that its slow rate of travel would make for a stability that was lacking in an airplane. He missed two problems that became apparent to him seconds after lift-off in Vancouver. The first was the rate of rise and, of course, the rate of descent in Victoria, combined with a spiraling rotation that gave his stomach an out of body experience. Second was the view through the forward bubble canopy—wonderful for anyone but the motion-challenged. The sight of the water rushing below, the sky flashing above, and the horizon distorted by the plexiglass created a vertigo that was the finish of the hapless inspector. Once again, he buried his face in the barf bag and didn't look up until the rotors shut down at the Victoria helipad. He was helped down by an attendant who handed him his carry-on bag and asked if he needed a taxi.

"I think I need an ambulance," he gasped, then, seeing the horrified look on the attendant's face, added quickly, "just kidding. No, thank you. I'm staying at the hotel behind the pad here. I'll just walk over. I can certainly use the fresh air."

Coswell handed her his barf bag.

Chapter 32

Blakemore, making full use of his siren and speeding privileges, arrived at the scene a full five minutes before Zachary and Heather. As he drove up he saw Ernie's cruiser and two pickups parked in a line. He recognized Clyde's vehicle but it was not until he pulled alongside that he saw the owner of the other. Karl Reinhart, Clyde's number one man on the inhalator squad, was standing a short distance away, his face frozen in disbelief, his eyes pleading silently for an answer. Ernie was standing beside his cruiser and walked quickly over as Blakemore skidded his vehicle to a stop and leapt out.

"Karl found him," Ernie said. "He organized the volunteers to fan out over the main logging roads and this one was his. He got me on his cell phone. The others just have the firehall pagers, so I radioed their dispatch and asked for the inhalator van to stand by. I also directed the searchers to check the area for people who are hunting right now and to question any about shooting. The volunteers are all members of the Wilderness Watch and know where to look."

"Karl's really shaken up, Paul," he added. "You'd better speak to him first."

"Okay," answered Blakemore. "But has Michelle been notified yet? That's a job I really dread."

"No," replied Ernie. "And I'll do it. I know how close those two are to you. It needs to be done in person, though, so I'll drive down right after you settle Karl."

"Paul," he added, softly. "I don't think a hunter's stray bullet killed him. I think we have another murder on our hands."

Blakemore looked at him, incredulous, but only for a moment. He went over to Karl and put his arm around his shoulder.

"Go home Karl," he said. "Go home to your wife. You've

done all you can here. Leave the rest up to us. Doc Bensen's on his way and Ernie's ordered up the van. You don't need any more of this right now. We'll talk later."

Karl nodded and allowed himself to be led back to his truck. He got in, started it up, and made a U-turn in the clearing, passing the two squad cars just as Zachary and Heather pulled up. He didn't stop, driving his truck slowly down the road back to town.

Blakemore's composure had returned. He cursed himself for not being more insistent that Heather stay at her apartment or, better still, that she go to the hospital to be checked up. She was a huge complication that he didn't need in all this. He got back to Ernie quickly enough for a whispered comment before Heather and Zachary got out of his car.

"Ernie," he said. "Let me deal with Heather. I don't want things getting out of hand before we make some sense of this. We'll stick to the hunting accident theory until you and I get a chance to talk."

With that he strode over to Zachary's car and stood at the passenger door to block Heather's exit and motioned to her to roll down the window. She did so with a suspicious look on her face.

"Heather," he said in his most authoritative voice. "I'm going to ask you to remain in the car until Doctor Bensen and I have had a chance to investigate. Constable Downs will stay with you. It appears that Clyde has been the victim of a random bullet, probably from a hunter below. The killing range of the bullet from a hunting rifle is five miles. You'll be safer in the car."

"Didn't help Clyde much, did it? And why isn't one of you down there looking for the shooter?" she retorted, but she remained seated. She would work on Ernie.

"Two of us aren't going to cover much territory, and besides, Ernie will call in the Wilderness Watch to do just that," he answered, haughtily.

He cautioned Zachary as they approached Clyde's truck.

"Doc," he said. "I want you to go real lightly here. Watch where you're stepping. Don't disturb any foot or tireprints. I have the luxury of a forensic team in town right now, as you know, and I'm going to bring them up here. I think that both of us better do no more than take a look. I don't think Ernie or Karl touched anything. The door's still closed. Can you delay the pronouncing of death thing?"

"Yes, of course," agreed Zachary.

Blakemore walked around the truck and looked in the passenger window. Zachary tried to peer through the bullet-punctured driver's side window. Clyde's head was leaning against it. The point of entry wound was readily visible through the cracks. His eyes were closed.

Both men knew instantly that they were looking at a murder. Blakemore called to Ernie, waving him over with one hand and holding up his other in a "halt" position to Heather, as though he were directing traffic. Ernie paused to say something to Heather, then walked over. She remained in the car watching the three men.

Blakemore summed it up.

"Correct me if I'm wrong," he said, "but this is no accident. Clyde was a stickler about safety. He's wearing his running shoes, which are strictly off-duty footwear. When he's on the job it's steel-toed work boots—always. And when have you ever seen him at work without his hard hat on? There's no sign of skidding or veering. It looks as though the truck was stopped when he was shot, but the emergency brake pedal hasn't been depressed. Clyde would not have removed his seat belt before doing that. Even if he had gotten out to check the fire and returned, the brake should be on. Most careful drivers around here use them because of the frequency that they park their vehicles on slopes. It becomes a habit."

"Yes, I noticed all that too," agreed Ernie. "And how can he be sitting in an upright position if the truck wasn't moving and he was hit on the left side of his head by a high-powered rifle bullet?"

"That's true," added Zachary. "Without his seat belt on, the force of the bullet should have knocked him over sideways on the seat. The other thing that's odd is that his eyes are firmly closed. Unless he was sleeping, his eyes should be open after a head shot like that. I think someone didn't like being stared at by a dead man and pulled them shut."

"And then he was driven up here. But why?" asked Ernie.

"I think I know," answered Blakemore. "Clyde's responsible for all of these slash burns and he has to check that they're thoroughly extinguished before they can be abandoned. His vehicle would be expected up here. But something's missing."

"What's that?" asked Ernie.

"There's no pump truck. There has to be one present at all times while the pile's burning. It's also used to douse the ashes afterwards. That's the law. This fire's still smoldering. Where's the truck?"

"Used by the killer to get away," answered Ernie.

"Exactly," said Blakemore. "Someone knew it would be here. We need to find it, then have a talk with Ross Crocker. This is his show."

Zachary interrupted.

"This is getting out of hand. We've had three murders here in less than two weeks. Heather's been attacked. They have to be related. Paul, you and Ernie need help. I think you should get that Vancouver Inspector back here as soon as possible and bring in more manpower. This rampage has to stop. I also think that the public should be made aware of what's happened. Secrecy will surely come back to haunt us all if it's continued."

The mention of Heather's name did bring Blakemore back to earth. He sensed that he was getting very close to solving this case on his own but he had run out of stall time. Zachary was right. He spoke first to Ernie.

"I want you to head back down and get the forensic crew up here pronto. Phone Coswell, or even Ward if you get any argument. Tell them it's all part of the same case. Then go to Michelle. She's at work. Try your damndest to keep her from coming up here. Tell her we're bringing him down and she can go to the morgue then. Leave it up to her as to who she wants notified. The two kids are in school. Suggest that she leave them be for the afternoon, at least. They'll know soon enough. I really don't know Clyde's parents. Barbara probably does. Call her. She'll know what to do."

"What should I do about the Inhalator crew and the Wilderness Watch guys? They're going to want some answers soon," asked Ernie.

"Tell them Clyde's been shot and we don't know by who and we are investigating. That's the truth. Leave it at that," he said, ignoring Zachary's stare.

With that he walked, head bowed, to where Heather waited. Once more, he told her everything.

"I'm asking you to put a lot of thought into how you're going to break this news to the citizens. I told you this afternoon that you wield a helluva sword with your pen. That's all I'll say. I only hope the next word I give you is the name of the son of Satan who's doing this."

She sat, stunned for a moment, then got out of Zachary's car, notepad and pen in hand, and walked towards the dead man's pickup. Blakemore stood briefly, watching, then ran quickly to overtake her. This was a crime scene, after all, and he wasn't going to let her bugger anything up.

Chapter 33

Despite the relative antiquity of its home city, the University of Victoria is young by Canadian standards. It grew from a regional college under its big brother, the University of British Columbia located in Vancouver, to gain full university status in the early 1960s. Unlike the majority of the older academic institutions, which added buildings and faculties harum scarum as demand and funding became available, the University of Victoria was planned to the *n*th degree. Rather than attempt to offer everything, specific faculties were chosen and the emphasis focussed on excellence in those disciplines rather than the creation of a degree mill. Law, Environment, Humanities, Native Studies, and Fine Arts lead the list. The physical plant comprises modern, aesthetically pleasing structures laid out in two concentric circles. Residences, library, faculty buildings, and even parking lots are optimally placed so that moving from one area to the other requires minimal legwork.

Victoria is the City of Gardens, year round, and the landscape architects had a field day with its university. The students live and study in a veritable park, filled with trees, flowers, and shrubs of diverse species, all flourishing. One wonders, even in the fall, how the scholars maintain their concentration with such beauty visible out of every window.

Coswell had no difficulty finding the registrar's office, and once he had identified himself and his purpose to the pleasant young lady at the reception desk the registrar herself was summoned. She emerged from a small office at the side, a short, matronly woman with snow-white hair. After checking Coswell's credentials, she looked at the name that he had written down for the clerk. Her eyes widened briefly, then turned and disappeared for less than a minute, returning from somewhere in

the back with a file folder in her hand. She gave it to him.

He took a seat on one of the waiting room chairs, opened the folder, and began to read.

The young activist was enrolled in environmental studies. His academic achievement fluctuated, and comments from some of his instructors hinted that Dietmar's anger had not tempered since his Edinburgh days. He listed a campus dormitory address at the beginning of his first year, but Coswell noted that the address was a postal box after that. His aunt's name and address in Germany was written in the "to be notified in case of" column— no mention of his father. There was no Victoria address or phone number. Despite it being his fourth and graduating year, he had not registered for the current semester. Coswell returned to the desk with the file. The registrar was waiting for him, presuming correctly that he would have questions for her.

"I am surprised at how little personal information is in here. Does the University not require more?" he asked.

"Times have changed," she told him. "The giving of any more than basic information is purely optional now. We require only a transcript of their high school or other college marks and a local mailing address. If they require student loans, then we ask for more details. This student funded everything himself, including his one semester in residence."

Coswell noted that she gave this information without consulting the file.

"Can you tell me anything you think might be of value to our investigation that isn't in his records?"

She paused, seemingly unsure of her ground.

"This is a murder investigation," he reminded her.

"Yes, of course," she said, then, with a sigh, she proceeded to answer his question.

"I wear many hats in this institution, not just that of registrar.

I'm chairperson of the student placement committee and I sit on the disciplinary board. I'm afraid that problem students, both academic and personal, come under my jurisdiction. Dietmar Kraus was brought to my attention shortly after he arrived. He was a difficult, angry young man. He had been in one of our student residences for only a few days when he clashed with the resident advisor. That was the first time I spoke to Dietmar. He registered by mail, not in person, you see."

"Can you recall that conversation?" asked Coswell.

"Vividly," she answered. "I think that I had an advantage, being a woman, during that session. He obviously couldn't deal with authority, even at the benign level of the resident advisor, but I do have counseling skills, and my gender I suppose tempered his hostility. He calmed down after his initial tirade at the perceived injustice he suffered in his residence and actually opened up to me. I felt sympathy for him and I suppose my motherly instincts took over. I contacted the head of student services and obtained the names of those that had applied for off-campus accommodation. It's expensive living on site here and many private homes offer much cheaper living for financially strapped students. I reasoned that billeting him with the right person would go a long way towards settling him down. I chose a first-year student who was two years younger than the Kraus boy and enrolled in the Honours English program. I reasoned that the difference in ages and interests would cause minimal conflict. It worked. Dietmar actually came by a month or so after he moved in and thanked me. He continued to have problems with some of his instructors, but I put that down to a healthy young mind not swallowing everything fed to it. Professors can be difficult too, you know. I did have to intervene a few times on his behalf, but I did it through the professors, not in a lecturing session with Dietmar. I knew I would lose his confidence if I did that."

"Do you have the name of his roommate?" Coswell said, interrupting.

"I can't recall," she answered, "but I'll go through the year book and see if it comes to me. Student Services may keep a list of names of those applying for accommodation, but I doubt it. We're all having to cut down where we can."

"That name would be invaluable to us, I suspect," Coswell stated. "We have such little personal information to go by. That roommate lived with him, possibly for the three years Dietmar attended the University. He must know a great deal and could very well be the key to our investigation."

"Leave it with me," she said. "I'll do my best."

Coswell thanked her profusely and gave her his card, requesting that she call him at any time if she could find or recall more information for his case. His next stop was the address of the Commonwealth Scholar that Hans Kraus had given him— Jeremy Witherspoon, 68 Linden Street, Victoria.

Rather than go directly through the city to his destination (68 Linden Street was less than a block from the water) he drove his rental car along the scenic route instead. The view of the ocean is spectacular. Affluence is reflected in the grand residences that are along the way, their grounds tended by professional gardeners who use native and exotic plants to generate blooming colour even in the late fall. The first half of the drive looks out on the Strait of Georgia and the Gulf Islands, with the Coast Range Mountains on the far shore. Abruptly, the road turns west and the Strait of Juan de Fuca lies to the driver's left. The extinct snow-capped volcano, Mount Baker, looms far south in the State of Washington, and the Olympic Mountains extend to the northwesternmost shore of the continental United States. Watercraft abound, particularly sailboats taking advantage of the steady winds that blow year round. Whitecaps are a common

sight from any of Victoria's shorelines. The posted speed limit is fifty kilometers per hour but rarely does the car travel that fast as the driver tries to navigate the narrow, twisty two-lane road while gawking at the vista surrounding him. Beach Drive is the slow route to be sure, but no one complains.

Linden, like many of the streets in the old part of the city, runs perpendicular to the marine route. It extends for a mere two blocks, then dead-ends at a crossroad. It begins again just past this point, but with a different name. Coswell was fortunate to have been given an excellent city map and so was able to find the Witherspoon residence without difficulty. The houses in this area were on much smaller lots than the mansions closer to the University, and were considerably older. Many had been built before the turn of the century. In their day they were probably mansions as well, housing the well-to-do of the era. Most were three storeys high, with bay windows, gables, and ornate trim. Number sixty-eight was typical. Coswell parked directly in front, walked up the short flight of stairs to the front porch, and rang the doorbell. A thin, athletic young man wearing a tracksuit answered, who, much to Coswell's delight, turned out to be Jeremy Witherspoon himself. After identification and purpose were established, Coswell was invited in. He was led from the tiny foyer through a set of leaded glass doors into a classic Victorian era sitting room. Heavy velvet curtains were drawn back to expose the bay window, which let in considerable light, but the dark wood paneling and the heavy leather chairs gave a somber feeling to the room. Coswell could imagine Queen Victoria doing afternoon tea here, sitting bolt upright, teacup in hand, discussing the British Empire with her advisors—men dressed in black morning coats.

"You just caught me," Jeremy said. "I was headed out for a run. I'm training for the Victoria Marathon and I'm up to fifteen

miles a day now. My folks are in England visiting relatives so I'm house-sitting for them. I actually live and work in Vancouver."

"Are you on holidays?" Coswell asked.

"No. I teach graduate students at UBC and right now they're on a reading break. I go back next week," he replied, glancing at his wrist watch. "But what can I do for you? You are probably aware that I roomed for a short time with Dietmar Kraus."

"I won't keep you long," Coswell said. He summarized the investigation to date, deliberately leaving out most of the details of the murder.

"Dietmar's father told us that you had had a falling out with him when you were roomates. Would you elaborate on that for me? We're trying to get a clearer picture of the victim and perhaps a reason that someone wanted to kill him."

"I understand. Well, I can tell you that he was no fun to live with. He was an arrogant son of a bitch in a place where arrogance was the norm, but his was nasty. He was like a pit bull with a chip on his shoulder. I tried to get along with him, especially after his mother died, but he was unbearable. It wasn't just me, either. No one could stand him. He put down everything and everybody."

"Did you ever come to blows?" Coswell asked.

"No. He was a scrawny little shit and, as you can see, I'm pretty big. I'm a bit skinny now from all my running, but over there I was on the rowing team. It would have been an unfair match, for sure, and as frustrated as I got at times, I never wanted to hit him. I really felt sorry for him, but I had to get on with my studies and he was too big a distraction. He took the news that I wanted him out pretty well. I think he'd made his decision to leave for Canada by then anyway."

"Do you know why he chose Canada?"

"Probably because of me. I'm a walking Chamber of Commerce guy when it comes to my homeland. Being over

there made me appreciate it even more. When we first bunked together, I guess I went on a bit about the forests, the wildlife, and all that, and he seemed really interested. He was, after all, planning a career in environmental work, and since Europe has fried off most of theirs, Canada must have sounded like paradise from my descriptions. My field is political science, so talking it up goes with the turf."

"He was an activist, as you know," said Coswell. "They usually try to bend people to their causes. Do you recall his mentioning anyone who might have come with him?"

"No. He was a loner all the time that I knew him over there. It was here that he picked up his followers."

"How do you know that?" Coswell queried. "Did you have any contact with him when you came back to BC?"

"I did. He must have realized what an asshole he'd been to me and felt guilty. My folks put an announcement in the Victoria paper when I got the teaching post at UBC. He saw it and phoned the house. I lived here for a few months before going over to Vancouver. I met him at a vegetarian café downtown and we had a really amiable talk. He actually apologized for his behaviour, but then went on about his activities. He was a zealot, all right. Christ, you'd think he was fighting the war to end all wars. I found it all a bit embarrassing, but I humoured him. No point in getting into an argument with him, I thought. I had a feeling that he was headed for real trouble. I caught the six o'clock news special when he was interviewed last month. He was condoning tree-spiking. That can be lethal, as you probably know. I figured some big, burly logger was going to get his number one of these days. Do you think that's how he met his end?"

"Could be. He lived and died in timber country, all right. I don't suppose he mentioned any possible candidates to you, did he?"

"No. The only person he mentioned by name was his roommate at UVIC, but I don't think he was an activist, just a friend. I might have that wrong, though. I thought he mentioned the roommate to impress me that he was capable of living with someone."

Coswell's heart gave a leap.

"Do you remember the roommate's name?" he asked.

"'Fraid not," Jeremy answered.

"I can't begin to tell you how important that name is to us," said Coswell. "Please try to remember it."

"I will, but I doubt it will come to me. I've got a photographic memory when it comes to something I want to remember, but trivia just zips through, and, I'm afraid, that name was trivia. I wasn't planning to strike up any relationship soon with Dietmar. He was too weird."

Coswell's hopes sunk.

"I might be able to help," Jeremy offered. "I drove him home from the café after our meeting. I actually remember the place. He and his mate rented an apartment in the 'Pink Palace.' That's an old building in James Bay, painted the most god-awful pink colour. I went with a girl whose father is one of the owners. He's the manager of the BC Forest Products sawmill and I thought it ironic that Dietmar stayed there. Hopefully he didn't know the owner. I don't know the address, but you can't miss it. It's still painted that horrible pink and it's right on the southeast corner of Montreal and Superior."

Coswell's spirits rose again. He thanked the young scholar profusely and headed back to his car. As he pulled away from the curb he saw Jeremy in his rear view mirror, skipping down the steps of the old house and setting out on his run.

The James Bay district of Victoria was for many years as close to a slum area as the city could muster. The shoreline there was

broken by huge grain elevators, freighter docks, and warehouses. The homes were tiny originally. Dockworkers and labourers made up the residents for the most part. The district's main claim to fame was the rugby team, aptly named the James Bay Animals. In recent years, the whole area has become gentrified. Small, low-level apartment buildings intermingle with historic old buildings restored and converted to condominiums. Rents in this area are reasonable compared to the university district and so it's popular with students. Bus service is good, and those who cycle use the adjacent waterfront route with its wide, dedicated bike lanes and are unhampered by traffic all the way to their classes.

Jeremy Witherspoon was correct. The Pink Palace stood out like a sore thumb. It was actually called Pacific Palisades. "Pee Pee" either way, mused Coswell. Two laps of the block did not yield a parking spot other than one or two between signs reading "Resident Parking Only." He pulled into one and parked. He noted the distinct lack of garages anywhere; the locals obviously parked on the street. This was early afternoon. He could only imagine the problems when the inhabitants returned from work or school.

He pulled a photo of Dietmar Kraus out of his briefcase, locked the car door, and walked the short distance to the apartment building. He scanned the names on the mailboxes at the front entrance, not really believing that he would see the name Kraus. It wasn't there. He rang the manager's suite. A gruff voice blared from the speaker above.

"Yes?" was the only word spoken.

"My name is Inspector Coswell of the RCMP. I'm here on official business and I'd like to have a word with you."

"Shit," was the reply.

Within moments, however, a grizzled old man appeared at the door and turned the latch. Coswell stepped inside. The foyer

was surprisingly large for a small complex such as this, but it had the musty smell of old carpets. The manager showed no inclination to invite the visitor into his apartment. It appeared that all business was going to be conducted right there. Coswell showed him the photo.

"Do you know this man?"

The manager did no more than glance at the picture before answering.

"Yeah, for sure. He and his buddy rented room 321 for a couple of university sessions, maybe three; I forget."

"I'd like you to think very hard about this," Coswell said in a firm voice. "I'm conducting a murder investigation and the information you give me could be very important."

The man picked up on the tone and lost some of his surliness. In his role as manager of a building with so many students, he probably had more than a few dealings with the police and knew not to mess with them.

"Actually, the guy in the picture was here for two sessions. His buddy stayed on one more or, to be exact, part of one more. He was killed in some kind of accident up-Island a few weeks after the start of this university year in September. I never heard exactly what kind of accident—car crash I guess, although I didn't see anything on TV about it. His father came and took away his effects. It was too bad the young guy died, but it created a real pain in the ass for me. Just you try to rent a suite after all the students are settled in. No chance in this place, I can tell you."

Coswell was dejected. So close, he thought, then this.

"When did you last see the boy in the picture?" he asked.

"On the six o'clock news two or three weeks ago," the old man replied. "He was some kind of violent tree hugger. I wasn't surprised. He was a moody bastard. Wouldn't give me the time of day if I asked and he always had a sourpuss look on his face."

Not unlike you, thought Coswell.

"The other kid was nice, though," he went on. "Always paid his rent on time. No parties. Real serious student. Complete opposite of the other guy. Strange that they roomed together."

Coswell sensed a dead end here but his training forced him to complete his questioning.

"Did the tree hugger leave anything behind, do you know, when he moved out?"

"Not that I know of. If there was I guess the other kid's father took it. The storage locker is empty and there wasn't anything in the apartment when I vacuumed it out for the new occupants— oh, other than the phone. The father said he didn't have any use for it and I could give it to the new renters. It was a good one with one of those tape answering machines built in, but he definitely didn't want it. It was nice of him, really, and the students who took over appreciated having it. The apartment's rented furnished—TV, cable included, but the phone's up to the tenants."

"Do you know the father's address? He might be able to give me some information." Coswell asked.

"No, I don't. He was really shaken up by his son's death. Hardly said a word. Looked like he was going to cry if he did. I asked him if he wanted any help carting out his kid's stuff but he just shook his head. He followed me like a lost sheep when I opened the storage locker for him and showed him the things in the room that belonged to his boy. He asked me if there was any money owing, and when I told him the damage deposit covered the one month's notice he settled the phone thing and that was it. I told him to take as long as he wanted—even stay overnight if he had a long way to go—and just lock the key in the room when he left. He just nodded and stood there. I went back to my apartment and didn't look in again until the next morning.

The key was on the kitchen table and the bed wasn't slept in. No notes or nothing."

"What was the boy's name?"

"Smith. John Smith. I guess you know the sour one's name—Deitmar is how he signed his half of the rent checks. I got to admit that they were always on time too."

"I'd like to have a brief look at the apartment," he said.

"Okay," the manager agreed. "But I'll have to go up with you. Two female students are renting it and one or both of them might be in. Classes these days seem to be morning, afternoon, or night. They come and go at all hours."

They proceeded directly up the stairs to the third floor. Coswell noted the large ring of keys on the manager's belt. A knock at room 321, however, was met with an answer and a pretty blond girl dressed in jeans and a shirt tied at the waist opened the door. When she recognized the manager she released the security chain.

"Hi, Pops," she said. "What can I do you for?"

The old man coughed and blushed.

"Got a respectable inspector of the RCMP with me, Sara. He wants to see your room."

"Jeez, officer," she said, eyes twinkling. "I gave up hooking last year and I swear I threw the pot plants out a month ago."

"Behave yourself, Sara," pleaded the manager. "This is serious business."

The exchange between the two cast a whole new light on the elderly man's personality. Obviously he was a pussycat—not the grump he first appeared to be.

"I won't take much of your time, Miss," Coswell said. "May I come in?"

"Of course," she said. "Especially because you've asked so nicely."

The occupants had made an attempt at livening up the basic furnishings provided by the owner. The artwork on the walls was a collection of abstracts, striking in the colours used, but suspect in the composition. Coswell surmised that one of the girls was an art student. The pictures were framed in do-it-yourself metal. The single bookshelf was stacked with magazines and CDs with labels of groups totally unfamiliar to Coswell. The ubiquitous sound system filled one corner of the living room. A large, multicolour braided rug broke the monotony of the blue shag carpet on the floor. A counter partition separated the main room from the kitchen, and on this was a small wine rack that held a few bottles of cheap wine. Glasses were hung upside-down from a holder above.

Overall, the apartment was tidy and clean. This was certainly not the den of hookers and drug addicts so commonplace in the Vancouver police scenes.

"Would you like some tea?" the girl asked. "I've just made a pot for myself but there's enough for you. Also, my roommate made some super brownies—Hashish-free, I can assure you."

Coswell smiled. He sometimes regretted his decision to remain a bachelor when he met a woman like this, but those thoughts had passed with the years. He was content letting his job take up most of his waking hours. The daily observation of the pain caused by marital strife, both for the public he dealt with and within the ranks, reinforced his resolution. She was a cutie, though.

"Why not?" he said. "That's very kind of you." He noted that the manager appeared to be in full agreement and so the two men sat while the girl poured the tea and offered them a plate of double chocolate brownies. The old man looked as though he had experienced this treat before, scooping up the largest piece for himself.

"What is this serious matter you're here for?" she asked, after they had all settled.

"I'm investigating a rather gruesome murder in the Nelson area and the trail has led here."

"That's weird," she said, looking accusingly at the manager. "I thought the guy who was here before us got killed in an accident."

"Yes, he did," confirmed Coswell. "It's his former roommate who was murdered and you needn't be concerned. This wasn't a drug or gang thing, I'm sure."

Relief showed on the girl's face. Someone had obviously cautioned her about big city life. Despite her initial flippancy about drugs, Coswell suspected that she was a small town girl. He continued.

"Did you or your roommate ever come across either of the two men at the University?"

"No, and not likely to. Janet and I are first-year students—frosh. The upper classes barely acknowledge our existence. I'm afraid we aren't going to be of any help to you."

"Possibly not," he agreed, "but there may be something you've forgotten. Did they leave anything behind other than the phone? Were there any calls on the answering machine? Was there any mail or subsequent phone calls concerning them—anything like that?"

"No, not a thing. But it's funny you asked about the answering machine. The whole incoming message cassette was missing. The outgoing one was there okay. The dead guy's voice was on it with the usual—'You've reached number so and so. I'm not in right now but leave a message after the beep'—nothing really personal or unique. We erased it, of course, and put our own on. The tapes for the machine are cheap so that was really no problem. We really do appreciate having it. Our social lives are improving."

If Sara's roommate was as attractive as she, Coswell mused, he knew they had no worries about that. The upper classmen

would not ignore the two girls for long. Twenty-something hormones aren't over-ridden by academic seniority.

"Any chance that the message tape may have been tucked away in the apartment somewhere—trash baskets, kitchen drawers, behind the couch?" he asked.

"No. We looked everywhere for it. Also, my roommate's of Dutch descent. She insisted that we polish this place from one corner to the next. We moved all the furniture, vacuumed, scrubbed, and cleaned every inch—the whole nine yards. I thought it was overkill. Pops did a good job before we moved in or else the dead guy was some kind of housekeeper."

"It was me," interjected Pops.

"Of course," she said, blowing him a kiss.

They drank up their tea and got up to leave. Coswell again went through the routine after thanking Sara for her hospitality.

"If you or your roommate think of anything or if something like mail or phone calls come up regarding either of the two men, please call me," he said, handing her his card.

"Gee, thanks," she said, taking the card. "I don't suppose you'd sign it for me, would you? It would make a great souvenir."

He laughed and took it from her, signing it, "To Sara, in appreciation of her cooperation, Inspector Mark Coswell, RCMP."

"Neat," she said. "Thanks again."

As he and the manager walked down the hallway, Coswell heard the door close and the rattle of the chain as she refastened it.

"Good girl," he said aloud. The manager nodded in agreement. Victoria was a long way from Vancouver so far as crime was concerned, but it was catching up.

The manager saw him to the door and said, as Coswell was leaving, "I'll keep my eye on the mail for you too. There was no tape cassette, by the way, in the trash or anywhere else in that apartment. I really did clean it out pretty good."

"Thank you," said Coswell, handing out yet another of his cards. They shook hands.

Coswell returned to his car, pleased to find that there wasn't a parking ticket under his windshield wiper. That was always a problem when using an unmarked vehicle and he detested the paperwork necessary to have the citation waved. He sat behind the wheel for a few minutes, going over in his mind his Victoria investigation so far. He felt that he had missed something vital, but couldn't put his finger on it. A methodical routine usually paid off and so he contemplated the loose ends. Smith's father needed to be tracked down. He could get that information through the registrar at the University, now that he had the student's name. The local TV station would have a tape of the interview with Dietmar. He especially wanted to see that. Coswell wasn't a morbid individual, but homicide was his field, after all, and seeing a corpse come to life again put a personal touch on the case that he found stimulating. He decided that he would do that first—view the six o'clock news tape.

The TV studios were downtown and were surprisingly blessed with ample parking, including stalls for visitors. Coswell pulled into a vacant one. The lady at the reception desk was not the least fazed by the intrusion of the RCMP officer in her workday. She gave the impression that she had dealt with many more bizarre requests. She looked about forty, her hair without a trace of grey (probably chemically maintained), and she was dressed impeccably in a dark blue business suite with a three-quarter-length skirt. I wish to God I could get the female civilians working in my department to dress like that, he thought. It gave a sharp, professional air to the whole office that was decidedly lacking in the casually dressed workers he was accustomed to. He didn't, of course, include his own dress habits in his thoughts.

"If you'll wait a moment, I'll get that tape pulled for you. It

would be helpful if you knew the date of the telecast, but the subject and the fact it was a six o'clock news broadcast will be enough, I'm sure. Lynn, in archives, has an amazing memory for things like this. I'll ask her to look for it."

She was right. Lynn, an obese girl with a bad case of acne, appeared within minutes, cassette in hand.

"Lynn, dear," said the receptionist, "would you take Inspector Coswell to the viewing room and run the segment he wants?"

Lynn merely nodded and, with eyes averted—giving the impression that she'd be happier in her records room—led Coswell through two sets of doors into a room that looked like a miniature theatre. A TV screen, even bigger than the giant ones in sports bars, was mounted in front of six rows of nicely padded seats. Coswell sat in the centre of the first row while Lynn disappeared behind the screen. The images from the tapes, it appeared, were rear-projected, leaving no obstruction to annoy the viewers. Nice, he thought.

Lynn emerged from behind the screen with what looked like an oversized TV clicker. She sat at the end of the row from Coswell and again, without looking at him, pressed buttons on the controller, dimming the lights and starting the tape at precisely the beginning of the interview. Coswell watched, fascinated.

Dietmar looked anything but a tree-hugging hippie. He wore a shirt and tie under a dark green sweater. His blond hair was cut short and groomed to perfection. He appeared to have inherited his father's build and blue eyes. He gave the appearance of a senior choirboy—clean cut, sincere, and very, very serious. Only his words gave away the ferocity inside.

The interviewer was a mature man in his mid fifties. He had adopted the *Sixty Minutes* technique—a calm, benign approach, with patronizing remarks interrupted by blunt, merciless

questions. He was good, but Dietmar responded with equal calm, quoting statistics and sticking to his cause with the resolution of a true fanatic. The tree-spiking segment was particularly well done by both men.

Interviewer: "I understand that you, personally, have been involved in the practice of tree-spiking. I understand from experts in the logging industry that this activity goes beyond simple protest and is, in fact, an act that endangers human life. While most of our viewers, I'm sure, are sympathetic to the protection of our environment and our forests, risking an innocent life to do so seems extreme—outside the bounds of reasonable behaviour. It has been suggested that your cause is harmed, not enhanced, by such violent action. How do you respond?"

Dietmar: "Forests are all about human life. They produce the very oxygen we breathe. They hold the water, vital to life. Without them, we die, burning up and choking to death. The industrialists—those that strip the forests and those that contaminate them, are killing us all. They must be stopped, just as the Nazis were stopped in World War II—by force, not negotiation. History has shown us that peaceful means rarely work, or if they do, the time required is so great that the very thing sought to be protected disappears with the waiting. Procrastination merely strengthens the destroyers."

Interviewer: "Comparing loggers and businessmen to Nazis seems a bit far-fetched, don't you think? But you're too young, perhaps, to realize how extreme that statement is."

Coswell looked for a change of expression, some body language to reveal anger, but there was none. If anything, the voice became steadier.

Dietmar: "I chose that analogy with great care. I have studied history very closely and I am quite aware what it means. To take it a step further, I could postulate that the Nazis were less

of a risk to the human race than our current day industrialists. A strong leadership might have made laws with teeth that stopped, or at least slowed, the death march our current anemic governments have us on. Hitler was an artist, a man of aesthetics with a summer home in the Bavarian forest. There was every chance that he might have saved all of Germany's forests had he won the war. The German industrialists who took power after him had no such preservation ideals and effectively killed the trees with their acid rain."

Wow! thought Coswell. Those remarks alone were enough to invite retaliation from loggers, industrialists, WWII veterans, or even those within the environmental movement itself. This guy really was a loose cannon.

The clip ran for about ten minutes, the producer cleverly punctuating the Dietmar interview with clips of damaged logging equipment, close-ups of spiked trees, and comments from angry woodworkers. The bias was obvious. The environmental movement was effectively painted with a tar brush.

At the precise moment that the interviewer thanked Dietmar for his time (with the sincerity of a cat in a canary's cage) and the young man nodded coldly, Lynn clicked off the projector and hurried to remove the cassette. Coswell assured her that he could find his way back to the front desk, since it was obvious she wished to return directly to her beloved archives. As he opened the last set of doors to the reception area he did a double take. There, leaning over the desk, was Dietmar's interviewer, in the flesh. The efficient lady with the business suit obviously contributed more to the station than merely running the reception area; she had a nose for news. The man walked quickly around the desk, hand outstretched.

"Inspector Coswell," he said, oozing good will. "I'm delighted to meet you. I've followed your exploits with the Vancouver

Homicide Bureau and I can tell you that I am an admirer. Harvey Robertson, the crime reporter for the *Vancouver Star*, is a personal friend of mine and he's told me good things about you. Presenting the facts to the public in these gruesome cases is a difficult job for us in the fourth estate, and cooperation from the police is so helpful."

Harvey Robertson is the world's biggest shithead, thought Coswell. This slippery bastard probably dropped Robertson's name knowing what a supreme pain in the ass the reporter was who bad-mouthed the hard-working officers if he didn't get what he wanted for his column. The Victoria man was actually threatening Coswell in a round-about-way. Neglecting to identify himself in his greeting bespoke the arrogance of the fellow. Coswell, presumably, was supposed to recognize the famous face.

"I have a special interest in the young man you just saw on the tape. I do my homework before an interview like that and so I know the boy and his background very well. The story goes on, I see, with his murder and I would like to do a follow up soon. Perhaps you would be kind enough to fill me in on your investigation to date? I have a cameraman who's just returning from an assignment with one of my juniors, but maybe we could do a prelim off-camera until he arrives. My office is upstairs."

Before Coswell could utter a word, the man turned to the receptionist.

"Betty. Would you get the Inspector and me a pot of coffee and some of those Peak Freans I know you hide under your desk? That's my girl."

Betty didn't even blink, jumping up to do his bidding, which surprised Coswell. He judged her to be of more character than that, but maybe she was related to the guy. Who knew? He repressed the urge to tell the pompous prick to shove it; he had too many years dealing with this type of individual and knew how bad that

move would be. The newsman was also one of the few people available to Coswell who had had some contact with Dietmar not long before his demise. He allowed the man to put his arm over his shoulder and lead him up the stairs. He congratulated himself for not flinching, although his stomach took a turn.

The office of the man, whose name turned out to be Robert Oughton (liberally recorded on photos, plaques, and trophies scattered about the room), was tiny. Coswell had noted much larger rooms down the hall, which probably were occupied by Oughton's superiors. Men of real power, he had observed, were much subtler in their dealings than this bully. Oughton was more the used-car salesman type than the dealership owner, he thought, although he had to concede that the interview with Dietmar was first class. As an afterthought, however, he realized that the producers probably gave the man a script. He wondered how much leeway Oughton was actually given. He decided to take the offensive.

"You were actually on my list of people to question in this case, Bob," he lied. "You are, after all, one of the last people we know of who actually spoke to the victim before he was murdered."

Oughton's mouth dropped. This was not the direction he wished to go. Being the interviewee was a role he did not envision, and he definitely didn't like the 'Bob' familiarity. Coswell pressed on.

"Let's go back to the homework you mentioned. The police are always looking to gather information from responsible citizens, especially in a murder investigation. In fact, such information is a legal obligation."

Oughton swallowed, and replied, "Of course, I'll help in any way that I can. Go ahead and ask me whatever you want."

"Perhaps you could start by summarizing the work-up you did prior to the interview. Were you the one to contact him in the first place?"

"No. The whole idea came from Reg Ireland. He's the producer of the six o'clock news. There was a lot of airtime being spent on the Carmanha Valley protest and he wanted an angle that was unique. He actually picked up on an article in the *Victoria Sun* written by an investigative reporter at the site. Tree-spiking is a big no-no in logging country and most of this island is just that. Reg sent a cameraman and my junior to meet the *Sun* guy and set up footage. There were protesters everywhere, I gathered, and Dietmar's name came up. My junior sent out word via the jungle telegraph and lo and behold, Dietmar called us. Reg set up the time and got our research team to get as much dope as possible on the guy before then. He looked it over and set up the questions for me."

"Was a hard copy kept of the research?"

"Everything's kept around here. We even microfilm stuff for future reference. I'll see that you're given a copy."

Betty arrived with a tray carrying a pot of coffee, cream, sugar, and an ornately painted tin containing the promised cookies. Coswell was delighted to see that the coffee was in a Bodem press, not yet plunged, and the cookies were, indeed, genuine English Peak Freans. With a glance at her watch, Betty pushed down the plunger of the Bodem and poured the coffee into two china cups set on matching saucers. I'll bet she's timed exactly four minutes to brew the perfect cup of coffee, he thought. He declined the cream and sugar and sipped the rich brew—dark French Roast, his favourite. He selected a Peak Frean and bit into the crisp cookie, feeling his teeth sink into the sweet cream and jam-filled centre. His enjoyment was short-lived—Oughton got his second wind.

"Betty. Would you get Lynn to pull the research file on Dietmar and make a copy of it for the Inspector?"

"Certainly," she said, and left the room.

"Now, Inspector," Oughton continued. "Could you bring me up to date on your end?"

Coswell finished his cookie, took another swig of coffee, and replied.

"I have a few more questions to ask you. Did you have any conversation with Dietmar before or after the interview, off camera?"

"Almost none. He arrived just in time for the make-up people to prep him before we went on air. When the interview was over, the bugger literally got up and left without another word. That's weird. Most people hang around for a bit. They want to know how they did and they like to prolong their five minutes of fame, so to speak. But not him."

"Did anyone accompany him to the studio or leave with him, do you know?"

"I'm sorry, I don't," Oughton answered. "But Betty would. You can ask her."

"Yes, I will," Coswell said, looking at his watch. "Goodness, it's almost five-thirty. Where does the time go? I'm afraid I must run. Vancouver is calling and I have to finish up here pronto."

He stood up abruptly, extending his hand to the newsman, who took it with a start.

"But, but . . ." he stuttered.

"Oh, don't worry," Coswell assured him. "I'll make sure you get an official update of the case in writing. My Vancouver staff will get on that as soon as I get back. You've been a great help."

With that, he turned and left the room, walking briskly down the stairs to where Betty waited, the research copy in an envelope placed on the desk in front of her. Way to go Lynn, Coswell mused. Oughton was scrambling behind him but Betty's interview had already begun.

"Thank you Betty," Coswell said, picking up the envelope.

"You're most efficient and I must tell you that you make a fine cup of coffee."

She beamed.

"Bob here suggested that you might be able to answer my question about whether or not there was anyone with Dietmar when he came to the studio."

"No," she replied. "He came by taxi, alone, and had me call him one when he left."

"I presume that it took some time for the taxi to arrive here when he departed. Did you have any conversation with him?"

"Yes, a brief one," she said. "Actually, the taxi service from here is very good. Being downtown, there are cabs on every corner. I was surprised that he didn't just go out and flag one down. It was raining though. Maybe that's why he had me call one for him."

"What did he say to you?" Coswell asked. He was aware of Oughton behind him, probably gesturing to her. She was looking over his shoulder as she answered.

"He just said that he was going to go back to the hotel to catch up on some sleep and then he was going out that evening to a friend's place. I got the impression that he'd travelled a long way to get here for the taping. We book all our guests in the Laurel Point Inn, which is very nice, and I told him a bit about it. I also encouraged him to take his meals at the hotel since we have an account with them. It makes the bookkeeping so much simpler. I did say that we would also cover sundry expenses related to his coming for the taping, including his travel costs, but he never did submit anything. We received only the hotel and taxi bill to and from the studio, nothing else."

Coswell wondered if she actually did the books in addition to all her other duties.

"Did he say where his friend lived, per chance?" he asked.

"Yes," she replied. "I asked him, and he told me James Bay. The Laurel Point Inn is also in James Bay and so he probably just walked over to his friend's place."

"One last question," Coswell said. "I noted that the Dietmar segment was aired September 28th. What was the date of the taping?"

"The same day," interjected Oughton. "He was perfect. Reg said it was a take. The film people spliced the clips we already had on to it and away it went—six o'clock news, September 28th—my birthday."

Coswell had turned to face Oughton and saw, through the glass front door, a van pull up and two people get out—one, a young woman carrying a clipboard, and the other a man wearing a jacket with a crest bearing the logo of the TV station. The man opened the sliding side door and gathered up his equipment—a shoulder mounted camera and a battery pack. The woman produced a microphone and a length of cable. Time to go, Coswell told himself, or I'll be on the six o'clock news. He looked at his watch again.

"Goodness," he exclaimed. "I'm going to be late. Thank you both again. You've been most helpful."

He moved quickly through the glass doors, brushing past the camera crew and ignoring Oughton who tried to follow him, babbling something he couldn't quite hear. He jumped into his car and drove off, waving out the window.

Chapter 34

Ernie drove his cruiser down the twisty logging road looking on either side for any sign of the water truck that was missing from the burn site. He wasted no time and almost caught up to Karl who was driving more slowly in front of him. They parted at the

main road, Karl heading for his home on the Cougar Creek road and Ernie to the Blakemore residence just off Main Street, downtown. He decided that Barbara Blakemore would make his job of facing Clyde's wife Michele a lot less traumatic. He prayed that she would be at home. As he drove up, he was relieved to see her unloading bags of groceries from her car parked in the driveway. She looked up as he pulled in behind her, expecting Paul.

"Ernie," she said. "What a pleasant surprise. Come help me with these bags and I'll reward you with a piece of Wendy Ewart's blueberry pie. I just bought it."

Her cheerfulness faded when she saw the expression on Ernie's face. Her first thought, ever in the mind of a policeman's wife, was that something terrible had happened to her husband. She froze.

"It's not Paul, Barbara," he said, understandingly. "It's Clyde Groat. He's been killed."

Barbara's emotions whirled. She felt instant relief, then shock, and finally guilt. Michele was the victim, not her. Paul was all right.

Ernie explained the circumstances of the death and asked her help in breaking the news to Clyde's wife.

"Of course, I'll help, Ernie," she said. "You go ahead. I'll take my car and meet you out front of the Credit Union. We'll go in together and break this to her."

No matter the severity of the blow of bad news to the survivors, the variation in reaction was something that Ernie found fascinating. He didn't know Michelle personally, as the Blakemores did, but she obviously came from tough stock. It seemed that she knew the worst already and had prepared herself for it. She stood up from her desk when they entered, Barbara leading the way.

"He's dead, isn't he?" she said, looking Ernie straight in the eye. He nodded. Barbara rushed forward and hugged her close. She

didn't respond, standing stiffly, staring into space. Her co-workers had all stopped what they were doing to take in the tragic scene.

"I must pick the children up," she said, her voice a monotone. "They'll be waiting at the after-school day care for Clyde."

"I'll drive you," said Barbara, "I have my car outside."

"I'll have to clear my desk and report to Mr. Spenser," Michelle replied as though she were reciting a duty list.

Spenser, the manager, was already beside her, summoned by one of the workers.

"Go, Michelle," he said, firmly. "I'll look after your desk. Please go."

Barbara helped her on with her coat and led her outside to the car. Ernie held her arm as she got in and Barbara went round to the driver's side. He watched them leave knowing that Paul had been right. Barbara knew what to do.

He drove quickly to the Thunderbird Hotel where he found the lab crew packing up to return to Vancouver. The Sergeant voiced no objection whatsoever to the request that his men get involved in Clyde's investigation. He merely asked for detailed instructions about the route up to the site and then ordered the crew back to work. No one complained. Ernie was impressed.

His next stop was the firehall where he knew the volunteers were waiting. They were all there, with the exception of Karl. No one spoke as Ernie walked in but all eyes were on him.

"Clyde Groat is dead," he said. "Shot in his truck by a high-powered rifle. Karl Reinhart found him at the slash burn a mile up from number three gate."

They all began to speak at once.

"How? Where? Who?"—all jumbled in a cacophony of voices. Ernie cut them off.

"We don't know, but we're trying our damnedest to find out and Paul and I need your help."

That brought instant quiet. Anger, vengeance, whatever the emotions, these were men who responded to a plan of action. Ernie had their undivided attention.

"I want you to fan out, exactly as you did earlier, but this time you are looking for two things. The first, of course, is anyone on those roads with a gun or anyone you even think might have a gun. Talk to everyone you see, ask if they saw or heard anything. Second, we're looking for the water truck that was parked up there. It's disappeared."

He saw the men look at one another. An accidental misfire was their first thought, but Ernie was obviously implying another possibility.

"Be careful," he cautioned. "We may be dealing with a sicko here. Don't put yourselves in any danger. That's a job for police. I hope you all read me on that."

This was an Ernie the men had not seen before, but his uniform and demeanor were unmistakable. This was a policeman, no doubt about that.

George Smith was leaning against the inhalator van, staring at the ground. He looked up when Ernie approached him. There were tears in his eyes.

"George," he said, gently. "I know you and Clyde go back a ways but I need someone to bring his body down. We sent Karl home, but I can get him back if you want him to help you."

"No," George answered, shaking his head. "I'll do it."

Ernie watched the big man, shoulders slumped, speak to two of the younger men who nodded assent and followed him to the van. As it drove out the great roll-up doors, the rest of the men dispersed, checking their pagers and arranging a pre-dusk rendezvous back at the hall. Ernie returned to his cruiser. He was going to find Ross Crocker.

Chapter 35

Blakemore, Heather, and Zachary watched as the Vancouver forensic crew literally swarmed the crime site. For Blakemore it was a repeat of the Dietmar routine, but for the other two it was a fascinating display. One man dusted for fingerprints and took plaster casts of tiremarks and footprints around the pickup; another gathered samples of just about everything—glass, hair, blood, and dirt; a third took photographs from every conceivable angle. The Sergeant gave few directions, each man appearing to go about his role automatically, but he made numerous notes and spoke repeatedly into a miniature Dictaphone as he walked round and round the truck, pausing frequently to look inside the cab. This process took considerable time, forcing George and his two volunteers, who had driven up, to wait at the side of the road until the lab men had finished. Blakemore walked over to join them, followed by Heather who hoped to gather more information and thought that the big cop might loosen up a bit with one of his cronies. The sight of George Smith had also triggered a memory in her. His son was one of Ethel Roberts's success stories and there was a wrestling connection. She would tell Blakemore when she had a chance. He was already speaking to George when she caught up to him.

"Good of you to come up, George," Blakemore said. "This is a hard thing to take. Clyde was a good man and a good friend. He didn't deserve this."

George nodded.

"You know the logging scene around here probably better than anyone. The water truck's gone and the slash is still hot. Clyde wouldn't have let that happen. Who knew it was up here?"

"Just about everybody," George answered. "Burning that

pile was one of the job assignments yesterday morning. I drove the truck up. Two of Crocker's boys, Derek and Clark, followed me in a company pickup. After we got the fire going Clark volunteered to stay behind and tend it. He brought his rifle up with him because he still has a mulie tag left and hoped a buck would cross the slash while he was sitting there. Derek drove me back to town."

"Did Clark stay up there all night?" Blakemore asked.

"No. I guess by the letter of the law someone is supposed to, but nobody does. There wasn't much wind and it would have burned down pretty good by late afternoon. Derek, I'm sure, went back and picked him up. Those two never miss happy hour at the Thunderbird, and besides they knew that Clyde would go up and check it once or twice in the evening and first thing in the morning."

Their conversation was interrupted by a beep from Blakemore's pager. He returned to the cruiser where he had left his radiophone. Ernie was on the line.

"A Crocker water truck has just been spotted at Bender's garage. Do you copy?"

"Right, Ernie," replied Blakemore, testily. "Cut the copy shit. Is it the one from up here?"

"Can't be sure," was the reply. "Jim Bender said someone dropped it off sometime before nine and just left a note under the wiper telling them to check the brakes. No one remembers it being driven in but I gather that's not unusual. Bender does all the service work for Crocker's vehicles and apparently they're often dropped off like that at any time of the day or night. Jim fixes them up and parks them out front when they're ready."

"Nice service," commented Blakemore. "But I want that truck impounded. Don't let anyone touch it. It'll have enough fingerprints on it as is and I don't want any more added. We've

got casts of the tire tracks and I'm sure these guys from Vancouver can do a positive ID for us. Tell Jim to send a tow-truck up to bring Clyde's truck down to our lot when George and his men have the body out."

"Roger," said Ernie. "I'll see to it. Meanwhile, I'm taking a run up to Crocker's ranch. He's there right now. I just spoke to him on the phone. I want to know where he and everyone associated with him has been for the last twenty-four hours."

Blakemore was beside himself. He wished he could be in three places at once. He wanted to stay for the results of the forensic crew's investigation; he wished to question Heather more thoroughly; the school interviews needed to be done; but at that moment he wanted most of all to have a go at Crocker himself.

"Ernie," he said. "I want an intersect with you at the bottom of this road. We're going to Crocker's place together. See you there in ten. Over and out."

He tossed the phone on the passenger's seat and approached the Sergeant who was still speaking into his Dictaphone. Blakemore explained the importance of the water truck to him. Once again, the Sergeant agreed to have his unit go over that vehicle as well. This guy is really something else, marveled Blakemore.

Zachary was standing beside the pickup, engrossed in the workings of the forensic crew. Blakemore spoke to him.

"Doc," he said, "this is your case after they're finished. Would you please supervise George and his boys getting the body down to the morgue? I'm going up to the Crocker homestead with Ernie. I think we're real close to getting our man and I've got a hunch that the answer is there."

"You think he did it?" asked Zachary, incredulous.

"No. But I think someone very close to him did and I'm going to wring Crocker's neck till I find out."

"Would you also ride herd on our lady of the flaming hair?" he added. "Try to convince her to go easy with the reporting, even if only for a day. I think this case will be busted wide open by then. Also, Ernie and I are very busy right now and really don't have time to do the protection thing for her. We need your help."

"You've got it," he said. He looked over at Heather who was talking to George. When she saw Blakemore leave in the cruiser, she came over to him.

"Where's Paul off to in such a hurry? Has something turned up? Is he leaving me out in the cold again?"

"He and Ernie are off to question Ross Crocker, but he's given me a very important job that I intend to do to my utmost. You've been assigned to my care—protectionwise I mean," he said with a grin.

She smiled at him and then they both, with twinges of guilt, returned to the macabre scene beside them.

"You've got work to do here when the men are finished," she said. "I can work on my story in the car. Don't rush on my account. I'll wait for you."

She walked over to Zachary's car and, with a word to George, got in and began to write.

The Sergeant had closed his book and put away his Dictaphone by the time Zachary walked back to him. His three crewmembers were packing up their samples and preparing to leave.

"You can have your men take the body away now," the Sergeant said. "He's all yours. Would you like to hear my summary?"

"I would indeed," answered Zachary.

"Your man was killed instantly by a high-powered bullet—likely a hunting calibre, judging by the size of the entrance and exit wound."

"Exit wound?"

"Yes. The bullet entered the left temple, just in front of the ear, and exited through the scalp on the upper right side. My man found what was left of the slug on the floor just inside the passenger door. It bounced off the side doorframe. The shooter couldn't have been very far away for the bullet to penetrate like that and with that trajectory. Usually the slug stays in the head. I would guess he was no more than twenty feet from his victim and probably standing. The distribution of the blood spatter coincides with that."

He went on. "The fingerprints on the door handle and the steering wheel are totally smeared. I suggest that the killer wore gloves and smudged the victim's own prints. The footprints beside the truck are likely those of the chap who found the body and, of course, Corporal Blakemore's and your own. The killer expertly hid his footprints all around the pickup and over to the water truck as well. Come see for yourself."

Zachary followed and squatted down with the Sergeant as he pointed out the fine scratches made most likely by a branch, obliterating the tracks.

"I'll bet the killer is a hunter," he said. "He knows all about hiding a trail."

"That, unfortunately," said Zachary, "includes at least 75 per cent of the males in this territory over the age of fourteen."

"That's why I love this job," the Sergeant said. "Everything I deal with is right here. No tedious questioning or going through piles of documents. Blakemore and his buddies are welcome to that. Just give me the crime scene."

Zachary waved to George, calling his men over. The Sergeant remained briefly, examining the seat after Clyde's body was lifted out, then, satisfied, joined his men in the lab van. The cavalcade then drove down the hill to town—the forensic crew, the volunteers, and finally Zachary and Heather.

Chapter 36

It was almost six o'clock when Coswell phoned the Registrar's office. All he got was a taped message stating the office was closed and would re-open at eight-thirty the next morning. The brownies and the cookies hadn't really suppressed his appetite and he was looking forward to his evening meal. When he booked his flight on the helijet he also phoned the Sooke Harbour House and made a reservation for dinner. Dining out at a gourmet restaurant was a passion with him. He rarely ate at home, his own cooking consisting chiefly of packaged microwave meals. His doctor had chided him about his eating habits—fast foods gulped down with coffee over the day—and so he considered the evening meal not only a source of pleasure, but also an integral part of his health routine. He planned to add some exercise when he felt up to it. He had no intention of returning immediately to Vancouver. His stomach deserved much better than that.

There were two items of business that he had to deal with first. He drove to the Laurel Point Inn, a magnificent modern hotel overlooking the entrance to Inner Harbour on one side and the Strait of Juan de Fuca on the other. He parked at the entrance and nonplussed the valet by flashing his badge (being perfectly aware that an on-duty RCMP inspector was an unexpected visitor to these palatial surroundings). He knew his car wouldn't be touched; it would stay right where he parked it. He entered and went directly to the manager's office located at the side of the reception counter. The door was open and seated at a desk was a young man dressed in a black suit and sporting a red rose in his lapel. He was startled to see Coswell appear in the doorway and as perplexed as the valet when the badge was presented.

"I'll just take a moment of your time," Coswell reassured, as

usual. "I am tracking the whereabouts of a Dietmar Kraus who, I understand, was booked into your establishment September 28th. Would you be so kind as to pull that information for me?"

"Yes, of course," replied the manager. He walked over to the reception desk and spoke to a clerk who disappeared through a door behind for a couple of minutes and returned with a slim folder. The manager glanced through it then handed it to Coswell.

"There's not much in this," he said. "Most of it is related to the booking and payment by the television station."

"I notice that Kraus did not supply an address. I believe that is a law in this province, is it not?" Coswell inquired.

"Yes, it is, and I am duly embarrassed. I can assure you that the clerk involved will be reprimanded. These commercial accounts are a bit too easy for those checking guests in and some slackness occurs, I'm afraid. I guess the staff presume the television station address is sufficient."

"Don't sweat it," Coswell reassured him. "I don't plan to make an issue of it. What I do want to know is if anyone remembers seeing him leave or return to the hotel that night. I also notice that there is no indication of him signing out the following morning, and what does this squiggle indicate in the corner?"

The manager did not look where Coswell was pointing. He had obviously made a mental photograph of the file when he glanced at it.

"I was on duty that evening. My shift starts at seven but I always come in early and eat a light meal in the staff lounge. Free food is one of the perks here. The kitchen sends a tray over for the night employees. I like watching the six o'clock news on the TV that's there," he explained. "That Dietmar guy was really something else. Imagine my surprise when I start my shift and there he was booting it across the carpet and out the front door."

Coswell interjected.

"So, am I correct in assuming that Dietmar left the hotel at precisely seven o'clock?"

"Exactly," he answered. "I was pinning on my ID."

"When did he return?"

"That was strange. I had my eye out for him because I wanted to talk to him and see if he was really as wild as he appeared on the tube. I'm a bit of an amateur psychologist and I find people really interesting. To answer your question—he didn't return, or at least he didn't before I left at two. I found out the next day that his bed had been slept in but he left everything behind—toothbrush, overnight bag, and some clothes. That's what the squiggle means—stuff left behind when a guest leaves. He never came back for it and, as you've noticed, we didn't have an address at which to send it to him. I presume that you want to see it."

Coswell nodded and waited for him to fetch the articles. The manager was correct: there was nothing other than hygiene articles, crumpled undergarments, socks, and the tie he had worn to the studio. There were no notes, addresses, or even a map. Dietmar certainly traveled light and obviously planned to return to wherever he came from with minimal delay. But Coswell had got what he wanted. He left the curious young manager with thanks and a handshake and went out to his car, nodding to the valet who hovered nearby.

Back in his hotel room, Coswell pulled out his notebook where he had written down the phone number of the manager's suite at the Pacific Palisades. "Pops" himself answered in his usual gruff tone.

"Just following up on a lead," Coswell explained. "Do you remember the exact date and time of day that the Smith boy's father came to pick up his belongings?"

"Yeah, I do," he answered. "It was the same day as the six

o'clock news had that Dietmar jerk on. The father came by just after lunch. It was a Friday. Just a minute, I'll flip the calendar back and tell you the exact day." There was a pause. "Here it is—September 28th."

Coswell's heart leaped.

"I thought so," he said under his breath. "I think that Dietmar and the senior Smith met that night in apartment 301."

"I'm going to ask you a huge favour," Coswell said. "I'm coming by in a few minutes. I'd like you to take a small clipping of the rug in Sara's apartment and put it in an envelope for me. I'm going to give you a photograph of Dietmar to show to all your tenants in case one of them may have seen him the night of the 28th. Would you also describe the Smith boy's father to them and ask the same thing? I know I can get a local police crew to do that, but you know the comings and goings of your tenants best and can catch them in. I also don't think the sight of uniformed cops swarming your building would be good for business. What do you say?"

"I'll do it," the manager agreed, with a degree of enthusiasm that surprised Coswell. Perhaps the old fart was a crime buff.

When he had dressed and checked his image in the mirror, Coswell drove to the Pacific Palisades and repeated his request to the manager, giving him a copy of Dietmar's picture. He also checked that the old man still had the business card he gave him with the main RCMP dispatch phone number on it. He then returned to his car and drove the twenty-three twisty miles of the Sooke Road to his evening of gastronomic ecstasy.

The Sooke Harbour House is a world class restaurant—part of a resort in the middle of nowhere. The hotel overlooks the waves crashing in from the Pacific and the little town of Sooke lies just down the road. Reservations normally have to be made months in advance, but Coswell was coming for dinner only,

and because alone, the restaurant accommodated him. He was met at the front door by a charming lady who, although casually dressed by Vancouver upscale restaurant standards, received him with a practiced grace. He was warmly greeted and led to a small table adjacent to the kitchen. This didn't faze him in the least. He knew this was the least desirable spot for most diners, but he loved it. Serving staff often overlook a single diner, but this location was hard to miss because they had to pass him each time they delivered their orders. His server arrived within moments of his being seated. She was a pretty girl with long black hair, neatly arranged in a French braid, and she radiated a beatific smile. Coswell suspected that she was the junior amongst the servers and probably didn't have many more tables other than his to serve that night. Perfect, he thought to himself. This was going to be a memorable evening.

"May I bring you something from the bar, sir?" she asked. Coswell was pleased that she had not given her name and made the usual "I'm your waitress for the evening" announcement. She was obviously going to be his waitress and needn't explain it to him.

He opened the wine list and noted those available by the glass. He was delighted to see that the list was considerable—a rarity even in the best of eating establishments.

"I'd like something light to start with," he said. "What do you think of the Lang Vinyards Riesling?" He was teasing her, knowing she probably hoped he would order a beer or a cocktail.

"Good choice," she said, then, blushing, admitted, "I'm supposed to say that, but the truth is I don't know these wines at all. You really should ask Suzanne, the Maitre d'. She knows everything."

Coswell chuckled. He loved the naïve "Maitre d'," although Mistress d' tickled his funnybone even more.

"Don't worry," he said. "Before this evening is over you're going to know a lot more about wines. I'm an expert."

Her face broke into a huge grin.

"Wow!" she exclaimed. "That'd be great."

"Alright," he said. "Now what you should say about this wine is that it's from the Okanagan—Naramata, to be exact. It has a nice flinty quality with a clean aftertaste. It's a perfect apéritif. That means a drink taken before a meal. A good second choice would be a Blue Mountain Pinot Gris. That winery is in Okanagan Falls, just south of Penticton. It's a bit heavier but full of citrus flavour. Stress the clean aftertaste. Wine connoisseurs love that term."

"I'll get the Riesling for you right away," she said, beaming.

She had only just left his table when Suzanne wafted by. She paused to tell him, "Cindy is one of our newest employees. If there is anything not up to your wishes, please have her come and get me. She has been told to do that, of course, but you know how the young like to forge ahead."

"We're getting along fine," he reassured. "Is there anything on tonight's menu that you particularly recommend?"

"No," she replied. "Everything, as usual, is fresh, and it would be presumptive of me to apply my tastes to your choice. If nothing on the menu appeals to you, just let Cindy know and the cook will prepare anything you wish."

Coswell was impressed. He hadn't received a good put-down like that since Jaques at Lili le Puce in Vancouver told him that requesting mustard on the side for one of his jambon creations was tantamount to treason.

Cindy appeared with his glass of wine and with a sidelong glance at Suzanne, placed it ever so carefully beside his plate.

"The cork?" Suzanne said, one eyebrow arched. Cindy blushed and quickly returned to the bar.

"The cork?" echoed Coswell.

"Yes," explained Suzanne. "That bottle was just opened and we like the recipient of the first glass to do the honours with the cork. We have no house ordinaire. A patron ordering a glass of wine, in our opinion, deserves the same treatment as someone ordering an entire bottle. With the strict drinking and driving laws these days, more and more people are doing that—ordering just a glass or two. We're happy with that since they usually order a more expensive vintage. Our profit margin is just as good and we take pride in the quality of wines we offer."

"What a great idea," he replied. "I hope that trend travels far and wide. My great pleasure in life is an evening of fine dining, and since I'm usually alone your policy suits me to a *T*."

She picked up instantly on Coswell's obvious savoir faire and, seeing Cindy hurrying back to the table with cork cradled in a napkin, she left him and moved smoothly from table to table, greeting regulars and newcomers alike, one eye constantly on the front door.

"The ceremony of the cork, Cindy," he told the young girl standing expectantly beside him, "is probably overdone by most. It's a bit gauche to stick it up to one's nose. A skunky wine is more esthetically determined by sniffing it in the glass. A real connoisseur just looks to see that the cork is not dry. If it is, then there's a good possibility that the wine has been affected by air getting in. Still, he will usually taste it before declaring it bad. Never argue, by the way. Unless the customer is a jerk, he's generally right about a wine being bad. Occasionally a novice ordering a grape with which he is unfamiliar makes a mistake. He misinterprets the strange taste to indicate that the wine is off. Have the bartender or your wine steward check it and, if it's okay, return to the complainer with a sweeter wine like a gewürztraminer or a more familiar one such as a Chardonnay.

Everyone will be happy. Now, off you go. I'm going to sip this nectar and study the menu. Don't feel you need to hurry back. Just keep a watch on my glass of wine. When it's half gone, I'll be ready to order."

Coswell had also noted with satisfaction that the usual recitation of "this evening's specials" did not exist here. He wondered how many microwave dinners were produced in the kitchens by chefs who had to fill a non-special request. The menu here was magnificent. The use of edible flowers began in this restaurant and the hot soup offering was "Shady Lane Tomato, Garden Basil Puree Garnished with Nasturtiums and Fresh Tuna." One of the cold appetizers was a "Garden Green Salad with Edible Blossoms Tossed in an Oregon Grape, Sunflower Seed, Pumpkin Seed Vinaigrette." Item after item was unique, imaginative, and mouth watering. As usual, he agonized over his choice, but, as promised, he was ready when half of his wine was gone. Cindy appeared before he could put the glass down.

"I'm going to start off with a cold appetizer instead of a salad. I'll have the 'Basil, Cold Smoked Salmon and Goat's Cheese Terrine with Seared Horse Mackerel Loin Toast Crisps and a Basil, Canola Oil Dressing.' The rest of my Riesling will go well with that. For my entrée, I've chosen the 'Brazed Osso Bucco and Ragout of Malahat Farm Veal on a Caramelized Shallot, Cabernet Sauvignon, Purple Sage, Rustic Arugula, and Veal Stock Reduction with a Sour Cream Parsley Potato Cake, Roasted Banana Squash, and Daikon Radish, with Snow Peas.' If all this tastes as good as it sounds, I'm in for a wonderful meal."

"I can assure you of that. Chef gives us little tastes of everything before the customers arrive and it's all so good. He's really a genius. I wish my boyfriend would learn to do something like that instead of cutting down trees for a living."

"Oh, I'll bet he's good at what he does too, Cindy," Coswell said. "The forest industry has been the lifeblood of this province for over a century. We need capable people working there too."

"Not if the tree-huggers get their way," she answered, a flash of anger passing over her face.

Coswell immediately regretted his remarks. He should have been more sensitive. Sooke was the first logging community to be hit hard by the anti-logging protestors. He recalled the television news clips he had just viewed. Some of the angry woodworkers probably came from this area. Before he could change the subject, she continued.

"My boyfriend is good. He's competing in All Sooke Day this weekend. Last year he won the top-rigging event and he's only nineteen."

Pride and love rise above protest he mused.

"I've always wanted to see one of those logger sports days. I guess this and the Squamish events are the biggest in the province. Pity I never seem to have the time," he lamented.

"All Sooke Day came long before the Squamish show," she said, haughtily. "We're still the best. Our guys go over and beat them all the time. Too bad you can't stay, but you know, after your dinner you could walk over to the fairgrounds. It's floodlit and some of the guys are practicing there right now. I know my boyfriend, Gerry, will be there till ten. That's when I'm off. He drives me home."

"You know, I think I'll do just that," Coswell replied. "I'm sure a little walk will do me good after I down all this fine food. Thank you for telling me about it."

"No problem," she said, and headed off to the kitchen with his order.

Coswell leaned back, feeling a lovely mellowing effect from the wine. He reveled in these moments of bliss. He took another

sip of wine, reminded himself to save some for his first course, and gazed over the heads of the other diners to the windows facing out to sea. The sun had set and the light was rapidly fading, but seagulls, searching for scraps, flew past sending flashes of white as the last few rays reflected from their feathers.

He thought about what he had gathered so far in his Victoria trip. His perusal of the TV station's work-up on Dietmar merely confirmed the fanatic that he was—tree-spiking, vandalism of logging equipment, hate messages sent in various forms, and only the one instance of his being caught at an illegal sit-in. Dietmar Kraus was a nasty little piece of baggage—bad enough to be murdered. It was too much of a coincidence that the paths of John Smith's father and Dietmar crossed so precisely in time and place. Something happened in that apartment—possibly the killing itself. The blue nylon fibres on the corpse's head and the carpet in the girl's apartment could be a match. Vancouver forensic would do the comparison quickly. But Dietmar was ignorant of his friend's death. Were his statements on the TV really enough to make someone kill him? And why would the senior Smith turn on the set anyway?

Coswell was so deep in thought that he was unaware that Cindy had arrived with his appetizers. He started as she spoke.

"Here you are," she said. "I stole a few extra toasts for you. They're really yummy."

He looked down at the plate and marveled. The presentation was a work of art. He noted two Nasturtium flowers on the top of the terrine—an extra from the chef. He ate slowly, relishing every morsel. He had never eaten a flower before and was surprised at its peppery flavour, blending beautifully with the salmon and goat's cheese. He rationed the last of his Riesling. When his glass was empty and his plate finished, Cindy reappeared. Coswell had the distinct feeling that she watched his

every move. He had not seen her serve anyone other than him. He wondered if Suzanne thought he might be a newspaper food critic. She passed by often, smiling at him, but not uttering the "and how's everything" phrase, for which he was grateful. He was into eating, not conversation, and appreciated her respecting this. Cindy had obviously been instructed to do the same, but she did ask him if he wished another glass of wine as she cleared away his plate.

"Yes," he said. "I've settled on a glass of the Grgich Hills Cabernet. I'm absolutely amazed that you have it, and by the glass no less. It's golden. There's no other word for it—simply one of the best red wines in California. Anyone who orders that and doesn't like it deserves to be shot. It's really too good to drink with food, so don't hurry with my entrée."

She laughed, not believing that anyone could be so enthusiastic about anything as mundane as a glass of wine. She didn't drink alcohol and her boyfriend was beer all the way. She waited, however, until she saw half the wine gone before she gave Chef the go-ahead to prepare his second course. There was only a finger left when she brought the plate to him.

"Perfect timing," Coswell said. This presentation is even better than the first course, he thought, or the 13 per cent alcohol in his wine was altering his senses. Every component was placed to compliment the others in colour and texture, and when he took a forkful the blending of tastes was superb. He closed his eyes and moaned with pleasure. Cindy suppressed a giggle and left him, a man transcended to gastronomy heaven.

He finished his dinner off with a cappuccino and gratefully accepted the complimentary dessert offered to him—a Belgian chocolate shell in the shape of a scallop, filled with cream and topped with fresh strawberries. Suzanne brought him his bill which he paid with a personal credit card, adding a 20 per cent

tip for Cindy. He never charged his eating indulgences to the Force, knowing that the sums and the names of the restaurants would cause bad vibes in the bean counters.

When he stood up to leave, he was glad that he had decided to go for the walk that Cindy had suggested. He was definitely feeling a little too mellow to get behind the wheel of a car, despite the fact that two glasses of wine were supposedly safe.

Late October in southern Vancouver Island is usually cold and rainy, but not infrequently a warm air mass pushes up from the south and a sort of Indian Summer results. It was this type of evening that surrounded Coswell when he stepped out from the restaurant. Cindy had given him good directions to the fairgrounds, but he could have found them easily. The tall floodlights were visible for blocks. He walked at a leisurely pace, feeling the fullness in his stomach, but enjoying the warmth around him.

The main gate to the fairgrounds was swung wide open, left that way by the young men who had driven their pickups into the competition area. A small group of young women and a few children were seated in an adjacent section of bleachers. Coswell ambled over and took a seat beside them. A few looked briefly his way but most were intent on watching the men practice. Two were hurling double bladed axes at large wooden rounds painted with bulls-eyes. As each man cocked his arm and let fly, the handle and head of the axe cartwheeled to the target with amazing accuracy. Coswell marveled at the number of revolutions and the unerring bite of the blade into the wood with every throw. Not once did the axes glance off the block. Other activities were taking place—log burling in a large pool, cross-cut sawing, choker-setting—but the main attraction was the high rigging area. Four seventy-five foot spar trees were erected in a tight circle, and at the base of one of these was a short, muscular young man adjusting some sort of

harness around his waist. Beside him was an older man holding a coil of rope and wearing a timing clock on a cord around his neck. When the younger man was ready, he took the rope, slung it over his shoulder, and approached the base of the spar tree. He flicked what appeared to be a thicker, shorter rope attached to one side of his harness around the trunk and, catching it, knotted it on the other side of the harness, loosely tethering himself to the tree. He nodded to his timekeeper to start the clock and began to climb, digging in with sharp spurs strapped to his boots. His rate of ascent was dazzling; the safety rope was flipped up intermittently as he rose to the top. There he quickly pulled the coil of rope from his shoulder and, with what appeared to be a magician's slight-of-hand, fashioned a loop that he flung through the air to lasso the top of the next spar. A sharp tug and two quick spins secured the line to the spar he was standing on. Coswell couldn't see what happened next, but the young man was suddenly airborne, sliding along the line held by something attached to his belt, his safety line trailing behind. When he slammed into the next spar tree he give a single yank and the rope released from his previous perch. He repeated this process until he had traversed all four spars. The instant he landed on the last one he looped his safety rope over the top and, to Coswell's horror, appeared to fall the full seventy-five feet to the ground, the loose end of the rope barely held in one hand. In actuality, his spurs nipped in every ten to twelve feet and he used the safety line for drag, applying pressure by pulling on it with his free hand. None the less, he landed with a thump on a pile of sawdust at the base of the tree. Coswell expected him to have broken both legs, or at least suffered a compression fracture of his spine. He had neither. He let his rope fall and rushed over to his timer.

"Twenty-five seconds!" Coswell heard the older man shout. "You're unbeatable, man!"

"We'll see," the climber said, modestly. "The Squamish boys won't be here till tomorrow. Abe Winslow's back again this year. Remember how close it was last time?"

The sight of a young man appearing to plunge to his death before Coswell's very eyes stunned him for a moment. As he recovered he came to a startling revelation.

He had just seen a solution to the body from Heaven mystery.

Chapter 37

The word "ranch" applied to Ross Crocker's spread was a misnomer. He did keep a few horses for hunting purposes but there was no sign of any livestock. Heavy machinery of every description was scattered about the yard—trucks, backhoes, excavators, graders, and the like. A helicopter pad occupied the centre of what originally was probably an orchard. A few scraggly trees still grew at the perimeter. Islands of fuel barrels, some on platforms, were dotted about the property like mushrooms. Various machine sheds and a stable were utilitarian metal structures, but the main house was imposing. It was a log building of Titan proportions, with dormers, gables, and a huge veranda. It looked every bit the picture-book hunting lodge on a grand scale.

Ernie and Blakemore pulled their cruisers into the yard and parked in front of the house. A half dozen dogs of various breeds greeted their arrival with a chorus of howls and barks. The animals sensed an air of authority in the two Mounties, however, and kept their distance. A small, grey-haired woman wearing an apron over a plain blue dress came out onto the veranda. Her age was indeterminate; she could have been in her forties or her sixties. She regarded the Mounties with a pinched, suspicious expression on her face.

"What do you two want?" she demanded. "Ross told me you were coming up but he didn't say what for."

"We'd like to speak to him," Blakemore said. "Please tell him we're here."

"Awe, come on in, then," she growled. "No one tells me anything. He's in the den with Derek."

She turned and led them through the house. The foyer was enormous, its vaulted ceiling rising forty feet from the red tiled floor. A wrought-iron chandelier hung down suspended by a crudely hammered chain. It looks medieval, Ernie thought, with real candles in each of the cups. Blakemore's silent observation was more mundane—I wonder how the hell they light the thing, he mused. Old World paintings of hunting scenes hung on the walls. A sitting room was visible through glass doors to their left, and to their right was a long hallway that presumably led to the kitchen and dining areas. Directly ahead was the biggest staircase imaginable—six feet across, with banisters and newels of yellow cedar logs. The woman proceeded to climb the stairs; the Mounties followed. At the top of the staircase was a mezzanine with rooms leading off from it. All the heavy wooden doors were closed but one.

Their guide halted at that point and announced: "Here are the two cops, Ross. They're all yours. I'm going back to my kitchen."

With that perfunctory remark, she turned and disappeared down the stairs.

Crocker was seated in a large leather easy chair, facing them. Derek stood at his side, an insolent sneer on his lips. Try as they might, neither Ernie nor Blakemore could hide their awe as they looked around the room. The head of every game animal in the province hung on the walls—moose, deer, cougar, bear, antelope, rams, mountain goat, bison, lynx, elk—and suspended from the

ceiling and mounted on stands were birds—ducks, geese, pheasant and grouse. Antique guns were hung between the trophies. A locked glass case in one corner held a virtual arsenal of rifles, pistols, and shot guns, along with their appropriate ammunition.

Blakemore was the first to speak.

"I don't see any trigger locks on those pistols," he said. "And that glass had better be burglar proof or I could write a helluva big ticket right now. You know the new gun laws."

"Fuck the gun laws," Crocker replied. "You know damn well they're stupid and no one's going to pay any attention to them. I'll bet those sporting things you got aren't under lock and key all the time. Anyway, I hope you've come up here for something more important than that. Derek and I were discussing business before we were so rudely interrupted."

"We're investigating a series of deaths in the community," Ernie interjected.

"What do you mean 'a series?'" Crocker asked. "I thought the German tree hugger was the big murder you were working on. Good riddance to him, I'd say. Our own Canadian loony-toon environmentalists are bad enough, but to have some Kraut prick come over here to tell us what to do is too much. He deserved to be wacked. But who else has been killed?"

"Clyde Groat, for one," Ernie replied.

"Clyde Groat! When did that happen? No wonder he didn't show for work this morning. Was he in an accident?"

"He was murdered," Blakemore answered, bluntly.

"Jesus H. Christ! What's going on around here?" Crocker shouted, then, suspicious, added, "And what brings you here? I sure as hell didn't have anything to do with any murder. Clyde was a good man."

Blakemore had looked closely at both men when Ernie made his announcement and noted both appeared duly shocked.

Neither would be good actors, he thought, and cursed the probability he was barking up the wrong tree.

Ernie was more methodical.

"There are some findings that concern your business and the people who work for you," he said. "One of your water trucks almost certainly was used by Clyde's killer to leave the scene. That leads us to believe that someone in your organization is involved. It would be unlikely for this to be a random act. More likely it was carefully planned."

"One of my men?" Crocker asked, incredulous. "Who and why? Nobody I can think of. Clyde didn't have any enemies I know of. Do you, Derek?"

"No," said Derek. "I sure don't know any murderers."

"Clyde was killed up at the burn above gate three. You were up at there yesterday with George Smith and your pal Clark," Blakemore said to Derek. "I understand you drove George back and left Clark to tend the fire. When did you go back?"

"I went back around four and picked him up. We doused what was left of the fire but we didn't move the water truck. Clyde has to give the order for that."

"Who was supposed to go up there this morning and drive it down?

"Clyde told me and Clark to do it when we met at the Thunderbird, but not to rush because he was going to check the fire first. We didn't hear from him so we went up to Cougar Creek."

"Why wouldn't he send George?" asked Crocker. "You and Clark were supposed to set chokers for the helicopter."

"George was doing the cleanup at Ethel Roberts's place," answered Derek.

"Where did you and your men go right after we saw you at the Thunderbird this morning?" Blakemore asked Crocker.

"Everyone except Clyde went up to the Cougar Creek site," he answered.

"Directly?"

"Well, no," admitted Crocker. "I went with the helicopter crew to my place and made sure they loaded up okay, then I drove to the site."

"Alone?"

"Yes," said Crocker. "But I got there in twenty minutes—ask the crew."

"What about you?" Blakemore said, looking at Derek.

"Clark and I hung around the Thunderbird for a little while. Clyde had a cell phone and we thought he'd call us there, but he didn't. So, like I said, we drove up to Cougar Creek. We got there not long after the boss."

"That's right," Crocker agreed. "And we were all there till late afternoon. Ernie got me on the phone just after Derek and I arrived at the house."

"Where's the helicopter, by the way?" Blakemore asked.

"It's back in Nelson. We're finished with it for now. I don't really own the damn thing. I just lease it. I built the pad because I use it a lot and it saves on the hourly rate if it flies to the jobs from here."

"Why wasn't George Smith at the meeting this morning?" asked Ernie.

"I've got nothing to do with George," answered Crocker. "Clyde uses him like a subcontractor for odd jobs. My contracts were with Clyde. I didn't care who he hired as long as he got the job done. George and I haven't exactly been buddies from the day he got here. This community needed another gypo logging outfit competing for the same dwindling timber reserves like a hole in the head."

"I have no more questions," said Ernie, looking at Blakemore.

"I don't either—for now," Blakemore said, and turned to leave, pausing to add.

"Oh, by the way, we've put an impound on that water truck of yours—any objections?"

"Be my guest," replied Crocker. "But don't keep it forever. I'll be burning more slash soon."

It was dark before the two Mounties reached the station. Ernie checked for messages. Central dispatch had several. The volunteers had all come up blank in their search for anyone who might be involved in Clyde's death. Zachary had overseen the deposit of Clyde's body in the morgue and said he would be back later that evening to do his examination. He was going to have a quick dinner with Heather. There was a message for them from the Sergeant saying that he and his forensic team were going to try to get half way at least to Vancouver that night. He left a written summary of the examination of the water truck for them in an envelope at the hotel and promised a full report within the next day or two. Barbara phoned to say that she was spending the night with Michelle Groat and had persuaded her to wait till tomorrow to view his body. Blakemore was to call her there.

"This has been a helluva day, Ernie," Blakemore summed up.

"Yes, but I think we're nearing the end. Don't you agree?" Ernie replied.

"I'm not so sure. I thought we'd get the answer at Crocker's place today, but he and that Derek cretin have two iron-clad alibis as far as I can see."

"But there's one name that kept coming up, didn't you notice?" Ernie asked.

"You mean George Smith, don't you?"

"Exactly. And think about it. He was on the scene at one time or another at all three murders and he was working the backhoe when Heather was attacked."

"But Clyde and George were partners in a loose way even after George sold out. And what possible connection did he have with Ethel Roberts and the Dietmar kid? As far as I can figure—none. What do you think?"

"I don't know," said Ernie. "But George, I think, is someone we need to look at. You know his history a lot better than I do. He's an old-time resident here. That's about all I know about him."

"It's funny, but I don't know a helluva lot about him either. He's a Vietnam vet I've been told. Came up here from Washington State in the early seventies and started his logging business with GI pension money. He keeps to himself except for his volunteer work, especially after his wife died of cancer a couple of years back. She was Canadian but I don't think she was a local. They had a son who went away to university, but that was also a few years ago. The family's always lived on that small holding off the Main Street extension. He must have been a logger when he lived in Washington because he was a one man show from the day he got here, according to the locals—didn't need anyone to show him a thing. He does odd jobs now, mostly for Clyde, but people also hire him for cleaning out gutters, brush-clearing, and the like. He can operate most machinery so that backhoe job is typical. He's never been involved in any protest stuff that I know of and I've never even had cause to give him a ticket. I don't think he's our man, Ernie, but I'll be damned if I can offer up anyone else."

"Who could give us information about him?" asked Ernie.

"Ethel Roberts, I'm afraid, would have known him the best. Now that I think about it, his kid was some kind of athlete scholar at the school. Someone there might give us a clue. I'd planned to question the staff about Ethel anyway. I'll do that tomorrow."

"What are we going to do about notifying Coswell? If he finds out he's off on a wild goose chase and no one told him he's not going to be a happy camper," Ernie said.

"I'll put a call in for him now," agreed Blakemore. "Our local dispatch would like nothing better than to patch through to the big city. I'll use them." He dialed the local number and, as he expected, the operator took on the task as a personal mission.

"Also," Ernie continued, when Blakemore hung up, "we mustn't forget about Heather. She's still in danger, and we certainly don't want a fourth disaster to deal with. We'd better get back on our rotating surveillance. I'll do the first shift starting when Benson brings her back here. He is sticking with her, isn't he?"

"He promised to do just that," said Blakemore. "Meanwhile, I'm going to check in with Barbara, then I'll drive out to George Smith's place and have a talk with him. I'm also hungry as hell, how about you?"

"Famished. I didn't get lunch either. We can eat here. Why don't you call Barbara and I'll see if the Thunderbird'll do up a take-out for us. I have to pick up that forensic report anyway. Any preferences?"

Blakemore replied, "I want a double cheeseburger with fries, gravy, and a Diet Coke."

"Diet Coke? You're kidding."

"Got to cut the calories somewhere," said Blakemore, self-righteously.

Chapter 38

Zachary and Heather changed their minds about a quick supper and chose, instead, a dinner at the Quality Inn. They lucked out by getting seated in the Library that Ernie had so admired during his lunch with Blakemore. Heather was still self-conscious about her swollen face, although it was beginning to subside. The waitress looked at her with obvious curiosity but made no comment.

"I walked into a door," Heather said by way of explanation.

"Poor dear," commented the waitress.

Zachary laughed, causing the girl to look at him suspiciously. They ordered light meals, beginning with wine—Merlot for him and Chardonnay for Heather. He lifted his glass in a toast; she responded by doing the same, lightly clinking her glass on his.

"To another evening together," he said.

"Yes, and I spent so long in the Salon, preparing myself," she answered mischievously.

"And a lovely result, too," he said. She laughed.

"Did you get your article written for the *Bulletin* while you were waiting for me?"

"Pretty well," she said. "I'll polish it up at home tonight and have it on disc for the editor tomorrow morning. You'll read it in the afternoon edition. I'd like to get more background on Clyde Groat, but George Smith gave me a lot of personal information and I really don't want to bother Clyde's wife. There is a limit to the lengths I'll go to for a story, despite what Blakemore has probably told you."

"I don't mean to interfere in your work, Heather, but Paul did put in a plea via me that you tone down the murder aspect as long as possible. He thinks he is really close to solving the case and doesn't want the public in on it just yet."

"I know. But that's what he said about Ethel's murder as well," she said. "Zachary, there have been three people found murdered here in less than a week. I'm sorry, but Blakemore hasn't got the job done and people, including me, may be at risk. I'll bet that bringing the public in solves a lot more crimes than the police will admit. Memories can be triggered and associations made when people are made aware of the circumstances."

"You could be right, Heather," Zachary replied. "But that brings up the subject of your safety again—you said so yourself. What do we do to ensure that?"

"I like the *we*," she said, eyes twinkling. "Are you suggesting that you might move in?"

He blushed to his very roots and stammered an apology.

"Don't worry," she said, reassuringly. "I listened carefully to Ernie's lecture about locking my doors and not going out alone. I'll be all right. Also, I've got a feeling that the boys in blue are keeping an eye on me."

"I'll remind them," Zachary said with determination.

The waitress brought their salads. Zachary declined the offer to bring more wine for himself, but Heather ordered another glass of the Chardonnay.

"I think this stuff's more effective for pain than Tylenol extra strength and it sure as hell tastes better. For a house wine, this is really quite good," she said, draining the last of her glass. "Besides, you're driving."

By the time their main course arrived, Heather was literally feeling no pain. The alcohol had moved swiftly into her system and she was totally relaxed. She became loquacious, which in a lesser individual would have caused some embarrassment, but in Heather it merely made her more charming, especially in Zachary's eyes.

"I think all three of these murders are connected in some mysterious way," she observed. "The first was likely premeditated and the others committed to avoid detection. Both Ethel and Clyde must have known something that resulted in their having to be silenced. But what? Ethel likely taught Clyde in high school. His age is about right, and from what George Smith told me Clyde and his family go back in this community a couple of generations. I don't recall Ethel mentioning him in our conversations and I don't recall that they were on any committees together. For the life of me I can't think of any common bond that would result in them both being killed. And Dietmar at the head of all this is the

weirdest of all. Did I say 'head?' How thoughtless of me."

Zachary laughed. The thought of an overnight with this delightful creature was creeping into his mind. He couldn't remember the last time that such lascivious visions danced in his head and he was enjoying the sensation. She was looking at him as though she were reading his thoughts. He blushed again.

"You know," she said, "in our two dates so far, I've done 99 per cent of the talking, including tonight. It's about time we got you going. Let's start with your love life. I know you're single, but a good-looking guy like you must have left a trail of broken hearts somewhere. Have you come to the wilds to seek refuge from the female hormonal horde?"

"Hardly," he laughed. "I've been Dr. Nose-to-the-Grindstone for so long I could probably qualify for monkshood. Most of the women I've spent any time with in the past few years have been in the medical field and I'm afraid that studying or practicing medicine tends to have a neutering effect. We're all just colleagues."

"What about the nurses. I thought they were sexual fodder for young interns, or have I just read too many novels?"

That was a tough question for Zachary. He knew that during his years as a medical student and intern many of his fellows did take advantage of the sexual opportunities their glorified status afforded, but he didn't partake. He played the role of professional physician-to-be at such a lofty level that now, looking back, he realized what a prig he must have appeared to the nurses and technicians who fraternized with the young doctors. His mind flashed back to the many intern and resident parties that he deliberately missed, preferring instead to haunt the emergency room, observe late night autopsies, or make rounds with the senior staffmen. What a one-dimensional creature he was!

"I'm embarrassed to say that I missed out on all that," he

answered. "I really was Dr. Do-right. But I'm going to start right now by turning over a new leaf. How would you like to go steady with a born-again wildman?"

"Oooh, 'go steady,'" she teased. "I don't think I've ever heard that expression before. What does it mean? The 'wildman' thing sounds good."

"Now be gentle," he said. "You mustn't frighten me off."

"Okay, Dr. Wildman," she said. "How about this? You go to the morgue and I'll finish my article at home. We'll skip dessert here and have it at my place with coffee and some liqueurs. I have half a decadent cheesecake I bought in a moment of weakness at Svenson's Bakery last Monday. Don't hurry; I plan to soak in a hot bath after I write the article. In case I'm still in there when you arrive, just give the doorbell an extra ring."

"It's a deal," said Zachary, fantasizing the image of Heather, nude, in a tub. "But I'll follow you to your apartment first and make sure you're safely locked in."

"Yes, master," she said, bowing her head in mock subservience.

Chapter 39

"The doc is taking a helluva long time grabbing a bite to eat," Blakemore complained as he read over the Sergeant's report on his crew's examination of the water truck. The tire casts confirmed that it was the vehicle used by the murderer to leave the burn site.

"Now this is helpful. Hear this, Ernie," he continued. "'Traces of bird droppings, probably domestic fowl noted on the floor of the driver's side.' Chicken shit. All they found was chicken shit, Ernie. Nothing else—no prints, no hairs, blood, nothing from the killer. There was no answer when I phoned George's place.

I really don't want to go to Michelle's. I'm no good in these emotional things—let Barbara do that. I told her I had to work late, but what the hell am I going to do? No answer from Coswell yet. He's probably having a late supper somewhere."

"I think you should track down George Smith," replied Ernie. "God knows where you'll find him. I checked in the Thunderbird Pub when I was getting the take out. The volunteers were in there quaffing beer, but no sign of George and no one I asked knew where he was. He delivered Clyde's body to the morgue, then went directly back to the firehall and parked the inhalator. The two guys who helped him said he left them without a word. One minute he was there, the next he was gone. No one was surprised at that, though. George has a reputation for being a bit uncommunicative."

"He's probably at home, then," Blakemore said, "and just not answering his phone. I'll drive out there. No need for both of us to sit around waiting for Benson and Coswell."

Once past the last Main Street light standard, Blakemore's cruiser was plunged into darkness. A storm was brewing in the mountains, the clouds rushing in just before sunset, obscuring moon and stars. There were no house numbers. Names printed on mailboxes were the only identifying signs of the inhabitants of the properties. Most of the houses were set well back from the road, behind trees and shrubs. If one did not have exact directions, finding a particular residence would require multiple stops to read the names on the boxes. Blakemore, however, had driven this road hundreds of times and knew every one by heart. He pulled his cruiser into Smith's property and saw George's pickup parked in front. The house appeared to be in total darkness, but as he got out of the car he caught the familiar blue glow eminating from a television set through the window. He knocked on the door, hesitated, and then pushed it open.

"George," he called. "It's Paul Blakemore. Are you okay?"

No answer. He stepped into the hallway and looked to his left where he had seen the television. George's bulky outline was barely visible, seated in a large easy chair in front of the TV. Blakemore felt for a light switch at the doorway, found it, and turned the room lights on. George's head was slumped forward, apparently asleep, but the sudden intrusion of light caused him to snort and jerk his head up.

"Who ishit?" he slurred. "Whaaja want?" He was, apparently, quite drunk. An empty bottle of whiskey and an overturned glass were on the table beside his chair. The room reeked of booze.

"Jeez, George. Looks like you've really tied one on," observed Blakemore. "How far gone are you anyway? Can you answer my questions?"

George lurched out of the chair and tripped over the hassock on which he had been resting his feet. He fell heavily to the floor.

"Leave me alone," he said. "Whole world's a crock of shit. Goway."

He made no move to get up, apparently deciding to go back to sleep right there. He closed his eyes and snored. Blakemore wasn't going to strain his back trying to lift the big man onto the couch across the room, and so went in search of a bedroom. The main floor, he discovered, contained a large kitchen, bathroom, and den, in addition to the sitting room where George had passed out. Upstairs there were three rooms—two of the doors open. One led into an enormous bathroom with a shower, a full-sized iron bathtub, and a vanity with double sinks. It could be entered from the hall but there was also a door on-suite to the master bedroom. The door to that room was also open and revealed a four poster king-size bed with a real canopy. George's wife was obviously a woman of some taste, thought Blakemore. The bed

was rumpled and various items of men's clothing were strewn about—underwear, dirty socks, and workpants. Blakemore grabbed a pillow and pulled off the comforter to take to the prostrate man downstairs.

As he headed to the stairs, his curiosity drew him to the room with the closed door. Balancing the comforter and the pillow in one arm, he pushed open the door. He felt for the switch inside and flicked it on. The room was obviously the son's. In contrast to his father's bedroom, in spite of a badly needed dusting, everything was neat and tidy. A double bunk bed was in one corner—the bottom bed, covered with a bright patchwork quilt, the top was apparently home to his sporting equipment— basketball, football, lacrosse stick, and a huge toy gorilla with a yellow and black muffler wrapped around its neck. On the walls were numerous high school pennants of the same colours, denoting championships in various sports. A shelf stretching across one whole wall was filled with trophies.

Blakemore draped the comforter and pillow over the banister and entered the boy's room. He was drawn to a large corkboard filled with pictures. From the hallway he had noticed that many of them were wrestling scenes. As he passed the trophy shelf he read the inscriptions: Provincial Bantam Wrestling Championships; First, Western Canada Junior Wrestling Champion; John Smith, Athlete of the Year Award; John Smith, Bear Creek High School. The photos showed the young man in action, receiving awards, and as a member of numerous teams. There were many family pictures as well: John and his dad fishing, the two of them hunting, and one of particular interest. It showed the son and George in a mock wrestling pose: the boy was probably about fourteen and had his skinny arms clamped around his father's great neck in a hammerlock. Underneath someone had neatly penned, "Little John tames the Kootenay Mauler."

A loud sound below brought an abrupt halt to his snooping. George was astir. Blakemore quickly switched off the light and closed the door just as a staggering hulk appeared at the bottom of the stairs.

"Who are ya?" George bellowed as he lurched forward; stumbling on the first step he fell face down on the carpeted tread. Blakemore rushed down the stairs to help him up.

"It's Paul," he shouted into the man's ear. "It's Paul Blakemore, George. Take it easy."

George looked at him, bloodshot eyes struggling to focus.

"Paul?" he said, bewildered.

"Yes, Paul," Blakemore answered. "Now if you managed to get this far, you can get up to your bedroom. Come on. Hold onto the railing and I'll help you up."

The Mountie's legs buckled as George leaned on him, but after a considerable struggle he got the man upstairs and to his bed where he fell onto his back. Blakemore swung George's legs up and retrieved the blanket and pillow, propping the latter under the man's head and throwing the comforter over him.

"For Christ's sake, stay here till you sober up, George," he said. "There's no use talking to you tonight, but I want to see you in the morning."

He was answered by a loud snore.

Blakemore went directly down the stairs and out the front door, leaving George's bedroom door open so that the sound of his departure could easily be heard. He had spotted two more pictures on the son's corkboard just before he rushed out—one was a photo of John in his high school graduation gown with his mother standing on one side and Ethel Roberts on the other. The second was a faded black and white of a young George in a wrestling costume. It was professionally done. Ernie was right: George's role in all of this was becoming highly suspect.

Chapter 40

If it weren't for the return of the pain in her forehead, Heather would have been in a state of total euphoria. One of the attractions that prompted her to rent the apartment was the antique tub in the bathroom. Although her diminutive size did not justify the generous dimensions of the tub, she enjoyed the extra luxury of being able to stretch out to full length and to feel her body floating in a sea of bubbles. Her favourite perfume company had just put out its new line of effervescent, scented capsules and she threw in a whole handful when she poured the bath.

She tried to let her mind go blank. The headache, she was sure, had returned in part from the effort she put into her article on Clyde Groat. She rewrote it three times. The first draft sounded like something from the sensationalist morning rags in Vancouver and it took her two more attempts to produce something that settled with her conscience.

There was a message from Alfred Fitch on her answering machine asking her if she could attend the reading of Ethel Roberts's will the next morning at nine in his office, and to return his call only if that was not agreeable. Heather suspected he would be shocked if she had said no. Ethel Roberts's face popped into her mind as it had done many times since the woman's death. It set Heather to thinking.

Why was the gentle old lady killed and why did someone attack me? Where does Clyde's murder fit in? We must all be connected in some way to Dietmar and each of us must know something that will give the killer away. Otherwise, we all must have done something awful to this person to make him act like that. I made some enemies, I suppose, on Vancouver Island, but no one followed me up here, I'm sure of that. Ethel wouldn't cause pain to a fly. She even agonized about her feeble

environmental protests, fearing that the loss of jobs might hurt some financially needy family. I really don't know anything about Clyde other than that he was a hard worker, a good family man, and an asset to the community doing his volunteer work. Then she remembered what Paul Blakemore had said—that the answer might be in her conversations with Ethel. Heather decided to focus on that.

She let her head sink a bit so that when the water came up to her lips she blew some bubbles. She watched the foam scurry down to her toes as she let her legs float to the surface. A faint rattle emanating from the kitchen broke her reverie. She felt her heart race as she strained to hear. Silence followed.

"Jeez, but I'm getting jumpy," she said aloud. "Now, where was I?"

She focussed again on Ethel and their many talks. She tried to recall the rare occasions that negativity entered the conversations. The most recent was the Cougar Creek Project. They both really got going on that one with the *Bulletin* article and the petition signing. Ross Crocker and his crowd were the only ones bothered, but would any of them kill over it? The protests got nowhere and the project is going ahead, so what the hell? That couldn't be it.

The only other subject she could remember Ethel discussing with any degree of anger was anything that adversely affected her students, especially her favourites. She had such lofty ambitions for them and was deeply disappointed if they gave in to "short term comforts"—which is what she called teen pregnancies, a job with Crocker or the mill, their own car, and all those items given so much importance by the young.

Ethel, despite her spinsterhood, understood her charges so well that she could influence the most hardened of them. John Smith was one of those, and his story was Heather's

favourite. She loved the way Ethel described their first meeting. John swaggering into his first English Class, a great hulk of a boy dressed in a logger's Mac, scruffy jeans, and wearing a Caterpillar hat with the brim curved perfectly in the baseball style and pointing forward. The hat-backwards fad did not exist in loggers' country. Ethel had read the boy's profile sent up by the Junior High School and knew he was a problem. Bullying, disrespect, vandalism, and truancy were notations made by his previous teachers. He ruled the schoolyard like a Mafia Don. The community had decided on a "no fail" system during a referendum and so John was moved up each year, regardless of his dismal academic record. He was every teacher's nightmare, but he met his match in Ethel Roberts.

She began the year's first class by making each student come to the front of the room and give a five minute talk on their activities over the summer. This was a powerful tool since most teenagers' bravado disappears when they are isolated from the group and forced to perform. They usually returned to their seats in a more humble frame of mind. John, however, wasn't fazed by the task. He marched up to the front, and with gross insolence sat on the edge of Miss Roberts's desk as he gave his report. Using the most grammatically incorrect speech he could muster, sprinkled with *ain'ts*, *me's*, *you know's*, and the odd cussword, he described his summer working with his dad in the bush. He returned to his seat without even a glance at his teacher. The class sat stunned, waiting for her response.

"I didn't bat an eyelash," Ethel had said. "I knew he would do something like that and I was ready."

She applauded him and said that John had given the best talk she had heard in ages. She pointed out that a famous writer had used words like that—simple and earthy and to the point. That writer had won a Nobel Prize. His name was Ernest Hemingway.

She made *The Old Man and the Sea* the novel to be studied for the first semester. She also gave out a list of Hemingway's other novels and a brief biography pointing out his military service, his passion for hunting and fishing, and the fact that he was "a man's man." John Smith's life changed from that point on. He read everything Hemingway had written and submitted a term paper that was legitimately first class.

"The boy was obviously bright," Ethel recounted. "But even I was surprised at his ability to learn. He almost taught himself grammar through his reading. I didn't do much more than just encourage him."

Heather knew that was not likely 100 per cent true, but her own writing skills had developed in a similar way, thanks to a kindly editor.

There was a blot on the happy ending of the story of John Smith. Ethel had mentioned it only once in response to Heather's comment that the boy's parents must have been proud of his academic achievements.

"His mother certainly was," Ethel had said. "She was a quiet woman but I know she was disturbed by the delinquent reports that his previous teachers had sent home. George, the father, was a different story, and he was definitely the dominant one in the family. He wanted young John to follow in his footsteps. He already had titled his company "George Smith and Son, Logging contractors." The only school activities he supported were sports, and John was outstanding in those. I know the boy struggled to try to please his father, but he was as stubborn as the old man was and he kept on with his academics.

"When he won the Governor General's Medal and all the scholarships that came with it, I have never felt so proud of anyone in my life. When he was accepted into the Honours English course at the University of Victoria, I wept with joy. I

was doubly pleased when he would come back in the summers and visit with me. Sometimes he even brought a university friend with him. Such intelligent young men."

George was obviously pissed off, thought Heather, but no father—family business or not—could hold a grudge against Ethel Roberts for the change she made in his son.

There was a knock this time. Someone was at the back door! Not even my neighbours come around the back when they want me, she thought, fear tightening her chest.

"Hang on," she shouted. "I'm in the bath. I'll be there in a minute."

She leapt out of the tub dripping suds and water, grabbed her robe, and ran barefoot into the living room where she snatched her keys off the coffee table. She unbolted the front door, flung it open, and raced nude, the bathrobe still clutched in her hand, to her car parked on the street. She unlocked the driver's door, jumped inside, and hit the electric lock button. Hands shaking, she had difficulty inserting the key in the ignition but finally slid it in and started the engine. In one motion she pulled on the light switch with her left hand and put the shift lever in drive with her right. Accelerator to the floor, the car shot forward with its tires screeching on the pavement. She didn't slow down until she reached the end of the block where she abruptly turned right and then right again at the entrance to the alley that ran behind the apartment complex. Her car lights on high beam pierced the darkness and caught a dark figure running towards her, then veering off into the wooded area. She braked and then backed up into the street. She felt the cold now and quickly pulled on her robe and switched the heater onto high. The front door of her apartment was ajar when she drove back, the light spilling out into the step. She parked the car facing the wrong way in front and, leaving the motor running, ran over and pulled the

door shut. The automatic lock clicked into place. Looking right and left, she hurried back to her car, got in, and headed for the police station.

Chapter 41

Coswell felt a twinge of guilt when he got back to his car and checked his cell-phone. He really should have taken it into the restaurant with him and left it on mute. (A cell-phone ring in a first class eating establishment should be punishable by death, he maintained.) At least he could have checked the visual display periodically. The operator's tone when he dialed in was one of barely disguised annoyance.

"I have an urgent call for you, Inspector, from Nelson dispatch. A Corporal Blakemore has been trying to contact you for some time," she informed him.

"I'm way out in the wilds of southern Vancouver Island," he lied. "Must be a dead spot for telecommunications. I just got your beep."

Slightly mollified, she made the necessary connections that eventually got him through to the Bear Creek Police Station. Ernie answered.

"Coswell here. What's up?" he said in a perfunctory manner.

Ernie related all of the events since the inspector's departure from Bear Creek, including the X-ray findings and the fact that Blakemore was currently looking for George Smith.

"Holy shit," was Coswell's unprofessional reply. "The guy's last name is Smith, did you say? How old is he?"

"Mid fifties, I'd say," answered Ernie.

Coswell's mind whirled for a moment, then locked in with a series of orders.

"We have to be careful here. If we rush in too fast we can

lose the whole thing. You know how airtight our cases have to be these days to get a conviction. Get a hold of Blakemore and tell him to back off with Smith. Put a twenty-four hour surveillance on him instead. I know it's tough with just the two of you, but it has to be done. Get a warrant so we can search his house and go over his pickup. I'll get Nelson to send you a couple of officers in plain clothes to relieve you, but in the meantime you and Blakemore have to hold the fort. Get the reporter lady in a safe place, even if you have to lock her up. She's the next victim, I'm sure."

"I think the local doctor will help us there," Ernie offered.

"Good," said Coswell. "But make sure he knows the danger involved. I don't want him going under too. Finally, watch Clyde Groat's wife. I don't think she's as much at risk, but you never know."

"Paul's wife is with her," Ernie said.

"Fine, but the same advice goes for her, and make sure she can reach the two of you in an instant if she needs to. Get a pager for her with a panic button on it. Have either of you questioned her yet?"

"No. Paul hasn't been home yet."

"Good. I want to be there, so tell him to wait on that too. There's no way I can get from here to Bear Creek any earlier than tomorrow morning. I remember the schedule when I flew in there the first time. Check with the airport. I'll get the first flight out from Vancouver to Castlegar and with the drive I should arrive mid morning. We'll all meet at the station."

"Roger," said Ernie.

"Out," said Coswell.

Ernie was in the process of putting the call in to Blakemore when Zachary came through the front door.

"Where's Heather?" Ernie asked, apprehension in his voice.

"Safely locked in her apartment. Don't worry, I made sure of it, and to further ease your mind I'm going back after I finish my autopsy. You two can take a well-deserved break," answered Zachary, hoping that Ernie would not ask the obvious.

"All night?" Ernie asked, without mercy.

Zachary blushed.

"Maybe."

Ernie laughed and then explained that in view of Coswell's orders there was a very practical reason for his question.

"Then the answer is yes; of course I'll be there all night. I won't take no for an answer. I can sleep on the couch," said Zachary. Thank God Blakemore's not here, he thought, or this conversation could really be embarrassing.

"I'm going to the morgue now to get started. The sooner I finish the better. You don't think I made a mistake leaving her alone, do you?"

"No. Heather's smart. I told her what to do and I know she listened. She'll call us if anything is wrong,"

Zachary headed for the morgue just as Blakemore checked in on his car radio.

"Got your message, Ernie," he said. "I'm on my way in and do I have something to tell you. See you in ten."

The radio clicked off before Ernie could reply. Ernie contemplated phoning Judge Rawlston about the warrant, but Blakemore knew him a lot better and that job would probably be best left up to him. Blakemore's ten minutes shrunk to five as the cruiser wheeled to a stop beside Zachary's car in front. The expression on his face when he pushed open the station door was one of triumph. He marched straight across the office to the phone, speaking as he moved.

"Ernie," he said. "I think we got our man. I can't believe it but it looks as though George Smith is the likeliest candidate.

I can't explain a connection with the Dietmar kid, but there has to be one. Maybe he had an accomplice. We need a search warrant fast. I'm going to get Rawlston right away."

He had the number dialed and was speaking to the judge before Ernie could open his mouth. It took Blakemore less than two minutes to present the facts and get agreement for the search warrant.

"I'd appreciate it, Judge, if you would word it so we can look through anything we think might be pertinent to the case," he directed. "I don't want some lawyer making any hay with the paperwork."

He hung up the phone and didn't pause for breath until he told Ernie everything that had happened during his visit with George and the significance of his observations of the photos.

"I've got some time," he went on, "before he comes around and destroys some important evidence. He was shit-face drunk, I'll tell you, but he's also a big tough hombre and maybe he'll sober up faster than average. I doubt if he heard anything I said—especially about coming to the station in the morning. In fact, he was so drunk he might not even remember my being there and presume he put himself to bed. If he was more alert than I gave him credit for, I made a big thing about stomping right out without snooping. That and my not sticking around might keep his guard down."

"I hate to put a downer on you, Paul," said Ernie when he finally had a chance to speak. "But Coswell has ordered us to back off till he gets here."

He related the telephone conversation to Blakemore.

"Shit!" he said. "No wonder the guy's the King of Homicide. He makes sure he's always leading the charge. Damn, damn, damn. Just when we're so close."

"I don't think you should look at it that way, Paul. After all,

Coswell has tons more experience than we do in handling cases like this. I agree with him about the legal challenges. You don't want a murderer to get off on some technical loophole that you and I might overlook. The victims deserve more than that."

"You're right, Ernie," Blakemore said with a sigh. "But I don't mind telling you I feel a letdown."

"But I do have some good news for you," said Ernie. "Doctor Bensen has agreed to look after Heather. It sounds as though they have something going and he's going to do an overnight at her place. That will free me up to start the surveillance on George."

"Well I'll be doggy-damned," said Blakemore, breaking into a grin. "I didn't know he had it in him—Doctor Dedicated and all. I hope he knows what he's getting in for. That Heather's a real handful."

"Actually she's a nice person and very intelligent."

"I prefer dumb, hot, and obedient, but don't tell Barbara I said that."

"On a more serious note," replied Ernie, "when do you think I should set up at George's and how am I going to look inconspicuous? Our vehicles are too easy to recognize."

"That's a problem all right, but the locals are used to us prowling around, so just do a patrol pattern and stop frequently. Those issue binoculars are good and there are enough vantage points around that you can keep a pretty good eye on the yard. But take a break first. From the looks of him, I don't think even the best alcohol-tolerant type would come around from that snootful in any less than a few hours—more likely, not until tomorrow morning. Keep me posted and don't move in on him yourself for any reason. Got that?"

"Roger," said Ernie, smiling. "Big brother has spoken."

"Fuck off," said Blakemore.

Ernie left with that encouragement, calling back over his shoulder.

"Don't forget to fill Barbara in and warn her to be careful."

Blakemore nodded and once more picked up the phone. His wife listened carefully to his explanation then declared firmly, "I'm staying here for the night, Paul, but I want you to come by. Michelle's sitting beside me, but I know we'll all feel better if we see you." The tacit demand was unmistakable.

Chapter 42

Heather thanked her lucky stars when she was a block away from the police station. A squad car was approaching her going in the opposite direction. She flashed her lights rapidly as she pulled over to the curb and rolled down her window. She had become acutely aware of the fact that she was dressed in nothing but a bathrobe and didn't relish the prospect of walking into the station in that state. She was even more delighted to see that the driver of the police car was Ernie, not Blakemore.

Ernie responded to the signal and, recognizing her car, pulled over and walked across the street to talk to her.

"Heather," he asked, "what on earth are you doing out here? Zachary told me that you were safely locked in your apartment."

She quickly related what had transpired.

"Can you describe the man you saw in the alley?"

"I didn't see his face, but he was white and large. It could have just been the clothing he had on, but I had the distinct feeling that he was a big man."

"Like George Smith?" Ernie asked.

"Yes, as a matter of fact, like George Smith. My God, do you think that's who it was?" she said, astonished.

"No. It couldn't be. George, according to Paul, is currently

at home totally inebriated," he answered. "Anyway, let's get you home. Zach Bensen should be finishing up in the morgue and I'll get him to go directly to your apartment. I understand that he has agreed to help protect you and it's obvious we need help—Paul and I aren't doing the job if something like this happens to you."

"You can't be everywhere at once," she said, touching his arm lightly. "You've both been very considerate of me and I appreciate it."

Ernie returned to his cruiser and radioed Blakemore as he followed Heather's car.

"Jesus," Blakemore shouted over the speaker. "The villains are coming out of the goddamned woodwork! Believe me, the attacker couldn't have been George. I know a piss-eyed drunk when I see one. You stay with Heather until the Doc gets there. I have to swing over to the Groats' place for a few minutes but I think the Doc will be over there in a flash as soon as I tell him what's happened. Get that surveillance going on George as quick as you can. If you see anything suspicious, call me. Bugger Coswell, we'll move in with the search warrant if there's even the slightest indication. I don't want to lose everything just because the big inspector told us to wait."

"Roger," replied Ernie. He was glad that he was on the first shift watching George. Paul was getting too riled up and could wreck everything by charging in like a bull in a china shop.

Chapter 43

Coswell hated dealing with bureaucrats, even though he was often a member of that fraternity himself—quoting rules and laws that didn't always make sense. He was face to face with the night duty officer at the main police station in Victoria.

"Don't give me that bullshit," he said to the hapless officer.

"I know it's after hours and the Coroner is probably at home watching *NYPD Blues* on the tube, but this is an urgent situation. I need those records right now, not tomorrow morning after nine. If you won't speak to him, I will. Give me his damn phone number. That's an order."

The officer was about to tell Coswell that he had no jurisdiction in the Victoria precinct, but decided it wasn't worth the grief, although he was tempted. He didn't like being pushed around by anyone, Inspector or no.

The personal phone call turned out to be a real time saver for Coswell. The Coroner, a cheerful fellow, despite his calling, remembered the John Smith case well.

"It was really a tragedy," he recounted. "The boy was just trying to earn some money between university semesters. He was working with a crew that was clearing trails in what is now the Carmanha Provincial Park. He was bucking a big windfall fir when his chainsaw hit a spike in the tree causing a tooth to break off the chain. Somehow the fragment flew under his face shield and lacerated his right carotid artery. He bled to death before anyone could help him. It was an absolute freak accident. No negligence on anyone's part other than the tree-spikers, of course. I was there when the father identified the body. It was pathetic. The boy was his only child."

"What was the father's first name?" Coswell asked.

"That I don't remember, but it will be in the file, of course. My clerical staff won't be in until nine tomorrow, but I can come down and find it for you if you feel it's necessary."

"No," Coswell replied, glancing at the duty officer. "But I would appreciate a complete copy of the report faxed to the RCMP station in Bear Creek. I'll be there late tomorrow morning."

He repeated his name to the Coroner and gave him the fax number, which he had jotted down in his notebook.

He made one more call from the precinct phone—to the University Registrar's office. Her name was also in his book—Mrs. Joan Cartwright. He left a message for her regarding John Smith's name and requested also that she fax his file to Bear Creek.

Either or both sources should have the father's name and address noted. No such thing as too much information in a murder investigation, he thought

With a nod to the officer at the desk, he left and headed back to his hotel to check out and make his way back to Vancouver. He noted that the wind from earlier in the day had abated and hoped the return flight on the helicopter would be less turbulent. He wasn't looking forward to depositing his wonderful dinner in the helijet motion-sickness bags.

He tried to keep his mind on more positive thoughts. A feeling of completeness was coming over him. He had motive, a probable suspect, and method. It was a matter now of tightening the noose. The killer was not going to escape justice for his vengeful acts. Some strands of blue nylon carpeting and possibly an eye witness would tie him to what could have been the murder scene.

Chapter 44

Blakemore was pleased to find the Groats' front door locked when he arrived and the familiar voice of Barbara demanding, "Who is it?" and waiting for his response before she opened it. She led him into the kitchen. The two children were in bed. Michelle was sitting at the kitchen table holding a cup of coffee in her hands. She possessed a face reminiscent of the figures painted on Dresden China—pale, flawless skin, coloured only by her makeup. Her jet-black hair was cut short but combed to produce curls and waves that sent highlights flashing as she moved her head. Her full figure had been kept in check

with diet and fitness programs that offset the usual slide to the German hausfrau proportions of her mother and her aunts.

She looked up as he entered and asked, "Why, Paul?"

Blakemore stood, cap in hand, struggling for something reassuring to say to her.

"I don't know, Michelle," he said. "But you can count on my finding out."

Barbara poured him a cup of coffee and motioned for him to sit at the head of the table. As he sat down he made a decision. He wasn't going to wait for Coswell. He'd just made a promise to Michelle and he intended to keep it.

"We need your help," he said gently. "I know you must be in shock, but I'd like to ask you a few questions if you're up to it."

"I'm up to it," she said. The blank look he had seen at the Credit Union office was being replaced by resolve. The people in Michelle's family were loggers for as far back as she could remember. Accidents and deaths happened. The survivors grieved, then got on with their lives.

Blakemore paused, trying to think of the best line of questioning. He began, "I want you to think back to this morning when Clyde rushed out of the house after something in the *Bulletin* set him off. Do you remember what part of the paper he was looking at? The front page or something further along?"

"I was trying to get the kids off to school and I wasn't really paying much attention to Clyde. He usually doesn't get past any more than a page. It's just something for him to look at while he has his coffee and juice. He's always in such a hurry, what with the seven thirty meetings at the Thunderbird and the fire watches. I can't even remember if it was a recent edition or not. I usually keep the last two or three because he does like to read them through when he has time, and he's usually behind that far. But let me look."

She got up and went over to a parson's bench next to the telephone. A stack of magazines and newspapers were at one end, children's lunch kits at the other. She rifled through the stack and found two copies of the *Bulletin*.

"It was Monday's edition that he took. The rest of the week's copies are here."

That's the one that contained Heather's article on Ethel Roberts and the composite of Dietmar, Blakemore noted.

"I know you told me that he didn't say who he was in such a hurry to see, but aside from the Thunderbird meeting and the Cougar Creek job, did he mention any other plans for the day, people he had to meet?"

"He might have, Paul, but nothing seemed out of the ordinary, and I guess I wasn't really paying a lot of attention. I'm sorry. But maybe some of the men would know. George especially. Have you spoken to him?"

"I went out to see him at his place just an hour or so ago but I'm afraid he was really into the bottle and couldn't talk to anyone."

"George, drinking?" she said, disbelieving. "That's really too bad. He hasn't touched a drop since his son was born, according to Clyde. He was a hell-raiser before then, I understand. Even his wife couldn't control him, but that child turned him around completely and he really dedicated his life to him. It's really a shame they had a falling out about that university thing."

"University thing?" asked Blakemore.

"George wanted John, his son, to go into the logging business with him. The boy was a chip off the old block until he was in high school. He was falling trees and driving a truck when he was fourteen. He and George used to disappear into the bush for days on end, hunting and fishing. They were inseparable. But the kid got religion, so to speak, in high school. He ended up

at the top of his class and won a whole bunch of scholarships. It was natural that he should go on to university. His mom was really proud, but George kind of sulked. No one had any sympathy for him. What kind of parent doesn't want their kid to succeed academically? I sure hope mine do that good. Anyway, John would come home in the summer and work with his dad but the relationship was never the same. It really soured when John brought some of his friends to go camping and fishing with him. George's nose got really out of joint. He picked arguments with some of the boys who were conservationists. John eventually stopped coming, especially after his mother died."

"Did you ever see any of the boy's friends?" Blakemore asked.

"No, but Clyde did. He told me the whole story. We rarely socialized with the Smiths. They kept pretty much to themselves. In fact, Clyde's probably the closest to any socializing they ever did, but that was mostly at work. George even hunted alone, which is pretty strange up here, and he wasn't a member of the Rod and Gun Club. We were all surprised when he became a volunteer fireman."

"How would you describe the relationship between George and Clyde? Were they close friends, do you think?"

"I don't think anyone other than his family ever got close to George, and he was Clyde's boss after all. Clyde admired George's skills but I don't think they were ever buddy-buddy if that's what you mean. When he sold out to Clyde he agreed to stay on to help him out, but he never was an employee in that sense. He did help Clyde a lot keeping the business going. Things have been tough, what with the drop in the lumber prices, and George works cheap. They didn't spend much time together because Clyde had to be in so many places at once trying to do work for Crocker as well as keep our company going. But why all the questions about George? Do you think he had anything to do with Clyde's death?"

"Just part of the investigation, Michelle," Blakemore stalled. "Everyone's a suspect until we can narrow it down."

He saw in her face that his answer wasn't entirely satisfactory, but she didn't take it any further. He made an attempt to distract her suspicions.

"Did Clyde have any real enemies that you know of? Anyone holding a bad grudge?"

"No. Clyde treated everyone fair. He hasn't got an enemy in the world. There was no earthly reason for his being killed. It must have been an accident—some hunter who missed a deer and panicked when he saw what he had done. He's probably still running."

"Yes," Blakemore lied. "It could have been an accident for sure and we're looking into that."

He finished his coffee and excused himself, pleading more work ahead for him before the day was over. He reassured Barbara that he could manage by himself at home but (at Michelle's bidding) agreed to drop by the Groat residence early the next day for breakfast. He got back in his cruiser and went to find Ernie. He knew exactly where to look. There was an old dead end road above the Smith property from which the whole yard was readily visible.

"No sign of life down there," Ernie said when Blakemore pulled up. "There's not a light on in the house, and if it wasn't for the yard light it would be pitch black. It's going to be a long, boring night."

Blakemore nodded as he looked down on George's front yard. Something was not right, though. He tried to visualize the scene from his earlier visit. What was out of place? He took the binoculars Ernie had laid on the hood of his cruiser and scanned the property. The light from the TV no longer glowed. Had George sobered up enough to turn it off? The position of the

pickup was different as well. He distinctly remembered having to walk around it to reach the front door. It seemed ever so slightly forward of that position now. He couldn't be absolutely sure, and he still found it impossible to believe that George could have been feigning his drunkenness. There was certainly not enough to disobey Coswell's orders and rush in. He stayed for several more minutes chatting with Ernie, feeling bone weary.

"I'm getting old, Ernie. I can't take these late nights like you young guys. I think I'll go home to bed. I'd like to get that school interview in tomorrow before Coswell gets here. But I'll find out about the Nelson relief that he was supposedly going to arrange and I'll send them up here as quick as I can. You going to be able to hang on till then?"

"Yeah, but that relief sounds good to me too. See if you can hurry it up and let me know when they'll arrive. It'll make the wait more bearable."

It wasn't much of a wait. As Blakemore drove past the station he saw an unfamiliar car parked in the lot. He pulled in and greeted the young officer sitting inside.

"I'm it," the Nelson Mountie said. "We couldn't spare anyone else. Where do I spend the night?"

Blakemore told him, but added, "Constable Downs, who you are relieving now, will spell you off at seven-thirty tomorrow."

"Thanks," he said, with little feeling.

Chapter 45

The Bear Creek High School was one of those rare accidents of good bureaucratic planning. The student population fluctuated very little from year to year, unlike the boom and bust situations in other communities. Logging, farming, mining, and now the service industry for the tourists and retirees kept young families

in the district. The school was large and well run. Blakemore was impressed by the number of cars parked in the staff lot an hour and a half before the school day began. He parked the cruiser in a visitor's stall and made his way to the administration office. The principal was waiting for him—a tall, portly man in his early fifties with a red face and shining bald pate.

"I saw you drive up, Corporal Blakemore. We've been expecting you. Ethel Roberts's death has been a shock to us all. We'll cooperate in every way with your investigation. Where would you like to start—her office in the library?"

Blakemore was impressed. He liked people who got down to business fast.

"That would be great," he said. "I presume that is where she would keep any private and personal documents."

"Probably," the principal agreed. "I have her dossier in my office, of course, as I do for all the staff members. I have hers already pulled for you."

He handed Blakemore the bulky folder that represented thirty-five years of Ethel Roberts's professional life in the Bear Creek School System.

"You can use her office to go over all of this along with anything you find there, of course."

The principal then headed off with big strides down a long corridor, Blakemore hurrying to keep up. The library was surprisingly large, no doubt due to Ethel Roberts's influence over the years. Her office was a tiny room behind the check-out counter. A personal computer took up most of her small desk. Built-in bookshelves contained a few old edition classics and numerous plaques and gifts from students. An open file cabinet and a well-worn swivel chair completed the furnishings.

The principal, reading Blakemore's thoughts, commented, "Yes, it's amazing that so much has been done from this little

room. Staff and students will sorely miss her. As you can see, she was a popular lady."

"Was there any member of the staff that she chummed with who might know more personal details?" Blakemore asked.

"Not really. Ethel was a very private person. She attended all the school functions, staff parties, and so forth, but she always seemed to stand apart—not in an aloof or antisocial manner— more a sense of aloneness. She was not a person who bared her soul and I've always found it astounding that she had such influence over so many students. They certainly opened up to her when they wouldn't do so with any of the rest of us. Of the staff members I'd say that Joanne Martin was the one with whom she associated the most. I've noticed them together at the breaks and they'd often sit beside one another at our various meetings. That, too, surprised me. Joanne is the Physical Education teacher and has a personality exactly the opposite of Ethel's. She's very outgoing and, if you'll promise not to repeat it, has quite an effect on the males in this institution. She's an attractive lady."

"I'd like to interview her," Blakemore said with a bit more enthusiasm than he intended. "I understand that she runs a wrestling program that has had a lot of success."

"Indeed, that's true," said the principal, the hint of a twinkle in his eye. "I'll arrange it right now before classes start. You stay here. I'll go back to my office and have her paged. Please feel free to ask me for anything else that might help you. In the meantime, I'd better get my school ready for the day."

He left with the same loping gait, closing Ethel Roberts's office door behind him.

Blakemore quickly scanned through the desk drawers and ran his eyes over the shelves, but there was nothing of value to the investigation. He had already presumed that she would not keep personal documents in an office like this, which would be

so easily accessible to anyone, from students to cleaning staff. He turned on the computer and met with a Microsoft screen demanding a password before it would open up Windows. He knew Ernie could find his way into it if needs be and so he flicked the off switch. He was reading the inscriptions on the plaques and student gifts when there was a knock at the door. He walked over and pulled it open. Ms. Martin stood before him. She was absolutely stunning. Her blond hair was cut short, setting off a perfect Scandinavian face with high cheekbones and azure blue eyes. She was wearing track shoes and a tight exercise suit that left Blakemore breathless. Her ample chest was heaving slightly. A towel was around her shoulders and she used one end of it to wipe perspiration from her forehead.

"Hi," she said, "I'm a bit out of breath. I like to get a few laps in before classes start. Mr. Cruchley said you wanted to see me."

Blakemore struggled to bring his mind back to the business at hand. He meant to start off by explaining his investigation but out came: "I understand you're a wrestler."

Her laugh was spontaneous as he reddened.

"Not quite," she said. "I supervise the wrestling program here. I'm the Phys Ed teacher."

Regaining his composure, Blakemore turned on what charm he was capable of.

"And a very successful one I've discovered. John Smith's trophy collection bears proof of that. I saw it the other day— Provincial and Western Canadian Collegiate champion. That's really something."

"John was a special talent. He'd have succeeded regardless of his coaching, even his father's, poor man. George was one of the parent volunteers. He had some professional wrestling experience but he was lost in the amateur world where wrestling ability and not acting is what's needed. Professional wrestling

is all show. Get a big body with steroids or whatever and know how to fake the moves and you're a success. Amateurs are the real athletes, and John was all of that. His father was more a hindrance than a help, but he meant well."

Blakemore winced at the acting reference. Damn, he thought, George could have been putting on the drunk scene. He should have gone down and felt whether or not the pickup's engine was still warm when he was there with Ernie last night.

"Have you seen John recently?" she asked brightly. "I haven't seen him for a couple of years now. Do you know how he's doing in university? I expect very well."

Blakemore told her the sad news about the young Smith's death.

"That's too tragic," she said. "What an awful waste. His father must be very bitter."

"What makes you say that?" Blakemore asked.

"I guess it was the change I noticed during John's last year at high school. George just seemed to get grumpier and grumpier. I think he was feeling left out, and Ethel Roberts agreed with me. We often discussed the family situation, Ethel and I."

"Did George ever show any open hostility to anyone here— you or Ethel Roberts?"

"Not really. He just seemed to get more withdrawn—quieter. I felt kind of bad about it but there was really nothing I could do, or Ethel for that matter. John was entering a whole new world and poor George was left behind."

"You've been very helpful," Blakemore concluded. "I'll let you get back to your work."

"No more questions?"

"No, and thank you again," he said.

Blakemore left the school with a feeling of frustration. George might have felt left out of his son's life, but he'd have to be a total

whacko to kill someone for that—and the George he knew was too solid a citizen to fall into that category. Much as he hated to admit it, he needed Coswell and the big city investigation team. He still wasn't sure who the killer was. He headed back to the station. Coswell would be arriving just before lunch.

Chapter 46

The offices of Alfred H. Fitch and associates were in an old two storey former rooming house across from the firehall. In truth, Fitch was the only lawyer in the firm. His associates over the years were few and far between. Younger members of the legal fraternity who joined him on a trial basis found small town law unchallenging and quickly returned to the bigger centres. His practice was low-key, comprising mainly wills, trusts, and smaller matters that essentially required an LLB stamp. More serious cases tended to seek the prestigious firms in Nelson—prestigious, at least, by local standards.

Heather was late. She and Zachary had made up for their long periods of sexual abstinence with a night of glorious passion that went on well into the early hours of the morning. They both slept in, which caused a mad panic when they awoke and had to get him to his hospital rounds and Heather to the lawyer's office.

Fitch's secretary, a middle-aged lady, frowned as Heather entered the front office and said, "Go right in. They are waiting for you."

"They?" thought Heather.

"The inner sanctum" was what popped into Heather's mind as she stepped into the lawyer's personal office. It had the ambience of a mausoleum. The walls were wainscoted in a dark polished wood. A thick, deep-red Indian carpet covered the hardwood floor, and heavy drapes virtually obscured the

windows. The only light on in the room was a large desk lamp with a green glass shade. There were two other people seated in the room besides Fitch—a man and a woman in their early fifties with pinched faces. They were so much alike that Heather was sure they were related. They both scowled at her.

She had met Fitch a number of times at various functions. He was very much involved in community politics and spoke with a powerful voice. He was a tall, thin, wiry man with an Abraham Lincoln countenance and an air of authority. He was seated in an antique leather chair behind the largest mahogany desk imaginable. Heather estimated its value was probably more than everything she owned. He rose and stretched out his hand.

"Heather, so good to see you again. Thank you for coming in on such short notice. Please have a seat."

She noticed his delay in introducing the pair to her. This was not going to be a friendly affair.

"Caleb and Martha Schmidt are here, at my request. Caleb is related to Ethel and he and his wife feel they have a claim to her estate. He is mentioned in the will and I thought it would be expedient for all parties to be present at the reading."

Heather returned the cold nods that the Schmidts directed to her.

Fitch, with practiced deliberation, perched his reading glasses on the end of his nose and, pulling Ethel's will from a folder, began to read:

I Ethel Jane Roberts, of sound mind, do on this 1st day of July in the year . . .

When he finished, Heather was stunned. Ethel Roberts had bequeathed the major proportion of her considerable estate (over a million dollars) to her! She expressed wishes for a scholarship fund to be set up at the school, and left money to the public and school libraries, but she left the amounts solely up to Heather.

I have the utmost faith in Heather McTavish. She will do what's right, but it is my abiding hope that she uses my bequest to further her own education and career. She can make a much larger mark on the literary world than she will in this little community and I want her success to be my ultimate legacy.

Caleb was dealt with in one damning sentence:

To Caleb Schmidt, my stepbrother, I will two hundred dollars, a sum, which reimburses him for the cost he incurred on my behalf so many years ago.

The man reddened.

"This is preposterous! Giving all that money to a stranger. How do we know she didn't just butter the old lady up? I'm Ethel's only blood relative and I should be the one inheriting the money, not this little tramp."

"Um, I believe Miss Roberts referred to you as a step-relative, not a blood relation," Fitch interjected. "Unless you shared one common parent, the words *blood relative* do not apply. Isn't that the case?"

Caleb's mouth snapped shut and his face became darker.

"We'll see about this," he said.

"Does he have a hope in Hell?" Heather asked the lawyer. She had recovered from her astonishment at the content of the will and now directed her attention to Caleb Schmidt. Her bruised face was now as suffused with anger as his.

Fitch simply shook his head in answer to her question.

She rose from her chair and stood in front of the enraged man, face to face.

"I don't know what rock you crawled out from under you miserable son of a bitch, but I know Ethel. She was the kindest, most considerate person on the face of the Earth and I don't even want to think what you did to her to make her cut you out like that. It must have been something awful. Why don't you go

back to your slimy cave and contemplate what a piece of shit you really are?"

The man lunged at her, but Fitch, with amazing speed had rounded his desk and wedged himself between the two combatants.

"That's enough!" he shouted, pushing Schmidt back in his chair and holding on to Heather who had her fists up, ready to fight. "This is an office of law, not a prize ring."

"We're getting out of here," Caleb said, jumping up and marching out the door, followed by his wife who blubbered behind him.

Heather calmed down as quickly as she had become irate.

"I'm sorry," she said. "I'm all right now. Do you know I used to do that all the time—get boiling mad, I mean. I thought I'd grown out of it but this guy was just too much. I'm sorry about the language, but I'm not sorry about giving him a blast. He deserved it and somehow I think Ethel would have approved. Anyway, I at least feel a lot better for it."

Fitch released her and they both retook their seats.

"Heather," he said. "He truly does not have a case. I know the circumstances that produced Ethel's actions and although I can't relate them to you, I can tell you that Caleb Schmidt is not a blood relative. Ethel was an only child, an orphan, adopted by the Schmidt family directly from the orphanage. Her childhood was not an easy one.

"Caleb's discovery that Ethel lived here was pure accident. He and his wife were looking at the Cougar Creek Development as a place to retire. Crocker advertised all over the province. They live in Langley, just outside of Vancouver, and the mountain air and cheap living advertised in the brochures enticed them to have a look—ergo, he finds Ethel and somehow discovers she might be worth some money. It's pretty hard to keep a secret in

this community, and her investing skill is common gossip. When she died, he showed up like a dirty shirt."

"How long has he known about my relationship with Ethel?" she asked, thinking about the man in the alley.

"I don't know. Ethel first mentioned him to me about a month ago. I think that's when he first discovered she was living here. I have no idea how many times he's been to Bear Creek. It's quite easy to get people to talk about their neighbours anywhere, and I suspect he could've learned a great deal. Why do you ask?"

"Someone has been stalking me recently," she said simply.

Chapter 47

Blakemore read the fax as it came through from Nelson. George Smith had a record, albeit an old one. Ernie had run George's name through a computer scan earlier in the week but netted nothing. In a flash of brilliance, realizing that computer data was only as good as its input, Ernie had then contacted the Nelson record office and asked them to manually check their pre-computers booking records, reasoning that more minor local offenses might be stored there still. It had taken forty-eight hours but the records clerk struck paydirt. She faxed the file to Bear Creek to the attention of Constable Downs, who was currently being rewarded for his brilliance by relieving the Nelson constable on surveillance duty.

George Smith, age twenty-two, had been charged with assaulting a police officer who was trying to break up a brawl at a Nelson beer parlour. It had taken three officers to subdue him. The assault charge was dropped at the request of the Mountie involved and so George was convicted on the much lesser charge—"drunk and disorderly in a public place." The only thing unusual in the report was a brief description of George's reaction to being placed in a jail cell: "The

prisoner exhibited an extraordinary panic during his confinement, brought on presumably by an extreme claustrophobia."

George's defense lawyer had used that, plus a first offense appeal, to request the judge be lenient in his sentence. The judge obviously agreed. George was fined and had to perform what is now referred to as "community service"—picking up garbage on the highway. It was hard to imagine quiet old George whaling on three Mounties, but that was thirty or so years ago. Blakemore chuckled to himself as he remembered himself at the same age— know-it-all rookie, itching for action. He began to have doubts about his revelations the previous night; tying up half the Bear Creek Police Force keeping George under surveillance seemed excessive in the cold light of day. Better put a call in for Ernie.

Ernie beat him to it. He was radioing in from his cruiser.

"Corporal Blakemore. Do you read?"

"Yeah, Ernie," he said. "What's up?"

"Subject is on the move. His vehicle is proceeding along the Main Street connector, headed your way. Will you pick up?"

"I've got him, Ernie. Jeez, you don't think he's actually coming in voluntarily, do you?"

"Correction," the radio crackled. "Subject turning left onto Church Street. I'll continue to follow."

"Shit," Blakemore uttered into the mike, caught up again in the chase, ridiculous or not. Maybe Ernie was right in his suspicions. "He's headed back to Heather's apartment. Ernie, I want you to stay well back. I repeat, stay well back. I'm coming over. Heather should be at work, but I'll phone and be sure."

Heather's voice on her answering machine was a relief—she wasn't in her apartment. Blakemore wracked his brain as he headed to the door. What do we do now, he asked himself? But before he got to his cruiser, he saw Coswell's rental car turning into the station driveway.

"Jeez," he muttered. "Everything happens at once."

Coswell looked like the wrath of God again. Obviously the air flight had been a bad one and the drive to Bear Creek wasn't long enough to settle his motion sickness. Blakemore hoped he could bypass him and get directly to Ernie.

"Be back in a jiffy, Inspector," he shouted to Coswell, who was getting out of his car. "Brief emergency just came in. Go on in and take a break. I'll be back in a jiffy."

"Okay," said Coswell. "It would be nice to have everything stand still for a few minutes."

Blakemore glanced in the rear view mirror as he sped off and saw the Inspector walking a bit unsteadily to the station door. Pulling on to Main Street, he heard Ernie's voice again over the radio.

"Subject has proceeded past the Huntingdon Apartments and has pulled up in front of a private residence at the end of the street. He is unloading equipment from the back of his truck. It appears that he is about to do a job. The home owner has come out to meet him."

Blakemore braked and pulled over to the curb. He could see Ernie's cruiser a block ahead, moving slowly.

"Pick up speed, Ernie and drive by looking like you're headed somewhere important. Keep your eyes straight ahead. I'll take over from here. Go back to the station. Coswell's just arrived and you might as well be the one to fill him in. Would you also tell him the backup he arranged from Nelson is only one man and if this case is so important to him he can get us at least one more?"

He hung up the mike and feigned interest in a clipboard he picked up from the console. Sitting there too long would guarantee a visit from one of the nearby residents—nothing like chatting up a police officer to collect some juicy gossip.

He hadn't been parked any more than five minutes when he was jarred to attention by Coswell's voice on the radio.

"You will be relieved, Corporal, momentarily. It seems that four hours sleep has been enough for our Nelson man and he will be pulling up behind you any minute. When he is in position, you are to return directly to base. Understood?"

Blakemore fumbled for the mike.

"Understood," he answered.

Damn, he thought, the bugger probably switched on the station radio the second he walked in. He must have heard the entire exchange between Ernie and me.

"Oh, well," he sighed. "I was going to be in shit up to my neck with this guy anyway. A little more won't make much difference."

Chapter 48

The atmosphere greeting Blakemore when he returned to the station was decidedly cool. Ernie was busily shuffling papers behind the desk; Coswell was on the phone. Both appeared to be ignoring his entrance.

"Thank you again for your cooperation," Coswell was saying to whoever was on the other end of the line. He hung up the phone and turned to face Blakemore. He pointed to a fax on the counter.

"Read that," he said. "Constable Downs and I have already discussed it but I would be interested in your remarks."

It was the Victoria coroner's report on the death of John Smith. He was puzzled for a moment as he scanned the information until he reached the last page. In the box labeled 'next of kin notified' was George Smith's name, his address, and his Bear Creek phone number. The boy had written it on his job application form. Blakemore was stunned.

"The phone call I just took was from the Registrar at the University of Victoria," Coswell went on. "It appears that John Smith and Dietmar Kraus were roommates. Do you see a pattern emerging here?"

The tone was decidedly sarcastic, and from the expression of embarrassment on Ernie's face Blakemore knew that this question was definitely rhetorical.

"I guess that makes the Bear Creek connection," Blakemore said lamely.

"I would say that goes beyond conjecture," was Coswell's terse reply.

"What do we do now?" Blakemore asked. "Arrest him?"

"Only if you can assure me you have an iron-clad case that you have prepared with absolute care in my absence. Perhaps you could run over it with me now—your case, that is."

Blakemore reddened. He was really getting his nose rubbed in it and struggled to reply.

Coswell cut him off.

"All right then," he said. "Let's get on with it. You did manage to get a search warrant and I want that exercised pronto. We need proof, and since the forensic team is back in Vancouver we'll have to get it ourselves. If Kraus's body spent any time at Smith's place there'll be traces somewhere and that's what we have to find. If he did kill the other two, he's covered up pretty well although the lab boys may still come up with something from Groat's pickup."

"I have a theory about the lack of evidence around the body up on the mountain. Ernie has already filled me in on Smith's vocation as a logger, but I'd like to know how skillful he is and whether or not he's capable of high-rigging work."

I wonder where that came from, Blakemore asked himself.

"At one time, I guess he could do everything," he answered.

"He built his company up from nothing all on his own, and in those days it would have meant doing most of the work himself. But I grew up in the city and I really don't know anything about the technicalities of logging. It's hard to imagine, though, moving a body with a machine from the road to where we found it. Those extendable arms with a bucket don't extend that far, and to my knowledge the Hydro guys are the only ones who have them around here. Some of the loggers have small davits on their trucks but they would just reach the first line of trees."

"Does Smith's truck have one of those?"

"Not his pickup, but he probably has access to one of Crocker's vehicles that does."

"In that case, I want you to do two things. Find out from Crocker's equipment man if Smith signed out a machine like that in the last two weeks. I also want you to go back up to the mountain where Kraus' body was found and check the surrounding trees for spur marks. If you don't know what those are, ask the logging people. Oh, and you'll need to take an extension ladder."

"You think he did a Tarzan-carry-Jane-through-the-trees maneuver?" Blakemore asked, suppressing a laugh.

"Exactly," answered Coswell. "Do it and when you're finished I want you to relieve the Nelson man so he can catch up on his sleep."

"Yessir, I'll get on that right away," Blakemore said, relieved that his reprimand appeared to be over. He secretly took satisfaction from the fact that Coswell couldn't come up with anything better than his ridiculous theory.

"Ernie, you and I will exercise the warrant. Let's go," Coswell directed. Ernie jumped up, warrant in hand, and followed as the Inspector breezed past Blakemore and straight-armed the front door, causing it to swing back with such force that it almost

caught Ernie in the face. Blakemore paused, watching the two get into the cruiser, then proceeded leisurely to his own vehicle, contemplating where he would get an extension ladder.

Chapter 49

Constable Pritchard was struggling to keep his eyes open. Eight hours of surveillance and four hours of fretful sleep in his hotel room, broken by Coswell's phone call, did not combine to encourage any degree of alertness. He watched the subject gather his equipment—chain saws, ropes, and some kind of harness. Prior to that, the owner and he had stood at the bases of two huge cedar trees that grew alongside the house. It became apparent that the subject was being hired to remove them. Pritchard had watched some falling done around his posting at Nelson and wondered how these trees could be safely brought down without crushing the fence or the roof. There was no obvious place for them to fall safely.

As the man prepared for the task, Pritchard's interest grew. The harness consisted of leggings and a large belt. When he had strapped those firmly on, the subject approached the first tree, flipped a safety rope around it, and began to climb, kicking his spurs into the tree's bark. Dangling from his belt were a chain saw, two coils of rope, and a longer line that fed up from the ground. When he reached the first branches, he jerked the rope holding the saw and, as if by magic, it appeared in his hands. With a single pull, the tiny motor barked to life. Pritchard was amazed at the man's grace and strength as he sawed through each limb, catching the heavy branch with one hand as it broke free and redirecting its fall onto an open area on the lawn below. He repeated the process on the second tree, again denuding the branches so far up that the watching Mountie felt the trunk must

surely snap as it swayed ominously with the considerable weight so near its top.

When the limbing was completed on the second tree there was a pause while the man tied the longer rope around it at face level. He did this so quickly that his observer couldn't detect exactly what had been done. While he was admiring all this, the saw whined again and the top of the tree was severed. Pritchard started as the heavy weight toppled and appeared headed straight for the roof. Its fall, however, was abruptly halted by a rope tied on both sides of the sawcut, allowing the butt end to drop only a few feet. The main trunk swung violently, causing the man to be thrown from side to side, but he hung on until the oscillations subsided then calmly lowered the massive top to the ground. He then, to Pritchard's astonishment, made some sort of connection with his rope to the other tree, and with a spider-like move swung across thin air, reappearing in perfect position to remove its top in the same manner. Swinging from one to the other, he brought down both trees in manageable sections until only two eight-foot stumps remained.

Stepping onto the ground for the first time since he climbed the first tree, he removed his harness and with a larger chainsaw, cut the stumps almost flush with the ground. He then turned to the fallen sections and bucked each into eighteen inch stove lengths. When he finished, the home owner, who had also been watching the performance, called into the house and a woman appeared with a tray holding a pot of coffee, cups, and a plate of cookies. The trio sat at a picnic table in the back yard, and as they began their repast Pritchard became aware that he had missed his morning coffee along with breakfast. It would only take him a few minutes to slip back to the hotel and get something— no need to radio in, he thought. The subject appeared settled for the moment and the clean-up of the branches would take

considerable time. He started the car and drove back to Main Street.

Heather left the lawyer's office and headed back to the *Bulletin* offices on foot. Halfway there she felt an overwhelming fatigue. The effects of the late nights, the trauma, and this latest emotional distress had drained her more than she realized. She'd promised Zachary that she would go to his office immediately after her session with Fitch and they'd do an early lunch, but she needed a power nap in the worst way. The shortcut to her apartment through the woods was beckoning, and after a moment's hesitation she broke into a trot and didn't stop till she reached the back door. She unlocked it quickly and stepped inside pulling the door shut, hearing the automatic lock click as it closed. She kicked off her shoes, went into the bedroom where she grabbed a pillow, and, returning to the living room, fell back on the couch, tucking the pillow under the back of her head. She closed her eyes and immediately went to sleep. She was oblivious to the fact that high up on a tree a pair of eyes looking down noted her dash through the woods and her disappearing into the apartment.

The police cruiser was in his front yard and he could see Ernie knocking at the door of the house. The Vancouver Inspector was looking around the yard. What should he do? He was sure they would find nothing. The corpse was never removed from the tarp, and as an extra precaution he'd scrubbed the floor and the inside of the freezer with Pinesol. The tarp went up in smoke on the slash burn pile, but he worried. Once again, his mind fixated on Heather. She was in her apartment now. He'd seen her when he topped the last tree. This time he wouldn't miss. He wished that he could have picked up the big game bags and his butchering tools. His plan was to dispose of her body in so many pieces

that no one would ever find it by accident or otherwise. He'd heard of corpses rising from the bottom of lakes or being brought up by police dragging the bottom. Burying the whole body left too many signs and there was always the risk that animals could dig it up. He'd wanted to humiliate the Kraus kid, but Heather was merely a risk to his freedom that he had to deal with. He simply wished her to disappear.

Chapter 50

Blakemore cursed as he tried to get the ladder steadied in the snow. The fact that it extended to seventeen feet made it even more awkward. He didn't want to look foolish inquiring about George's borrowing a cherry picker if he didn't have to and so chose to inspect the trees first. He reasoned that if they showed no sign of spur bites it would be enough to dispel Coswell's theory. He climbed, praying the ladder wouldn't slip. He'd chosen the tree where the head had been placed and after checking the bark as high as he could go and finding nothing, carefully descended, his hands clutching the rungs. What's the point of checking any more of these damn trees, he asked himself? I'm not risking my neck. It's pointless.

With that he collapsed the ladder and dragged it back to the cruiser, tying it onto the rack and beginning the drive back to the station, rehearsing the report he would give to Coswell. First, though, he'd better check on Pritchard. Blakemore felt a bit guilty that it was on his account that the Nelson man had been dragged out of bed by Coswell and he felt a need to make amends. Relieving him as quickly as possible would be the best way.

He was puzzled, therefore, when he drove into town to see the unmarked car Pritchard was using for surveillance speeding towards the station. He followed him and saw the car come to a screeching halt at the front entrance. The Mountie leaped from

the car and frantically began flipping through a notebook. He was obviously trying to find the code to punch in to gain entry. The look of relief when he saw Blakemore's cruiser approach was considerable.

"What's up?" Blakemore asked, getting out and walking over to the distraught policeman.

The words came tumbling out. Pritchard had returned from his break to discover that George Smith had left. The owner had arranged to do his own cleanup and so Smith departed after a quick cup of coffee, stating that he had urgent business elsewhere. The ghost car's radio broke down and so Pritchard had rushed back to the station to report in.

"I wasn't gone anymore than fifteen minutes," he moaned. "I needed a break in the worst way and it really looked like it was going to be okay. Shit! Coswell's going to have my head over this."

"Don't sweat it," Blakemore reassured. "These things happen even in the best of circumstances. The perp gives us the slip. Hop in. You and I will find him before Coswell gets back. He's with Ernie going through Smith's place right now."

As he said that, Blakemore suddenly realized that George was very likely headed there and would see the policemen at his door. He wondered what the big man would do. He hoped that George would walk in on Coswell and give him what for, especially if he was innocent. If he is guilty, God knows what he will do, he thought. He was only five minutes from the Smith residence and so he headed directly there, not bothering to call them on the radio.

He'd stayed off Main Street and looked down from the logging bypass road above as Blakemore sped by. Good, he thought. All the Mounties are in one place, but I'll have to hurry. The hunt will be on soon.

He parked again in the woods behind the Huntingdon Apartment, using his four-wheel drive to back into the heavy underbrush. No one would see him here. He reached into the truck box and pulled out the large canvass duffel bag he used to carry his harness and climbing ropes. He dumped the contents onto the driver's seat and selected two short sections of rope, which he replaced in the bag. Reaching across, he opened the glove compartment and pulled out a roll of duct tape, which he also added to the bag. Swinging it over his shoulder, he set off on one of the forest trails that led to Heather's apartment. When he reached the tree line behind her garage he paused, deciding what course of action he would take. As he contemplated, the back door opened and she appeared.

"Damn, damn, damn!" Heather exclaimed as she pushed the back door shut. She'd slept for over an hour and she knew Zachary would be starting to worry. She decided again to risk the shortcut back to her office where her car was parked. She cursed herself for not driving it over to the apartment like she'd promised Ernie, but she'd been so tired she wasn't thinking straight. She paused, and listening and seeing nothing of concern, set out at a run past Ethel's vacant lot and cut into the short section of woods to Church Street. She didn't hear the phone ringing in her living room or the slight rustling in the trees behind her.

Chapter 51

Zachary listened to Heather's apartment phone ring on the other end. For the second time there was no answer. He'd phoned Fitch's office and was dismayed to learn that she had left there well over two hours ago. She was not at her desk at the *Bulletin*. Her car was still parked out front and she'd ducked in shortly after nine, according to Susan, just long enough to say she was late for an appointment and would be back later. Where was

she? He phoned the police station and got the Nelson dispatch. They said that both Blakemore and Ernie were off their radios at the moment but that they would keep trying. The operator sounded harassed and Zachary felt that he was probably a low priority on a busy police day. Nelson demands would naturally come first.

His own day was also busy. The extra hospital work had caused a backup in his office. Iris had booked him to the teeth and he was running forty-five minutes late. He'd instructed Iris to phone Heather so that she wouldn't come over and waste her time sitting in his office. She would have lots to do, he was sure, at the *Bulletin* while she waited for him.

The office pressures, however, diverted Iris's attention and she simply forgot. Zachary did not discover this fact until after noon and was horrified at the time that had elapsed since Heather's appointment with Fitch. With apprehension gripping his chest, he called Iris into his examining room and told her to rebook the entire afternoon's patients. In response to her moans, he agreed to do a clinic that evening and any emergencies in the meantime were to be sent to the hospital. He was out the rear exit before she could stammer a reply.

He drove to Heather's apartment and let himself in with the spare key she had given him. He was mildly relieved to see the back door locked and saw nothing indicating a struggle. He saw the pillow on the chesterfield in the living room and the apprehension returned. If she'd come home for a nap she'd come on foot. My God, he thought, she's taken the trail through the woods! He picked up the phone and called 911. Nelson dispatch answered. This time he was forceful.

"This is Doctor Zachary Benson. I want you to get me one of the Bear Creek RCMP immediately. There is every chance that an abduction or even a murder is in progress here and I want action

fast. If you can't get anyone local give me someone there."

In less than ten seconds Paul Blakemore's voice came on the line.

"What the hell is going on?" he shouted. "Who's been kidnapped and murdered?"

"It's Heather. She's disappeared. I've tried everywhere—the *Bulletin*, her apartment—she's gone. We were supposed to meet for lunch. I'm afraid something terrible has happened to her."

Blakemore shuddered. Heather and George Smith gone at the same time did not evoke pleasant thoughts. He did not convey this to Zachary, however; the Doc was hyper enough as it was, he thought.

"Calm down," he said. "She's probably got a lead on a story somewhere and is out following it up. Go back to your office. She'll either show up there or call in. Best you be there."

"I told my secretary to stay and page me the moment she hears from Heather. We need to get a search party going and I want to be in on it. What should I do?"

"Damn," Blakemore said under his breath. "I need an agitated civilian in all this like a hole in the head."

"You're not much use running all over in your car. If you want to help, go back to your office like I said and do some phoning. Check with the *Bulletin* and see if there's any story she was working on. She might have gone out to the school or over to Michelle Groat's place, or she might just be sitting in Keat's Korner drinking coffee. Be optimistic. I'm meeting up shortly with Ernie and Coswell. I'll inform them and we'll all get on it pronto if we need to. Don't worry."

"Okay," Zachary answered. "I'll do it, but phone me the minute you get any news and I'll do likewise. Would you also please call the Nelson dispatch and let them know how serious this is."

"Roger," Blakemore said and switched off his mike. To

Pritchard beside him he added, "I've got an awful feeling that the shit is about to hit the fan. We'd better bring Coswell in on this right now. We do need a search party and a damned good one at that."

Chapter 52

Heather's neck hurt most of all. The smell of the canvass bag over her head and the sensation of being trussed up like a pig on a spit were unpleasant, but the back of her neck ached unmerci-fully. A rabbit punch had effectively rendered her helpless on the ground while her mouth was taped and the bag pulled over her head. Her arms and legs were tied with amazing speed. She was then lifted and slung over her abductor's shoulder. He moved quickly through the woods and deposited her with a thump in the back of a vehicle. A tarp was thrown over her, cutting out all light. The motor starting up was obviously that of a truck and she heard the low gear whine as it bumped through the woods. The ride smoothed out as pavement was reached and the truck shifted to higher speed.

She struggled to keep oriented and make reasonable estimates about the direction and distance of travel. Concentrating on this helped to lessen the terror in her heart. She felt the left turn and knew the vehicle was headed towards Main Street—then a quick right after a few moments, and a stop. She guessed they were at the railway crossing. The double bump as the truck passed over the tracks confirmed she was correct. Another stop and a right turn, plus the sound of freeway traffic, let her know that she was going east towards Nelson. She tried to wriggle into a position where she might sit up and attract someone's attention but she was held down by the tarp that was lashed tightly to steel eyes welded onto the side of the box.

She no sooner discovered this fact than the truck made an abrupt turn to the left and her smooth ride was over. The pings of gravel in the wheelwells and the bumps that threw her about meant they were now on a side road. From the sound of gearing down and the twisting from side to side she knew it was a logging road and they were travelling up into the mountains above Cougar Creek. She prayed that someone would see them but knew the farther up they went the less likely that was to happen. This area had been logged off during her short time in Bear Creek and the second growth was still years from harvest, rarely visited now by anyone other than hunters and hikers. The hunting season was virtually over and the end of October was not prime hiking time.

If she wasn't going to be rescued then she needed to shift her concentration to the fact that it was now her against him—one on one. He had the upper hand, no question of that, but she was still alive—and since he hadn't killed her outright as he did with the others, she still had time to fight. Her bravery required her to suppress the fact that her situation was more akin to a lamb being driven to the slaughter than that of a caged tiger waiting to strike.

Chapter 53

Coswell was not happy to see Blakemore and Pritchard arrive as they pulled up behind Ernie's cruiser. The looks on their faces when they got out confirmed his assumption—they had screwed up.

"All right," he said, "give me the bad news. We've found nothing here so you might as well ruin my whole day."

"Smith gave us the slip," Blakemore said. "He's gone and so is Heather McTavish. Doc Bensen thinks she's been abducted. She was supposed to meet him for lunch and didn't show. He hasn't been able to track her down."

"I checked the trees, by the way, and didn't see any spikemarks," he added quickly, hoping Coswell would let that matter pass unchallenged. The Inspector didn't oblige.

"How well did you check them?" he demanded. "How many did you check and how high did you look? A good logger—and Smith apparently is one—could move across just below the top twenty feet of those pines. They're all trunk from there down. I've seen that from the highway."

"Smith's good, for sure," Pritchard blurted out. "I spent an hour watching him today. He's like Spiderman up there, swinging from tree to tree."

Coswell, Blakemore, and Ernie, who had come out of the house to join them, all turned and stared at him.

"Why didn't you mention this before?" Coswell asked. "It virtually pinpoints our man."

"You didn't ask," Pritchard answered simply.

"Holy shit," said Blakemore. "That's how he did it. You were right. My ladder only went up seventeen feet. His marks would be fifteen feet at least above that, but how did he tie the head on without leaving a mark?"

"Didn't you ever go down to the docks in the big city and watch sailboaters check their masts?" Coswell asked him. "It's called a bosun's chair, and anyone good with a rope could rig one up and lower himself down from the top of anything."

"Do you have any doubts now as to who our chief suspect is?" he continued.

Blakemore shook his head.

"Then Doctor Bensen's fears are more than justified. What do you propose we do at this point?"

"Get the firemen mobilized like we did for Clyde," Ernie interrupted.

"We've got a good tracking dog in Nelson," Pritchard added.

"Get something with their scents on and he'll find them."

"Commandeer Crocker's rental helicopter," Blakemore finally chipped in.

"Good. Let's go," Coswell said. "The command post will be the Bear Creek station and I'll man that. Each of you take your suggestions and act on it. I'll deal with the officer in charge at Nelson. I'm sure he'll add to our manpower."

"One last thing," he said, looking at Blakemore and Ernie. "Think of someone who might know where Smith would run to under these circumstances."

"Michelle Groat," Blakemore answered quickly. "I'll go there right now. Pritchard here can go back to the station with you."

In moments, both cars were lost in a cloud of dust as they sped out of the driveway, scattering chickens in every direction.

Chapter 54

It seemed an eternity but it was probably no more than twenty minutes when Heather's uncomfortable ride came to a halt. She was cold, stiff, and had a full bladder. When the motor was turned off and she heard the driver's door slam she yelled out.

"For Christ's sake get me out of here. I've got to piss like a racehorse. Don't make me do it in my pants."

Whether it was Heather's innate intelligence or divine intervention, she couldn't have done anything more effective to humanize herself in the eyes of her abductor. He quickly untied the tarp and pulled her out of the truck. Gathering her in his arms he began to run. The jostling further challenged her bladder but she didn't complain. He stopped abruptly and slid her to her feet and untied her hands.

She heard a door creak open and she was pushed inside. The smell let her know she was in an outhouse even before she pulled

the bag from her head. The single hole was huge and she had to be careful not to fall back as she perched herself on the edge. One of life's ecstasies, she thought, is relieving oneself from an over-filled bladder. She was still urinating when the door opened a crack and a large hand appeared holding a roll of toilet paper.

"Thanks," she said as the door closed quickly and the outside latch slid into place.

He was confused. His anger was gone now and he felt tired. Killing the Kraus kid and Ethel Roberts gave him a high. Even shooting Clyde seemed part of a plan, but he knew now that was wrong. He was acting like a wounded bear, lunging and pawing at anything in its path. But he couldn't face jail—ever. He had to deal with Heather. She would be the last.

Chapter 55

Coswell was delighted. He really hadn't expected to get this degree of cooperation so fast. The helicopter, the tracking dog, and the search party were organized in less than an hour. Michelle Groat couldn't give them an exact location, but her husband had told her of a hunter's cabin high up above Cougar Creek that he knew George had used. The dog had no difficulty finding the scene of Heather's abduction and the trail leading to where George had parked his truck.

The Inspector felt like a general directing a D-Day invasion. He let Ernie command the volunteers and gave him specific orders to keep his men out of danger. They were to locate the suspect and no more. The RCMP would make the final approach. Blakemore was in charge of that group—officers from the Nelson detachment. He, Coswell, would arrive on the scene when everything was in place.

The helicopter made the first sighting—the glint of a vehicle deep in the woods, five miles north of the highway. The pilot thought he saw a building but was too high to be sure. He had strict orders to stay above two hundred feet to avoid spooking the suspect. An hour later, one of Ernie's volunteers confirmed that the pilot was correct—George's truck was spotted parked at the hunter's cabin. The man pulled back quickly and notified Ernie by a pre-arranged signal on one of the cell phones that had been provided. Blakemore was promptly informed and he organized his men to move in and surround the cabin.

"Don't do a thing till I get there," Coswell ordered over the police radio, speaking first to Blakemore. Then, switching to Ernie's frequency, he said, "Come and get me. I don't want to miss the location and all those roads look the same to me."

"Roger," said Ernie.

Zachary could stand it no longer. He tried to do some paperwork in his office to ease the worry in his mind but he had no success. He simply could not concentrate. He hadn't heard from Heather and the people at the *Bulletin* had no idea where she might be. He even phoned the school but was told she was not there and was not expected. He didn't want to bug Blakemore, but he had a distinct feeling the Mountie had given him the quick shuffle. Something was going down and he, Zachary, was being left out in the cold. He phoned the station. On the fifth ring the Nelson dispatch answered.

"This is Dr. Benson again," he said, expecting that Blakemore had filled them in on his importance in the case. "I'd like to speak to Corporal Blakemore, please."

"The officers are currently unavailable," the woman replied. "I'll tell them you called as soon as they check in."

"Where have they all gone?" Zachary asked feeling a bit miffed.

"I'm sorry," she said. "I have strict orders not to divulge their location to anyone, Dr. Bensen—not even you."

"Did Corporal Blakemore not inform you of my involvement in this matter?"

"Yes," she said.

He knew he was stonewalled so far as this lady was concerned, and so after a curt thank you he hung up. Damn, he thought. I was right. I'm being kept in the background. Well, that was not good enough.

He put on his coat with an aside to Iris as he headed to the door: "I'm going to find out what's going on. Page me if Heather calls. I'll check back with you in an hour."

He was less than a block from the Police station when he saw Ernie and Coswell leave in the cruiser, its lights flashing. He couldn't hear a siren but they were obviously in a hurry. They were pulling away from him fast but he was determined to follow them, and since they were clearing the way, he was not concerned about getting in an accident. He just hoped that Ernie would not notice him.

He could hear her banging on the outhouse door. He wished she would stop. He was having trouble deciding what to do with her and the noise was not helping. He could shut her up quickly, he knew, by choking the life out of her in seconds. It would be humane, he thought. In all his hunting he never let an animal suffer. His kills were sure and quick. Even in 'Nam, he fired only when he had a target he could hit. He laughed at his fellow soldiers who held their automatic weapons over their heads and fired off clip after clip into the foliage. The 'Kong weren't so wasteful. Their shots usually spilled blood. He admired them for that.

Why was he stalling? Time wasn't in his favour, and the sooner he dealt with her the better. He'd heard the helicopter and knew it shouldn't

be in the area. Crocker had shut down the operation at Cougar Creek.
Where was the cat-person? The mouse was cornered and the kill should
be inevitable, but he wasn't ready to pounce. He wasn't cool anymore.
He was becoming more and more fatigued. He wanted to sleep and to
dream. He wanted to see his boy and his wife again. He wanted to lie
down and let his tormented mind rest. Bang, bang. She was hammering
again and shouting.

"For Christ's sake, let me out of here. I'm freezing and I don't
want to die in a shithouse. What did I do to you, you mother-
fucking bastard, whoever you are?"

She hoped her anger would hold. It helped warm her slightly
and stifle the fear she knew would soon take over. It was getting
dark and she'd heard nothing after the crunch of his steps in the
snow retreated to whatever habitation sported this lavatory from
Hell. The truck hadn't started up again and so she knew he was
still around, thank God. She tried to form a plan. There was a
stout pole in the corner—used to knock down the mountain
of feces from time to time, she surmised. She found she could
stand up on the seat and still have some headroom. This place
was built for giants, she thought. There wasn't room to swing
the pole, but she sure as hell could get in one good poke with
it. Maybe get him in the mouth with the shit end, she visualized
with some satisfaction.

"If I'm going out," she said aloud. "I'm going out fighting."

Her resolve lasted twenty more minutes, then collapsed.
She began to cry. Her sobs hid the sound of his return to the
outhouse. She started at the sound of a familiar voice.

"I'm sorry, Heather, that I have to do this."

"George!" she said. "George Smith."

The door opened and he stood there, a look of deep sadness
on his face. She cowered into a corner and began to whimper.

Chapter 56

Zachary braked as he saw Blakemore running towards him on the logging road waving frantically for him to stop.

"Get your fucking lights off," he hissed as Zachary rolled down his window. "Why the hell didn't you stay in town like I told you?"

"You promised to keep me informed," he answered. "And you didn't. Where's Heather and what's happening?"

"This is police business, Bensen," Blakemore said. "There's no call for a coroner yet, and you, quite frankly, are just going to be in the way."

Coswell appeared, obviously overhearing the last of their conversation.

"Let him stay," he said. "I sincerely hope not, but we might need a doctor's services here if there is any shooting. Doctor Bensen, I will ask you to stay back and not interfere in any way with the activities of my officers. I know you have a personal interest in Heather McTavish, but you must understand that her safety is paramount to us as well. We're all trained to deal with hostage-taking situations, and I, personally, have been involved in several. Trust us."

Zachary, feeling a bit sheepish, nodded and followed the two men back to the police vehicles, leaving his own car parked where he had stopped. When they reached the other officers, Blakemore gave his report.

"There've been no shots fired and Heather has been heard shouting up until a half hour ago or so. I have men in place for three hundred and sixty degrees around the cabin, with orders to move closer when it gets dark. They have to go slow because the cold and the dry snow give a real squeak to footsteps. Three of the men are sharpshooters with nightscopes. They'll take

George out if the situation demands it. You can't really time that sort of thing and they know their job. If Heather's still okay, I'd suggest the negotiation route and start it as soon as possible. Do you agree?"

"Yes," said Coswell. "Give me the bullhorn and let's go."

Zachary watched as the two men advanced up the road to the cabin, disappearing into the dusk. A few moments later he heard Coswell's voice blare from the loudspeaker.

"George Smith. This is Inspector Coswell of the Mounted Police. We know that Ms. McTavish is with you and we ask that you direct her to us. She has done you no harm and does not deserve to be detained. Please let her go."

In one motion, George reached in, grabbed the front of her coat, lifted, and spun her around. As she came down his arm went across her chest, clamping so tightly it knocked the wind out of her. He ran to the cabin holding her like a rag doll, arms and legs flailing. Once inside, he kicked the door closed and slammed home a crude iron deadbolt.

"Put me down, George," she wheezed. "I can't breathe."

He looked at her as though he just realized what he was carrying. He released his hold and she slumped to the floor gulping for air.

"This is Inspector Coswell. Do you hear me? Please respond."

The voice from the jungle was like that.

"Let man go. You go back to friends. We no hurt you. Let man go." He felt the 'Kong officer squirm under his knee, but he was going nowhere. His hands were tied behind his back and he'd made sure the man had seen the pin pulled on the grenade before he jammed it into his mouth. The tall eelgrass hid them as he dragged his prisoner back to the platoon hidden in the trees. The lieutenant was mentioned in dispatches for that one.

But this time he wasn't in control. He had no weapon other than the buck knife on his belt. There was no platoon to back him up. How could he escape?

"Now what do we do?" Blakemore asked as Coswell's pleas were met with total silence.

"This is the tough part," the Inspector answered. "We don't even know whether or not he has a gun. He could have killed the woman already but I think that's unlikely. From what you told me she was shouting, not screaming. We have to find that out first. Is she alive and, if so, what is the degree of threat to her life at this point? If Smith's still thinking rationally, he'll either let her go or use her as a hostage—probably the latter."

"One of us has to go in," Blakemore said. "And I'm the logical one. He knows me the best and I've got a gut feeling he wouldn't kill me in cold blood. I still find it hard to believe that George has done all this. Obviously I didn't know him as well as I thought I did, but I don't see him as a totally evil man."

"You realize this is totally voluntary, Paul," Coswell said quietly.

Blakemore nodded.

"All right, then. Let's get going. We'll move the cars in and floodlight you. You've got your flak jacket on under your coat, I presume."

"If George has a gun and wants to kill me, I'll get it right between the eyes. Nope, I'll go in stripped—no weapon. He needs to see that."

"You're calling the shots," Coswell said.

The voice was back again.

"George Smith. This is Inspector Coswell again. Corporal Blakemore is with me and is going to come forward. He is

completely unarmed and will do you no harm. He wishes to talk with you. Please let him advance."

The lights were blinding. He could see Paul's dark figure moving towards him, arms held up in the air, palms turned forward and his fingers spread.

The Vietnamese woman had done that too but he was ready for her. When her hand suddenly dropped and reached behind her back his bullet blew her backwards into the mud; the grenade remained strapped to her belt.

Heather was still sitting on the floor but he could barely see her in the dark. A light would give away his position. He grabbed her again and put his arm across her chest. With his free hand he pulled out his knife and flipped it open. She saw the glint of the skinning blade and whimpered. He squeezed and she stopped instantly. He waited for Paul to approach.

Blakemore stopped at the door to the cabin. So far so good he thought.

"George," he said. "It's Paul here. A friend. Please answer me. I know you can hear. Heather. Are you okay?"

Even through the door, Blakemore could hear the grunt as Heather's chest was squeezed.

"Don't hurt her, George," he said. "You and I can talk. I'd sooner come inside because I'm getting awfully cold in this skinny tunic but I'll stay here if that's what you want."

Coswell watched Blakemore's figure standing at the cabin door. He'd wasted no time after the Corporal had begun his slow advance. He quickly gave orders for all personnel to move in as close as possible. He was sure Blakemore would get nowhere with Smith but the Corporal would be a useful diversion. His plan was to suddenly extinguish all the lights and have the men storm the building, pulling their fellow officer to safety as they broke through the door. He'd been at too many incidents where the police assault had been delayed, causing needless loss of life. Giving the abductor

too long to think was a mistake, in his opinion, although most of the so-called experts thought otherwise. Action beats talk, nine times out of ten was his motto.

He was only six. That was a long time back but he remembered, like it was yesterday. He wasn't supposed to have a pet. His father said animals were animals, and when you lived on a farm they were good only for eating or working. His mother knew. She said the calf could be his, though, and it would be their secret. She was foolish and her husband said so when he found out.

"The boy has to learn," he told her. "A farm's no place for this kind of nonsense. That calf's marked for veal and you know it."

His father took him to the barn. His mother was crying and he was scared.

"Son," his father said. "We raise animals for food. We got all the milk cows we need and this calf's a little heifer. She's going to be meat—real fine meat we call veal. You know how you like the cutlets your mom cooks? Well, this is where they come from."

He took out his big knife, and grabbing the calf by its forelock slit its throat in one vicious slash. Blood spurted and the calf kicked for a few moments, then when limp. His father hung the carcass up on a meat hook.

"She didn't feel a thing," he explained. "One second she's eating hay and the next she's veal chops aging on the hook."

He laughed at his own humour.

George didn't cry, at least then, and his father was pleased.

Blakemore was shivering.

"George," he said. "I've got to come in or go back to the car. I'm going to freeze standing here."

He heard a slight sound of movement and then the clink of a bar being slid back.

Ignoring the tightness in his chest, he lifted the latch and pushed the door open.

"I'm unarmed, George," he said. "And I'm coming in slow—nothing sudden here, okay?"

They were in the dimness but there was enough light from the cars through the windows that Blakemore could make out George's bulk and Heather clutched in his arm. The brightest reflection came off the knife blade held at her throat. She was alive. He could see the whites of her eyes wide with fear. He almost jumped when George spoke.

"Close the door and lock it Paul," he said softly, menace in his voice. "And keep your hands where I can see them."

Shit! Blakemore thought. Now he's got two hostages.

Coswell echoed the curse. He hadn't expected this. His officer was inside and that was going to complicate matters to say the least. He wished he'd insisted on Blakemore taking in a concealed weapon. He held up his hand and watched the order pass down the line. Ernie appeared beside him.

"If anyone can talk him down," he said, "Paul can. Please give him the chance."

"Ten minutes, Ernie," Coswell answered. "And if we don't hear from any of them by then we blast in. Believe me, that's the only way."

"I don't agree with you, sir," Ernie said with surprising firmness.

"Don't agree all you want," Coswell said. "But that's the way it's going to be. This is war now and I mean to keep the casualties to a minimum."

Blakemore was talking at a staccato pace.

"George," he said, "don't compound things by doing this. Christ, with a good lawyer these days you got a chance. I'm sure you had a reason for what you did and the judge might see it your way. Let

Heather go and I'll see that you get every consideration I can get for you. This is insane, George, don't you see that?"

Silence.

Blakemore grasped for straws.

"You've been a good man in this community. No one has anything against you. They remember what a fine son you brought up. There are a lot of people who will be on your side. Think about it, George, for God's sake, think about it."

He saw the blade move and he gasped. But George had only shifted it to his other hand—the one across Heather's chest. He backed up with her to what appeared to be a stove. He bent down, forcing her to crouch with him. Blakemore heard the hiss, then smelled the propane as it permeated the room.

"Holy Jesus!" Blakemore exclaimed, forgetting his negotiator role. "What the fuck are you doing? Are you going to kill all of us you crazy bastard?"

George rose and moved towards Blakemore, pushing Heather in front of him.

"Open the door, Paul," he said. "And start running. She'll be behind you."

Blakemore hesitated for a second, then did as he was told. As he swung the door open, Heather was shoved violently into his back, sending them both headlong into the snow. The door slammed shut behind them and the bolt clicked into place.

Immediately the lights were extinguished and men in dark clothing appeared from all directions. Blakemore staggered to his feet and screamed.

"Get back. The place is full of propane. It's going to explode."

He felt Heather beside him and grabbed her coat, pulling her with him as he ran.

Mass confusion followed. Two men crouching at the windows with their stun grenades hesitated and saved their lives in the

process. The fireball went over their heads. Two more at the front door were blown straight back when the door blasted off its hinges.

Coswell and Ernie, one hundred feet away, stood in amazement as the flames lit up the scene in front of them. Heather and Blakemore, who'd been knocked down again, were picking themselves up and staggering towards them. Officers were appearing from all sides and dragging their comrades away from the fire.

Zachary, waiting at his car (Coswell would not let him come forward with the police vehicles), heard the thump of the propane explosion, and as he ran up the road he saw the glow from the fire through the trees. He arrived just as Blakemore and Heather reached the police vehicles. Ernie was helping them.

"Jeez! What a show," Coswell said. "I guess that ends that. George Smith ain't walking out of there. Justice has been served."

Zachary held Heather close as they all watched the cabin burn. It took only minutes for its frame to collapse in a shower of sparks. A few of the trees adjacent were burning, but in the windless air the blaze was obviously going to be confined.

"Call the volunteers," Blakemore said to Ernie. "They might as well mop up and get the body out now. It's still early evening."

Chapter 57

He was still the cat. My nine lives aren't nearly used up, he thought. The rear door of the cabin led directly into a woodshed built onto the back. That was his invention—he could step out in the coldest weather to get more logs for the fireplace and never even have to put on his coat. His timing was perfect. The policemen moving down from behind the cabin flattened with the explosion, just as he'd done, and in that instant he'd pushed open the shed door and dove into the snow, just ahead of

the flames. He heard the men rush past to the front of the building, completely unaware of him lying there. When they were gone he got up and slowly moved away, walking backwards into the forest, the flames giving him light to find his way and hiding him from his pursuers. He felt exhilarated and moved effortlessly. When he was sure he was far enough away, he switched on the flashlight he had picked up at the cabin. The footprints of the police team were easy to spot and he continued walking backwards until he reached the road where they had been dispatched. He set off at a trot, running easily down the hill and taking care to stay in the tire tracks. His footprints would be erased by the vehicle traffic that would follow. Just before he reached the highway, he was forced to step into the bushes as the firetruck and the inhalator van roared past. He took time to brush away his tracks with a pine branch.

The semi driver was tired, fighting drowsiness that hadn't been lessened by the coffee he had downed in Nelson when he fueled up. It had been a long day, leaving Spokane at six AM, travelling the slow, twisting highway all the way up to The Kokanee Glacier in BC and the dinky little town of Silverton that was thriving on selling bottled "Glacier Pure" water. Why the glacier water in Washington State wasn't as good was a mystery to him, but his one-man trucking business did well by it. He should have stayed and caught some sleep, but he'd promised his girlfriend he'd be back that night. Traffic and a flat tire had slowed his return but he was so close now. Spokane was only a couple of hours away. He needed someone talking to him. That always worked. The big man with his thumb out at the top of the hill was just the ticket.

"Heading for Spokane," he told the man. "Where are you going?"

"Same place," the man answered. "I'm going home."

Epilogue

Coswell suffered yet another miserable, bumpy flight back to Vancouver. His discomfort was compounded by the message he heard blaring over the airport PA as he made his way to the baggage area.

"Would de-planing passenger Inspector Coswell please call the switchboard immediately." The message was repeated continuously until he reached a service phone and dialed 0. Blakemore was trying to reach him. The operator patched him through within seconds.

"Thought I'd better give you the news before you checked in with headquarters," he heard Blakemore say. "I'm afraid to report that there was no body in the cabin. George has given us the slip again."

Blakemore had to hold the phone away from his ear as Coswell screamed his incredulity into the mouthpiece. Blakemore answered the myriad of questions with a simple "Yep, 'fraid so. We checked everywhere, including every inch of snow for tracks leading away from the cabin. There was nothing. He's disappeared into thin air and I can tell you this time he didn't swing away in the trees. We scoured the woods all the way back to the main road."

Coswell forced himself to calm down and think rationally. George somehow must have made it back to the highway.

"He's hitchhiking," he concluded. "Since Bear Creek is out of the question for him, I can tell you he's running for the border. I remember you told me he was originally from the backcountry of Washington or Oregon somewhere. Get on the blower to the nearest FBI office. This is their thing now, with George crossing international borders and all. They've got the clout to get the US border guards and Washington State Patrol on the alert fast.

I presume that you've already notified our units and have RCMP officers headed for the nearest border stations. He could cross on foot through the hills, but my guess is that he'll flag down an American vehicle and go through with them."

"Gotcha," answered Blakemore. "Yes, our boys are already there and checking all vehicles on the Canadian side. So far they haven't spotted him. I've made a poster of George from a photo I got at his house and we've faxed that to the stations. If he hasn't crossed yet, we'll get him."

"Right," said Coswell, a tone of obvious doubt in his voice. "When did you discover there wasn't a body?"

"It was after nine. It took that long for the heat to die down."

"It's almost ten now. By my calculations he's had almost four hours to get away. Even on foot it wouldn't take him more than an hour to reach the highway. If he hitched a ride right away, then he's gone. We've got to make the effort though. Keep me posted. I've got my cell-phone back on. Talk to you later."

Blakemore mused as he hung up. He had gotten the distinct impression, as their conversation had gone on, that Coswell was making a silent decision within himself that his inspector's role in this case was over. The identity of the killer had been revealed (that had been his job) and the apprehension of George was someone else's responsibility, particularly if he was now in the United States. Blakemore had to confess that he, too, had lost much of his motivation. It all seemed totally over now. He wondered at his lack of anger towards a man who had murdered three people, but that was how he felt. He'd even seen some good come of it all. Barbara seemed to have a new purpose in life, and that life was in Bear Creek looking after Michelle and her two children. He didn't see a promotion coming his way

any time soon, what with George slipping through his fingers. It looked as though the Blakemores would be sitting put for a good while (no tears from him). He suppressed a guilty chuckle and went to find Ernie.

Heather sat, fingers poised over the keyboard of her computer, contemplating Zachary's call. He'd returned to George's burnt-out cabin, after he'd dropped her off at the *Bulletin,* to supervise the removal of the killer's remains. She'd virtually finished her article for the paper when Zachary phoned her the news that George had escaped. Ernie, he'd said, was on his way and she was to lock herself in until he arrived at the front door. She knew this was unnecessary although didn't say so to Zachary. She'd let him play the protective male for her. She felt no fear of George now and believed neither she nor anyone else in Bear Creek would ever see him again. She, too, analyzed her lack of antipathy for her abductor. If she had to put her finger on one thing that might explain her feelings it would be the toilet paper. That wasn't the act of a fiend. A picture of George emerged in her mind of a decent man twisted by a bizarre combination of emotions—love, grief, anger, fear—who acted out against what he saw as an unfair and threatening world. Her hand reached for the mouse, clicked "new blank document," and she began to type: **The Making of a Killer—the true story of the Monashee Murderer**.

He was so very, very tired. He'd tried to carry on a conversation with the driver because he knew that's why the man had picked him up, but once they'd checked through US Customs, fatigue had overwhelmed him. His head nodded and he dozed fitfully.

The crossing had been so easy. He was prepared. When the officer asked him for ID he pulled out his old honourable discharge card with

the field commendations listed and his years of service in Vietnam. There was almost a tear in the official's eye as he handed it back and said, "That's good enough for me, man. Nice to welcome a patriot home instead of having to keep my eye out for chickenshit draft dodgers sauntering back across the line."

He was jolted awake by the hiss of airbrakes as the driver pulled into a truck stop.

"I need one more coffee to get me home. Can I get you one too?" the driver asked, kindly.

George saw the sign Kettle Valley Mobil. It was time to turn west.

"No, thanks," he replied. "I think I'll just stretch my legs. You go ahead."

The driver was astonished when he returned to his truck and saw no sign of his passenger. He pulled open the cab door and spotted his clipboard on the seat with a note clamped to it and a wad of Canadian bills.

The note read, "Thanks a lot for the lift. Go ahead without me. The money's yours. I won't be needing it."

More great mysteries

from NeWest Press . . .

Undercurrent

a mystery
Anne Metikosh

Conservation officer Charlie Meikle's peaceful life in the wilderness of northern Ontario is shattered when she finds the body of an old friend face down in the lake. Jim Griffith's death is ruled accidental, but to Charlie things don't add up. A bizarre discovery in the fisherman's cabin leads Charlie to suspect he was murdered. A desperate hunt for answers turns into a life and death struggle when Charlie stumbles across an illegal toxic waste dump that has the potential to destroy the lake and the town around it.

Like a powerful current, this book will pull you swiftly into its conspiracies and fascinating intrigues from beginning to thrilling end.

1-896300-87-1 • $10.95 CDN • $7.95 US

AVAILABLE AT FINE BOOKSTORES

WWW.NEWESTPRESS.COM

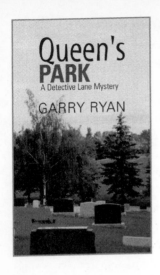

Queen's Park
A Detective Lane Mystery
Garry Ryan

Detective Lane has a knack for discovering the whereabouts of missing persons. But the city's latest victim has disappeared without a trace. After a brutal attack on his young nephew, ex-mayor Bob Swatsky has gone missing along with 13 million dollars of taxpayers' money. Is he on the run with the cash, or is it something far more sinister? A zany cast of characters, a love doll, and a chain-smoking grandma with an oxygen tank, lead Detective Lane on a thrilling romp through the streets of Calgary. The chase is on, and alone, Lane must uncover the truth before someone ends up visiting Queen's Park cemetery . . . permanently.

1-896300-84-7 • $10.95 CDN • $7.95 US

AVAILABLE AT FINE BOOKSTORES

WWW.NEWESTPRESS.COM

Watch for the stunning second book in the Detective Lane series

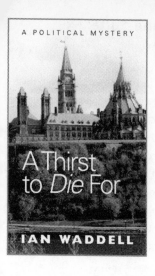

A Thirst to Die For

A Political Mystery

Ian Waddell

Water has been called Blue Gold: the most indispensable commodity on Earth.

Tipped off by a court case, Clayton Greene, Member of Parliament, discovers that a faction of high government officials have secret Orders-in-Council, allowing water exports from Canada to the United States. The Prime Minister of Canada denies any knowledge of the orders, but then the captain of the freighter that was to carry the exported water turns up dead and large amounts of money appear in a Caribbean bank account in the Prime Minister's name.

Fast-paced action including car chases and death-defying escapes, along with Parliamentary tricks, mark this thrilling mystery.

1-896300-55-3 • $9.95 CDN • $6.95 US

AVAILABLE AT FINE BOOKSTORES

WWW.NEWESTPRESS.COM

Beyond Spite
R.F. Darion

There is a rapist on the loose in the small town of St. Michael, and Staff Sergeant Dan Laurenson is on the case. The victim is alive, but Tiffany Skoreko, who has been beaten and violently raped, is found wandering barefoot and incoherent on a country road and Laurenson must track down the rapist before he finds a new victim.

1-896300-52-9 • $9.95 CDN • $6.95 US

Tip of the Halo
R.F. Darion

The offices of the Catholic School Board in the quiet community of St. Michael seem an unlikely locale for a murder, but when a body is found, Staff Sergeant Dan Laurenson is on the scene. Laurenson soon discovers that the board offices harbour a dark underground of sex, lies, and jealousy. There is much more at stake than discovering how someone could be killed in broad daylight without anyone noticing.

1-896300-39-1 • $9.95 CDN • $6.95 US
AVAILABLE AT FINE BOOKSTORES
WWW.NEWESTPRESS.COM

ROY INNES is a long time BC resident, growing up and attending university in Victoria, BC, before going on to the University of British Columbia to earn his MD. Innes remained in the bustle of Vancouver working life until retirement led him to Gabriola Island where he reads and writes to his heart's content. He ventures from home only occasionally to hunt and hike in the wilderness throughout the province.